FATES CURSED

GODS CURSED BOOK 5

LEISL LEIGHTON

Published by Leisl Leighton as Permien Press. For more information, email: leisl@leislleighton.com

Cover design – Samantha Marshall

Editor – Marnie St Clair

eBook ISBN: 978-1-922836-19-9; Print ISBN: 978-1-922836-20-5

 Formatted with Vellum

PRAISE FOR THE GODS CURSED SERIES

Was really hard to put this one down once I started! I can not wait to see what this new series ... Gods Cursed Series.... Holds in the future!

— DIANA K – GOODREADS & BOOKSPROUT

Loved this and it's Easter orientated. Check this out.

— WHITNEY – GOODREADS AND BOOKSPROUT REVIEWER

"So good! I will always love paranormal romances, they just have so many different types, and themes, and never get boring. Leighton delivers a great one!"

— TAPNCHICA – GOODREADS AND BOOKSPROUT REVIEWER

I absolutely love this ... Leighton brilliantly weaves in Greek and Nordic Mythology, and a HUGE splash of her rich and thrilling imagination. She is a master at world building, character, plot, and oh...those sex scenes are pretty damn hot. You'd be crazy not to read this series!

— LAURA BADHUS – GOODREADS REVIEWER

This was magical and captivating throughout. Thoroughly enjoyed the storyline and characters and how they overcome things.

— PAT'S REVIEWS - GOODREADS REVIEWER

I loved this! ... This is a very good book and is most definitely worth reading.

— A SCHOFIELD - GOODREADS & BOOKBUB REVIEWER

FATES CURSED

This is for my Mum who shared her love of the fantastical with me.

Love you Mum.

CHAPTER

ONE

"Is she asleep?" Korinna asked Jules as she entered the kitchen, Ilia following close behind.

Jules nodded as she joined Korinna at the kitchen table then looked back at Ilia who stood behind her. "Thanks to Ilia."

"No thanks necessary." Ilia patted Jules on the shoulder. "Just doing what I can to help." She gestured at the pot of tea Korinna had in her hand. "I'd love a cuppa though. Should I put the kettle on?"

"Don't bother. This pot is fresh. It's Violetta's relaxation blend. I thought you might need it to help you sleep." She checked the clock on the wall behind her. "It's only just after midnight so we could all still get a decent night's sleep with a little help." She began to pour it into the mugs that were already on the table.

"You're a Goddess," Jules said, reaching for one. "I'm so tired." She gave Ilia a gimlet stare as the ancient witch took a seat next to her. "I'm not quite sure why you're not given you're up every night helping me with my baby girl." She put one of the steaming mugs in front of Ilia. "What's your secret?"

Ilia shrugged as she picked it up and cupped it in her hands. She was exhausted, but not because her sleep was constantly interrupted by little Dawn's nightmares. It had more to do with the fact Trip, her soulmate, couldn't keep his hands off her, just as she couldn't keep hers off him. Every night was filled with the kind of glorious lovemaking she'd never known was possible. If not for how it filled her with energy, particularly when their fangs grew and they shared in each other's blood as Trip pounded into her in the way she needed him to, she would probably be worse off than Jules.

Although, if Trip stayed away any longer in his search for Loki, she was going to be in trouble. The sexual energy from their last encounter a week ago had been waning over the last day or so.

But she didn't say any of that. She simply followed up the shrug with an, "I have no idea."

She lifted her mug to her nose and took in a deep breath. The fragrant scent of jasmine, chamomile and a hint of lavender flowed around her, soothing her as much as the warmth from the tea-heated ceramic.

"Perhaps we're all used to a lack of sleep," Korinna said, her eyes dancing as she lifted her cup and blew across the hot liquid. "I don't know about you, but Tamuel keeps me up most nights." She waggled her brows. "In the best way."

Jules snorted. "I'm not sure I should hear that about my soul-son."

"It's no worse than him hearing you and Bas testing the springs on your bed every night. Or the way sexually tinged power zaps through the air every time Ilia and my dad are at it." Korinna shuddered dramatically

"What?" Ilia's mug thunked down on the table, tea splashing over the rim. "That does not happen! You're making that up."

"I'm afraid I'm not." Korinna laughed. "You should see your face!"

Horrified, Ilia turned to Jules for confirmation.

Jules chuckled. "Umm, I have to admit what Korinna said is 100% true."

Ilia's cheeks heated – and the rest of her along with it. Hades' balls. She wanted to sink under the table and never be seen again. Gaze firmly on the liquid in her mug she said, "Hells, I'm so sorry. I had no idea."

Jule's snort of laughter had her looking up.

"Don't be sorry," the other witch said, patting her hand. "The sex after your energy hits us is even better. Bas already had stamina, but now …" She waved her hand in front of her face. "It's spectacular."

"Oh Hells!" Ilia said, dropping her head into her hands. Then a thought hit and her head whipped up, gaze searching Korinna's smirking face. "That doesn't happen to you and Tam, does it?"

Korinna grimaced comically and said, "Yep."

"Argh! This is beyond embarrassing," she wailed, hiding her face in her hands again. Gods damn it! It wasn't only embarrassing. It was wrong.

Korinna might be over 2000 years old and only recently had found, and was getting to know, her father, but his sex life really wasn't something she needed to know anything about. Especially if said sex life was creating a situation that affected her and her mate in a way that made them horny. Not that they really needed help in that department – she'd spent months with them when she was in the HeartsBlood Gem and embedded in Tam's chest to keep her close and safe. She'd had to shut off her awareness many, many times while Korinna and Tam were having sexy-times after they mated.

But still … She lifted her head and forced herself to look at her daughter-in-law. "You shouldn't be pushed into having sex because of something your father and I are doing. That must be so … scarring."

Korinna snorted. "In the scheme of my life, not really."

Ilia couldn't stop her chin from wobbling as tears pricked her eyes. "I'm so sorry. I didn't mean to make things worse for you."

Korinna leaned forward and grabbed Ilia's wrist. "Please don't be sorry. Honestly, it's not that bad. Sure, it was a bit uncomfortable at first, knowing where the energy was coming from and why, but now …" A smile blossomed on her lips and her eyes turned a little dreamy. "I knew Tam was creative but …" She coughed a little and came back to herself. "Jules is right. Something about what you're both putting out there makes things even better. It's like he's in me spiritually as I'm in him and it's even more than the mating bond and yet it *is* the mating bond." She waved her hand, frowning in consternation. "I'm not explaining it very well."

"I think you're explaining it exactly right," Jules said as she leaned over to pat Ilia's hand. "We're not worried about it and you shouldn't be either."

Ilia grimaced. "I'm not sure about that. And I don't think Trip will be when I tell him." She knew he'd be as horrified as she was. "I knew we shouldn't have stayed." She stood up, her chair screeching across the parquetry. "As soon as Trip comes back, we'll go."

"No!" Korinna and Jules shouted at the same time.

Ilia looked between them in surprise. "But … we've been

here for months and we always intended to find a place nearby or go back to Trip's farm." The only reason they hadn't was because Trip needed to be where Korinna was after having chosen to have his memory wiped and be separated from his unborn daughter to safeguard her. Now he had his memories back and was recently reunited with her well ... There was so much he wanted to know about her; so much he wanted to make up for.

And Ilia hadn't argued the point because, apart from feeling his need, she felt her own need to be close to Dawn. Despite the spell at Christmas she and Trip had performed that separated her life-force from Dawn's and saved both hers and the baby's lives, the need to be around the growing toddler hadn't abated. In fact, it had grown as Dawn had grown – growth that wasn't normal physically or mentally. Not only had Dawn's ability to use mind-speech increased, her powers were beginning to manifest strongly – unusual in someone so young – and she was growing physically much faster than she should.

If one counted things as the humans did, she was about to turn one – her birthday was in two days' time – but she was about the size of a three-year-old and had the mental capacity of a child a few years older still. And every time she had one of her fits at night – seizures that gripped her entire body and filled her mind with nightmares that spilled out into all of them through her mind-speech ability – she aged a little faster.

Yesterday she'd been about average height and weight for a two-year-old but now ...

She shook her head and took a sip of tea, not caring that it was still too hot. It scalded her tongue, but she swallowed it down and took another. The fleeting pain was nothing to what poor little Dawn endured too many nights.

As if Korinna could read her mind, she placed her cup on the table then took Ilia's hand in hers. "We need you here." Her gaze flickered to Jules, who nodded. "Not just because you seem to be able to help Dawn come down from one of her fits faster than the rest of us can, but you are family."

"Not all families live in each other's pockets."

"This one does," Jules said. "We are stronger together. And as to you being embarrassed over the sexual power that you and Trip spill out into the world ... you don't need to be. I think it's happening for a reason."

"Why do you say that?" Ilia asked, frowning.

"Because everything has. Every event that has occurred since Bas came into my first incarnation's life has led to something necessary. And while you and Trip might be horrified that your sex life is affecting all of us, it's also strengthening us. It's creating tighter bonds between us and our soulmates."

"But how can that be?" The mating bond was unbreakable by anything but death – and came only second in strength and power to a soul-bond. Which was what Jules and Bas, and Korinna and Tam, and she and Trip all had.

Jules shrugged. "I know it seems an impossibility, but it's true."

Korinna nodded. "It is. And I think Jules is right. It's important. Besides ..." She ran her finger around the rim of her mug, "I need my Dad here. Plus over the last year, you've become more than a friend and family member, so I can't do without you close by either. But it's more than that." Her eyes lifted to meet Ilia's and something shifted in their depths. Her voice deepened as she said, "It's not only blood that binds and strengthens us."

Ilia shivered as the words echoed through her mind.

There was the touch of ancient power in Korinna's voice that pierced right into her very soul and made her new-found powers sit up and listen. If Korinna was right, she and Trip couldn't leave. And ... aside from that, she really didn't want to go – which was kind of surprising given how she used to feel about family and losing those she loved.

Slowly, she took a sip of her tea, swallowed and then voiced the thing that had been worrying her the last few days. "But ... what if it's me? What if my presence is making Dawn worse?"

Jules' and Korinna's eyes went wide and they looked at each other briefly before they both started shaking their heads. "Are you crazy?" Korinna asked.

"Maybe." Ilia looked down at her mug again and said softly, "But it wouldn't be the first time my presence was bad for her. I almost killed her last Christmas."

"You kept her alive last Christmas, despite the danger to yourself," Jules said, reaching across the table to grasp Ilia's hand. "Your energy has never been anything but positive towards Dawn."

"But how can you be certain?" she said, looking up into her friend's eyes. "We don't even know how my power works or where it truly came from. How can you be certain it's not made to hurt rather than heal?"

"Because, you've done nothing but help since you came to us. And Dawn loves you. She trusts you. She asks for you. She needs you. I don't think any of that would be true if you were the cause of whatever is happening to her."

"Jules is right," Korinna said, reaching to grasp her wrist and squeeze gently. "You always make Dawn better. There is no way you are causing Dawn's nightmares or her strange growth. That is something else entirely."

"But what?"

Korinna shrugged. "I don't know." She glanced at Jules then back again. "But I don't think we will discover what it is if you leave. I feel like you are essential to helping her. So you have to stay. Okay?"

Ilia met Korinna's firm gaze, then looked at Jules whose eyes pleaded with her. Tears swam in her vision and she looked down, covering the emotion. After a moment she said on a rasp, "Okay. We'll stay."

A loud sigh erupted from Jules as Korinna said, "Good."

Ilia glanced up to see the two women smiling at her in obvious relief. She began to return their smiles until a horrible thought hit her. "You don't think Dawn is being affected by Trip and me ... you know? Maybe her fits are being caused by—"

Korinna squeezed her hand again. "There is no correlation. Tam and I have already looked into that."

"You have?"

She nodded. "It wasn't hard to put together. You and Dad are blood-sharing most nights, right?"

Ilia blushed at the fact Korinna knew that, but nodded. "Yes. It feels ... necessary."

"Right. That's because it is." She waved her hand to forestall any questions that popped into Ilia's head. "We can go into that later. Right now, you need to know that what you and Dad are doing is not affecting Dawn at all."

"But how do you know for certain?"

"Simple. She's not having her fits every night," Jules said, getting up to fetch the biscuit jar from the counter behind them.

"That's not conclusive proof though. It could be building up in her until she has a fit."

"I don't think it is," Korinna said. "I mean, look at tonight."

"What about it?"

"Dad and Bas and Tam have been away for a week now searching for Loki to try and get some answers, so there's been no sexy times going on – for any of us."

She was more than aware of Trip's absence, the ache inside only assuaged by the fact she could feel their bond so strong and warm inside her – and the multiple face-time sessions a day because neither of them seemed to be able to go more than a few hours without seeing the other's face or hearing their voice.

Ugh, she'd never thought she'd be so pathetic and yet ... it was the most wonderful thing in her life. But that was beside the point. She pulled her thoughts back to their conversation. "Ah, I get your point. With Trip gone this last week there's been no special power leaking through the house. Yet Dawn's had some of her worst fits this week."

"Correct." Korinna nodded, a huge smile on her face.

But she didn't smile back because ... "That is so disappointing."

"What do you mean? You don't truly want to move out, do you?"

Ilia blinked at her friend, surprised by the panic in her tone. "Oh, no. I didn't mean that." She leaned forward so she could take both Korinna's and Jule's hands in hers. "Last year I felt crowded in because all of this was so new and this new body was ... well, alien to me. Plus I really just thought I was a pain in the arse to you all, complicating matters."

"I'm so sorry you felt like that," Jules said, hand turning over in Ilia's to grip tight.

"You don't feel like that now, do you?" Korinna asked.

"No! Not at all. And my feeling like that had nothing to do with you," she said, gaze moving from one to the other. "Or anyone here. You were all so welcoming and did everything you could to make me feel like this was home. No, it was more that I ..." She stopped herself, collected her thoughts. "It was fear. Fear of coming to love you all, to want to truly be a part of this family and then losing it when you all figured out I wasn't one of you."

"You *are* one of us," Korinna said, grip tightening on

Ilia's hand. "Always. Even if you'd never mated to my dad, you are family. Okay?"

Ilia nodded, blinking the tears from her eyes and swallowing down the lump in her throat.

"So, if you don't feel like that anymore, why were you disappointed that you're not causing Dawn's fits?"

She met Jule's gaze. "Because if our ... nightly activities ... were causing Dawn's nightmares and fits, then moving out would have been a solution. And ..." She shrugged. "Even though I don't want to move out, I'm disappointed that's not it. Aren't you?"

"No."

Her gaze jerked to Jules. "Why?"

"Because you both moving out would *not* have been a solution," Jules said, meeting Ilia's gaze and holding it with an emotional intensity that took Ilia's breath and made her heart pound. "As Korinna said, you're family. You belong here. With us. Okay?"

Tears threatened again and the lump that had grown in her throat made it impossible to talk, so she just nodded. She was still unused to this intensity of emotion after having spent thousands of years locked in a gem where she mostly felt numb — or raw, unfiltered fury at those who used her and abused her. This warmth of love and friendship was ... difficult. But wanted even though it still terrified her.

It was that uncomfortableness — and terror — that had her breaking the moment of soft smiles, love and camaraderie. She cleared her throat and said huskily, "I think my tea is getting cold."

"The inhumanity!" Korinna let go of Ilia's hand to pick up her mug as she said with a cheeky smile, "We wouldn't want to waste such bloody good tea!"

They all chuckled and Ilia's awkwardness slipped from her. She sipped her tea – it was actually the perfect temperature now – and took a biscuit from the tin Jules handed around.

"Yum, lemon drops. My favourite," Korinna said, putting the whole thing in her mouth.

"Please don't do that around Dawn," Jules said, looking a little horrified. "She's prone to mimicking you, and Bas and I really don't want her to learn how to do *that*."

Korinna winked as she chewed and swallowed, then after a big swig of tea to wash it down said, "The kid has to have some normalcy."

"Choking on a biscuit she's stuffed into her mouth whole isn't normal."

"But I'd teach her the art of stuffing and chewing appropriately, of course."

"Of course," Jules said, rolling her eyes. "You and Tam are going to be such bad influences."

"No. We're the best of influences. We're going to bring the fun."

"Bas and I bring the fun!"

"Yeah. But you're her parents, so it's not the same kind of fun as her brother and sister-in-law bring."

Ilia's mind flickered to her twin boys, who she'd never got to know after they were taken from her at birth and dumped in the Tyber by that bastard, Amulius. Thankfully they'd survived, but because of what had happened to her after that, the mythologies about her boys, Romulus and Remus, were the only thing she had of them. She couldn't help wondering what their lives might have been if she'd been there for them like Dawn's family was there for her. Blinking back the rawness of emotion-laden tears, she said roughly, "I think Dawn's the luckiest child in the world to have all of you."

"And you and Trip," Jules said. "If you hadn't done what you did, she wouldn't be here."

"She was only in danger because of me."

"Not true," Jules said. "You didn't tie yourself to her."

"Yeah," Korinna said. "That was entirely mine and Tam's fault when we did the spells to make you corporeal."

Jules shook her head. "No. You're both wrong to take responsibility," she said, shooting an admonishing look at both of them. "Dawn being linked to you was the influence of a higher Being. You can't deny it. She wasn't due to be born for another month and there were no signs of labour until the Void opened. It came on so quickly and the labour was over just as quickly, as if it needed to be done by a certain time." She pointed at each of them then herself as she said, "We've all been manipulated and at the mercy of wills greater than our own, so you know the feeling." Ilia and Korinna both nodded. "No, whatever is going on with Dawn, it's not any of our faults. She was born when she was, in the way she was, for a great purpose. I know this deep in my soul, but even if I didn't, the magic that's been Goddess-gifted to me is screaming that this is true."

"Your magic is telling you that?" Korinna shifted in her chair to stare at her friend and mother-in-law. "You never said this before!"

Jules looked down at her tea. "That's only because my powers are so new to me and I'm still figuring it all out, but with Bas' help and all the research I've been doing, I've come to realise that my powers react to meddling from higher Beings. And they have been unhappy for weeks."

"So, you think maybe what's going on with Dawn is causing that?"

Jules nodded at Ilia's question. "Absolutely. If the speed of her development and her extraordinarily strong powers weren't a giveaway, the fact that I feel a constant itch under my skin every time she has a fit is confirmation." Her hands gripped around her tea mug, knuckles turning white. "I don't want it to be so. I don't want her caught up in things beyond her control like we all have been. I wanted her to be free of that. But I don't think what I want for my child matters in the grand scheme of things. She wasn't born to have a normal life – I mean, she was born to a cupid with magical powers he shouldn't have and a Goddess-gifted witch after all." She chuckled, but the sound held an edge of fear. When she looked up, her eyes were swimming with tears. "I just really hope that whatever is happening, whatever the Fates or whatever Being that's manipulating all of this has in store for us, they won't use her up. That they'll let her live. Regardless of what happens to the rest of us."

"Demeter wouldn't let anything happen to her," Ilia said, reaching out to grab Jules' hand again.

"I don't think this is Demeter. I've felt her meddling since I got my power back and this isn't that. It's more ... vast."

"Do you think it's Perses?"

She sucked in a breath. "No. This doesn't feel evil. Not that it feels good either. It just ... is."

"Then how do you know Perses isn't doing this to her?" Korinna asked.

"Because everything he's touched has been utterly evil – like Clodia." She shook her head. "No, the meddling in my daughter's life, making her be born at Easter ... it isn't him. But it's an old power. And it doesn't feel about things in the same way we do. I know she is here for a greater purpose, but I'm also afraid that she's nothing but a pawn to whatever this is that's manipulating things behind the scenes and she'll be used up and spat out at its whim."

Ilia squeezed her hand, tears welling again at the sound of utter agony in the other woman's voice. She knew too well that fear; knew too well the grief of being unable to help your own child. "She's essential. I saw it in the visions of the future Loki showed us. Whoever is responsible for what's happened to Dawn, what's happening to her, they won't let her die."

"You only saw until the coming conflict, not after it. None of us know what's coming after. We don't even truly know what's coming before or how we're supposed to face it."

"Dawn *is* essential," Korinna said softly.

"You see, Korinna agrees," Ilia said, her gaze flickering to Korinna, staying there as she noted the strange look on the ancient witch's face. "Korinna?"

"Dawn *is* essential," Korinna said again, her voice echoing in the space around them.

"Korinna? Are you okay?" Jules asked.

"Dawn *is* essential," Korinna said one more time before her eyes turned pure black. Her mug fell from her hand to smash on the floor, liquid splashing everywhere. Then she slumped in her seat.

"Korinna!" Jules dived for her as she began to slip sideways, pulling her upright before she fell off the chair.

Ilia leapt from her seat, slipping in the liquid on the floor, slamming down onto her knees, but managed to help Jules hold Korinna up just as the witch began to shudder and shake.

Then Korinna's black eyes rolled back into her head until only the whites showed.

"Tamuel," Jules yelled, her power prickling in the air

around them in a summoning spell. "Something's happening to Korinna. Come now!"

CHAPTER

THREE

"He was here not long ago," Tam said, turning in a circle in the empty cave. "I can feel his energy still vib—"

"Tamuel! Something's happening to Korinna. Come now!"

Tam jerked to a halt, eyes wide. Even though the call was only meant for the cupid, Trip heard it too. And by the looks of him, so did Bas.

Something must have been terribly wrong at home for Jules' summoning to reach all of them despite its call only being for her son.

Tam raised his hands to open a portal, but before the purple and blue power – Tam's unique dual power he was still coming to terms with – could swirl into existence, Trip said, "This will be faster," and put his hand on both men's shoulders and jumped them through space.

More used to portal travel, Tam and Bas stumbled when they arrived in the kitchen of Stevens House and didn't immediately see the chaos.

Across the room, Korinna snapped upright from where

17

she was sitting, the violence of the movement bringing her to her feet, shoving Jules and Ilia aside so hard they slid across the kitchen floor. The chair she'd been sitting on flew backwards towards the two cupids he'd just transported with him.

"Duck!" he cried as he darted towards his mate and daughter.

"Help her!" Ilia shouted, already getting to her feet, her gaze firmly fixed on Korinna. Knowing she was okay, he skipped through space to materialise beside his daughter. He was about to reach out to her but then snatched his hands back when he saw her face, her eyes.

Fuck!

Quickly he threw up a shield around the house, not wanting anyone who might be listening to hear what could come out of her mouth. This looked like she was experiencing a major prophecy, and they were always written in the Hall of Prophecy for anyone in the Pantheons to read. His shield would stop it from winging its way there for a while, but it wasn't a permanent solution. Somehow he had to find a way to stop this one from being written there because then they'd know Korinna had the Sight and nothing good could come from that.

Ilia arrived at his side at the same time Tam pushed in front of him, arms stretched out to wrap around his mate.

Trip grabbed him, pulling him back before he could make contact. "No. She's having a vision."

"How do you know?" Tam's eyes were wide, his worry an almost physical brush against Trip's senses.

He understood – this was the last thing he wanted for his daughter – but it was out of their hands. It always had been. "I've seen this before. You can't get in the way of it. You've just got to let it play out."

"But look at her! She's in pain."

It was true. His daughter's skin was stretched over the muscle and sinew and bones of her face, making her look almost skeletal. The tendons in her neck, shoulders and arms stood out, caught in mid-spasm, her hands clenched at her sides, knuckles so white it almost looked like the bone was about to burst through the skin.

And her eyes – open too wide and filling with swirling gold – were inhuman.

If that wasn't bad enough, her mouth opened on a never-ending scream none of them could hear.

Tam reached towards her again, but Trip wrapped his arms around his son-in-law and held him back. "I know it's hard, Tam – believe me, I know – but you can't stop it. And touching her will only make her hurt you. You saw her throw Jules and Ilia aside as we arrived. And that was only when the vision was coming on. Now she's in the full-throws of a major prophecy, she could seriously hurt anyone it deems might be trying to stop it from being Seen. You have to let it play out."

"This is ..." Tam said, trembling as he watched his mate, his worry playing Trip's nerves like a violin. Not that Trip let anyone see that. He pulled a cloak of calm around him – helped by Ilia's touch, the grip of her hand – and tried to project that calm out to everyone in the room.

Out of the corner of his eye he saw Bas help Jules to her feet then. Jules winced as she put weight on her leg. Damn, she'd been hurt. Korinna would emotionally whip herself for hurting the woman who had become her closest friend and confidante outside her mate. Hopefully Bas would be able to use his healing powers on his mate as soon as he could and Korinna wouldn't know anything about it.

"I don't understand what's going on," Tam said, his

voice lost and echoing the pain his mate currently experienced. "How is this happening? She's never had visions like this before. She's had knowings. But nothing like this."

Trip's mouth twisted as he said, "She was always meant to have them. It's one of the reasons I left, because with me not in her life, her power would never fully manifest. I'd hoped because it had been dormant so long that it would stay that way but ..." He gestured at his daughter. "It seems that hope was foolish."

"What can I do?" Tam asked, obviously holding himself back with everything in him.

"Nothing. You just have to let it play out."

Ilia put her arm around Trip, snuggling up next to him, her presence a comfort he'd never thought to have. He wrapped his arms around her, needing her like he'd never needed her before as he stood back and watched his beloved only child suffer because of what he had given her:

His blood.

His powers.

His genesis.

She was in danger because of those things. He could wish it otherwise, but in his experience, wishes led to nothing but disappointment. There was nothing he could do about it. The alternative was to have the Eternal Well blink her out of existence – and that was absolutely not happening.

He wished he could have it blink him out of existence, but that was impossible. He'd tried too many times to end his life to know he was immortal in a way all other immortals weren't. It was why he, Loki and Demeter had come up with their insane plan to keep him out of Korinna's life until she was strong enough to deal with the danger of them being in this world together.

"This is bad, isn't it?" Ilia whispered.

He nodded. "More than you could know."

Ilia's arms tightened around him as she said, "Perses can use her now, can't he? Her Sight … it allows him access in a way he couldn't get before."

"Yes," he said roughly, tortured by the fact and that there was nothing he could do about it. Just as there was nothing he could do to stop Korinna's suffering right now as the prophecy shook through her, rising to be told.

Ilia looked up at him, her expression grim. "We'll keep her safe."

"Yes, we will." If it was the last thing he did, he would keep all of them safe

The only problem was, he had no idea how. Not without some clue from Demeter. But she was missing. As was her protégé, Loki.

"Korinna!" Tam yelled, as his mate shook violently and began to rise into the air. His hands jerked as if he was going to grab her, but he managed to hold himself back before Trip had to.

Then his pained gaze met Trip's as if pleading for him to do something.

But there was nothing Trip could do but watch as Korinna's arms stretched out wide, her eyes full of golden, swirling madness.

It was about to happen. Her neck was arching, her face raised to the ceiling so she could speak her prophecy straight to the Heavens, the words to be written in a fresh book in the Halls of Prophecy the moment his shields faltered. All because he'd failed to find Loki and make him tell them where Demeter was.

"If you mean to help us, Demeter, make it now!" he

demanded with his God-voice in his mind, hoping she might hear it despite his shield.

There was no response.

"Damn you, Demeter. Damn you!" He wanted to sob, wanted to scream at the Heavens, but none of it would do any good. This was happening and there was nothing he could do to stop it.

Ilia's arm tightened around him as if she could sense his torment – she probably could, given they were soulmates.

Korinna opened her mouth. A harsh hiss of air left her, then she began to speak in a voice as ancient as time and space – a voice he'd heard before, long ago; one that made his bones ache:

> *"A babe of witch and demi-God born*
> *Product of two souls bound and sworn*
> *Will shape and grow the greatest power*
> *For Gods to beware in the reaping hour*
> *A babe with magics to shape and See*
> *Protecting all she loves for eternity*
> *This I proclaim three times three times three*
> *It starts in the womb, so mote it be."*

THE WORDS RANG on a fae wind that whipped around his daughter, loosening her dark curls from their topknot to tumble around her face.

There was a high-pitched whining sound as the wind got stronger and stronger, tearing at Korinna's clothes.

Then it stopped and the wind died away as suddenly as it had come.

Korinna dropped.

He and Tam dove to catch her, managing to grab her before she hit the floor.

For long moments, after the wind and the echo of her prophecy faded to nothing, they stared at each other in the shocking silence.

Ilia was the first one to move. She ran to the sink, grabbed a cloth, wet it then ran back to wipe the spittle from around Korinna's mouth and the blood that had dripped from her nose and eyes – it was something he wouldn't have thought of doing, but he was so glad his love had.

"Here, let me," Tam said, holding his hand out for the cloth. Ilia gave it over to him so he could minister to his mate, then, without saying a word, encouraged Trip to let go of his daughter to settle her fully in Tam's arms, before pulling him up and away.

He didn't want to move away from his daughter, but Ilia was right. He wouldn't want anyone else tending to his mate either. It was Tam's right to look after Korinna and he had to respect that no matter what his parental concern and protectiveness might be pushing him to do.

So he let Ilia pull him over to where Bas had sat Jules on a chair, shock written all over their faces.

It was a disturbing thing to see a grand prophecy being told, especially if it was someone you cared about – and they cared for Korinna like a daughter. Thankfully, they were so shocked they obviously hadn't yet realised the prophecy was about *their* baby daughter. He'd been through the same when Cassandra had croaked her prophecy about him and his daughter. Thankfully Demeter had stopped that prophecy from being written into a book in the Halls of Prophecy so his daughter hadn't been killed.

He swallowed hard, gaze returning to Korinna's pale, sweat-and-blood-streaked face.

Once he took his shield down – and he would have to at some point – how long would it be before the Gods in all the pantheons came for Korinna because of what she had just foretold? Would they kill her or would they choose to take her and chain her to her prophesising in the way that Cassandra had been? Use her up until she was nothing but an insane husk of a woman croaking about futures that may or may not come to pass?

He couldn't let that be her fate. Not that he had any idea how to stop the pantheons if they came for her. Other than to kill them. And that would open another can of worms that, like Pandora's Box, should never be opened.

Maybe they wouldn't come for her. Maybe the only one they'd be interested in was Dawn once this prophecy became known. Fuck. That was no better. For they wouldn't simply kill her or use her like they would Korinna. No, they'd take her before she could protect herself and they'd throw her beyond the Void and into the section of the Beyond known as the Nowhere, where nothing good could ever survive.

It's where they would send him if they found out what he truly was.

It's where higher Beings were sent to die. And if they didn't die, they went totally and absolutely insane.

Just like Perses and the other surviving Titans had when they'd been sent there after they lost the war with their children.

If the horror of Dawn being ripped away from her parents and sent there wasn't terrifying enough, the thought that she wouldn't be given the relief of death, but could turn into something else as Perses had done, made his mind go temporarily blank with something greater than terror.

For if Perses was a danger, a power like Dawn would be an even greater danger if she turned to the dark.

More uncertain than he'd ever felt in his life, even when he woke not knowing who he was or where he was thousands of years ago after Demeter had taken his memories, he stared at the others in the room, waiting for understanding of the prophecy to creep over their faces, and the horror and panic he felt deep inside start to take them over.

He should say something.

He should come up with a plan.

Instead he just stood there, clenching Ilia to him, his only source of comfort, and intoned one word deep inside him over and over:

Fuck! Fuck! Fuck! FUCK!

FOUR

"What in all the Hells was that?" Ilia asked into the shocked silence. "Did that mean what I think it meant?"

Nobody answered. Their gazes were still pinned on Korinna as Tam wiped her face and neck clean and then rocked her to him, crooning, "You're safe, Rinna. You're safe. You can come back to me now. You have to come back to me now."

Ilia wanted to repeat her question but then thought better of it. Not only was all their attention on Korinna – where it should be – but they needed time to process.

So did she if truth be told.

Korinna's words had left an ominous shroud on the room that weighed heavily on her; especially because she had a knowing that it wouldn't be the last time Korinna intoned something that put Dawn – and all of them – in danger just from the speaking of them.

But she couldn't think of that right now. She had to concentrate on the prophecy that had just been spoken. There was so much in it that she had to understand before Trip's shields failed and the prophecy was released.

She went back over it. It said Dawn was a child of incredible power – a fact she already knew, so no prizes there for dropping new info – but that power *would* bring danger because she could be a God Killer.

Ilia had always been worried that Dawn's powers, gifted to her by a Goddess like they were, would bring the kind of danger and attention they'd brought to her mother, Jules, who had also been Goddess-blessed with power that no mortal should ever possess. But this? To have the power to kill Gods, just like Trip and Korinna?

Not that she wasn't all for killing Gods – many of the bastards deserved a good killing – but the pantheons certainly wouldn't be happy about it when they found out. Which was why that particular aspect of Trip and Korinna's powers had been hidden by Demeter and Persephone. But they didn't have either of those powerful Goddesses to hide such a thing now, so when Korinna's prophecy got written into the Hall of Prophecy, everyone would know. Which meant more danger than they were already in from Perses and his minions would be heading their way very soon.

She harrumphed. Why couldn't Korinna's prophecy be about fluffy bunny fun stuff? Why did she have to be a Doomsayer?

But she was getting sidetracked. The purpose of a prophecy wasn't just to be doomy and gloomy: they mostly spoke of major players and events that would bring the attention of the higher Beings. And this one would do that in spades.

She didn't have to look at Trip to see if he had recognised all the dangers too for Dawn and for Korinna. His entire body was vibrating with tension and worry. She wished she could do more for him than hold him tight. Wished she could come up with a plan.

Hells. She hated to say this but they needed Demeter and Persephone and Loki and anyone else they could muster.

She couldn't believe *she* was thinking of calling on the help of a God and Goddesses. She'd had more than enough attention and 'help' from those that ruled the pantheons and lorded over all the Realms. She really didn't want any more. Trip's search for Loki was a bitter pill she'd endeavoured to swallow every day because she understood the necessity – they did need to know more about what was coming – but truthfully, she was afraid if she saw the smiling bastard again, she'd punch him in his smug, patrician nose; or maybe worse.

Probably worse.

Fuck she hated the Gods. And Goddesses. They were often just as bad – or worse – than the danger Perses and his minions posed. Selfish. Fucking. Arseholes!

She wanted to scream at the universe, to let her words carry to those who used and abused those they considered 'lower beings'. But looking at Tam with a still unconscious Korinna in his arms, and then at Jules and Bas, she couldn't do that. They needed her to stay calm. They needed her.

And she wanted to be there for them.

Hells.

She couldn't believe she was so concerned about two demi-Gods who she once would have tarred with the same dickish brush she tarred all Gods with. But Tam and Bas had changed her mind – about them at least. She ... loved them. Like she imagined she would have loved a brother.

And then there was Trip.

Although, he wasn't a God. Or a demi-God. He was something else entirely – a gift of difference he'd given to his only daughter.

Right now though, he thought it was more a burden than a gift if the look on his face was anything to go by.

She hugged him tighter and looked up at him.

His gaze collided with hers.

Her breath froze in her lungs as it always did when he looked at her like that – as if she was his sun, his centre, the only thing in the universe that could make his world right.

It was too much sometimes and yet, she felt the same. Which could also be too much. Despite that, she would never wish it otherwise. For this ... this love she never thought to have and a devotion that still took her breath away every time she felt it from him, or felt it for him, was more precious to her than her life.

She still couldn't quite believe he'd come into her life and that he was hers in the same way that she was his.

Such a gift she never thought to have or want.

But now ... now it was everything and she would never, could never, want to live without it.

His gaze lingered on hers before he bent down to give her a fleeting kiss she felt to her core. He smiled at her briefly, then his attention returned to Korinna. As it should. Because now was not about them. It was about Korinna and the prophecy she'd just intoned and the impact it would have on the rest of them when they finally took it in and realised what it meant.

She wished these stupid new nebulous powers she couldn't figure out would do something useful – like change time. She could go back and try to change things so the prophecy would never have been told. But she couldn't.

Frustrated, she jumped on the only thing she could hope for. "What if we're wrong? What if the prophecy isn't about Dawn?"

His gaze met hers again, his eyes wide with pain and sorrow. "It is though. You know it is."

"Do I? Do we? It's not like Korinna said her name. I know prophecies are usually spoken to or in front of someone associated with them, but given we're all here, it could be about any one of us. Or maybe someone us-adjacent that we're not thinking of."

The sadness in his eyes deepened. Then he repeated the first line of the prophecy, "'A babe of witch and demi-God born.' Who else could that be about other than Dawn?"

He was right. There were few children in history who had been born of a witch and demi-God, and all were dead except for the one in this room – Tam – and the little girl asleep upstairs. But could she be forgetting something?

Her gaze flickered around, taking them in as she sorted through the facts she knew about each of them.

This was definitely not about Jules or Bas. Jules was born of two witches and Bas was born of a witch and a God. So they were out. It wasn't about her either – she wasn't sure where her magic had come from, because her parents were completely and disappointingly human, her father a particularly arseholish one at that, her mother too obedient to stop him from doing what he'd done to his daughter. Not that her ability to use magic had ever done her any good. She'd barely known how to use it, nor knew anyone who could teach her. And she'd only ever managed small spells, like doing some minor healing or repairing a vase she'd accidentally broken so her father wouldn't whip her for her clumsiness – which was a kind of healing too, she supposed. It wasn't until she was embedded in the Hearts-Blood Gem as the spirit fuelling it that she'd ever been able to do anything – and most of that not of her choosing.

Then after she was released from it ... well, who the Hells knew where her current powers had come from? They should have been Dawn Goddess powers, but she couldn't seem to use them for regenerative purposes or healing or even for procreation. Although ... maybe that's why she and Trip were giving off the energy they did when they made love.

Which wasn't helpful in any way and definitely not something she could seem to control.

So the prophecy was definitely not about her.

It wasn't about Korinna either – she was born of a witch and a ... well, whatever Trip was, which definitely wasn't a God or demi-God even though Demeter had encouraged him to be known as both. But Tam ... he was definitely in contention. "Tam's the product of a witch and demi-God."

"He's no longer a babe though."

"It could have referred to him when he was born. That was a pretty significant event."

"Yes, except the prophecy very much seemed to be about the present, not the past." He gripped her hands tightly. "I'm sorry, Ilia, but it can be about nobody other than Dawn."

She knew he was right, but still, she couldn't stop her mind from going over the rest of the prophecy again as they stood there and waited for Korinna to come out of the post-Sight unconsciousness.

What was the second line? Ah, that's right. *'Product of two souls bound and sworn.'*

Once again, that could be about Tam, and yet, while Bas

and Lianna – the original spirit who ended up being rein-carnated into Jules – were soul-bound at the time of Tam's birth, they were not sworn to each other in any official way. They couldn't be because she was a Vestal Virgin and he was a cupid, bound by cupid law – which Eros had broken to be with Psyche, but still bound his cupids to. Apparently what was good for the goose at that time was definitely not good for the gander in Eros' eyes. Look what he'd done to Tam to keep him from following in his father's footsteps. So much pain and suffering just because of some Godly hubris and jealousy that saw Eros wanting to keep the possibility of love for a cupid to himself.

Prick.

Thankfully he hadn't shaped his curse very well and had left a loophole that allowed Tam and Korinna to mate. Her heart filled with warmth for them, because now she knew what utter joy that was and she was so happy her two best friends in all the world had that too.

Her gaze landed on them again.

Korinna was still out of it, her face deathly pale, body limp as Tam held her, rocking and crooning, trying to bring her back to him. Devastation and desolation were clouding his usually bright eyes.

Ilia knew why. He probably couldn't feel her like he usually did – a consequence of the Seeing. Ilia had never had more than knowings herself, but even then, there was a disconnect with reality when they occurred. Trip had told her it felt like she was not quite with him when they happened. So after what Korinna had just endured, it must feel like his mate was barely there, if at all.

Just the thought of what that must be like had panic fluttering in her chest.

She pushed it down, dragging her thoughts back to

trying to decipher the prophecy. What was the next part? Oh yes.

'Will shape and grow the greatest power
For Gods to beware in the reaping hour.'

Well, that wasn't good. This was the line that would bring the pantheon's attention to the precious girl and not in a 'we want to embrace her and love her and make her one of us' way.

Fucking jealous megalomaniacs, the lot of them.

Her lip curled as her chest filled with her hatred for them, but when Trip's arm tightened around her, a grimace pulling at his lips even though all his attention was on Korinna, she realised she was leaking those negative feelings into him and had to stop.

Pushing that hatred right down as far as she could, she returned her thoughts to the prophecy. Okay, so the next section ...

'A babe' – Trip was right. It couldn't be Tam because he was not a babe –

'A babe with magics to shape and see.
Protecting all she loves for eternity.'

This was rather positive for a prophecy, because it indicated something beautiful and good could come from her terrible power. Not that higher Beings would take any note of that at all, concepts of good and evil didn't matter to them at all. Humph. Truly bastards.

Before she could let her rage overwhelm her, she concentrated on the last part of the prophecy.

'This I proclaim three times three times three
It starts in the womb, so mote it be.'

The last part was more like the end of a spell – not unusual given Korinna was a witch – except for the 'it starts in the womb' bit. Normally when a witch had a Seeing and bound it into the world like a spell, they ended with 'This I proclaim three times three times three, By the power of the mother, so mote it be' just like they would a spell. So 'it starts in the womb' was very unusual and seemed once again to point towards Dawn being the central figure of the prophecy – fuckity-fuckity-fuckity-fuck! – because what happened to the baby had started when she was still in Jules' womb. The magics of Oestra and the Goddess Ostara had sunk into her body and soul in a way they couldn't if she'd already been born into this Realm.

She almost slapped herself in the head. She should have realised this already. Because if the powers had been bestowed on her after she was born, Dawn would never have been able to give Tam the power to turn Ilia from spirit to corporeal. She would never have been able to help Ilia trap Clodia into the HeartsBlood Gem as Ilia had once been trapped.

Although, unlike Ilia, Clodia deserved and needed to be imprisoned – crazy, evil bitch that she was.

The gem in her chest where Clodia was trapped heated a little as it always did when she thought of the ancient High Priestess witch. She touched where it rested between her breasts as it had once rested in Tam's when Ilia had been its prisoner, willing her to be quiet. The gem listened to her as it always did – while it had been her prison for almost 3000 years, the part of the gem that was something close to sentient had loved her and protected her as much as it could. And it protected her even now from the evil witch trapped inside it.

The Well only knew she didn't need to be subjected to Clodia's ravings about eternal power and setting her Lord and Master free so she could have said power.

Ilia shook her head at the lunacy of such thought. As if

Perses would share his power with anyone. When he said he wanted to have dominion over all and would kill all the Gods and Goddesses in all the pantheons so there was no one to challenge him, what part of that did she not understand? If she managed to set him free, he'd suck all the power she had and use it as his own, leaving her as nothing but a dead husk at his feet that he would crush into dust.

"Ilia?"

She startled and then looked up at Trip. "Yes?"

"Where did your thoughts go?"

It was then she realised her grip on him had tightened to the point her nails were digging into him. "Sorry. My thoughts ... I don't seem to be able to control them. They're wandering all over the place."

"You're still not trying to make the prophecy about someone other than Dawn, are you?"

She shook her head sadly. "No. You're right. It's about her. I wish it wasn't, but it is."

He nodded sadly before asking, "So what were your meandering thoughts about?"

"Nothing important."

"I doubt that," he said, smiling at her wryly. "I'm pretty sure everything that goes on in that head of yours is important."

She loved that he thought so and leaned up to kiss him so he'd know. Words of love still didn't come easily to her, but the physical show of it – *that* she could do, and did, with relish. She pulled back before it could get serious though, because now was quite literally not the time.

Especially given what she'd learned this morning from Jules and Korinna about them all feeling the power of Trip and Ilia's sexual connection – bloody useless gift from

Ostara that it was. She'd like to have words with the Goddess about—

Korinna jerked up out of Tam's arms, spun around into a crouch, her eyes – wide and pleading – going to Jules and Bas.

"I'm sorry. I'm so sorry." Then she burst into tears.

FIVE

Jules stared at Korinna for long moments, her face holding the same stunned expression it had been holding since the witch had uttered the prophecy.

Korinna, seemingly unable to hold Jules' gaze, turned to Bas, lips trembling, tears spilling down her cheeks. "I'm so sorry. I never meant ... I wish ... I want—"

"Shh, my love," Tam said, reaching for her. "We know it's not your fault."

Korinna skittered back like an injured animal afraid of being hurt again. Trip felt terrible for his son-in-law – to have your mate skitter from you would cut deep – but he felt even worse for Korinna; that she was feeling so raw she couldn't stand to be touched by anyone. It took everything he had in him not to go to her and gather her up and take her away from here and the people she knew her words had hurt the most.

Ilia's arms tightened around him, helping him not to give in to that urge – for Korinna would not like such heavy-handed tactics now – or later when she was more herself.

Tam blanched, but he softened his voice and tried again. "Korinna. The prophecy you spoke ... nobody blames you for it."

"No. Nobody blames you," Trip agreed.

"They are not your words," Ilia said.

Bas and Jules stood there, rather like Lot's wife – except rather than statues of crumbling salt, they were crumbling emotionally as understanding hit them.

Obviously unaware of what was happening to his parents, Tam glanced back at them. "Mum. Dad. Tell her it's not her fault. That nobody blames her."

Bas shook his head slowly, realisation so patently a living beast tearing at his expression of shock until there was nothing but raw, naked pain. Trip thought the cupid was about to completely crumble but he glanced at his wife, then back to his son and daughter-in-law, and visibly pulled himself, if not together, then something closer to that state of being.

"Dad," Tam implored.

Bas blinked then said, "I ... no. Korinna. We know you didn't ... we know ... you have no control ... over what you said."

Tam nodded. "See." But Korinna's gaze was glued to Jules' ever-paling face, as if she'd heard nothing of what anyone else had said, if all that was going on in the world for her was with the Goddess-touched witch – Dawn's mother. Tam's gaze flickered between his mate and his mother and then he said imploringly, his voice breaking, "Mum. Jules. Please tell her she's not to blame for what she said."

For a long moment it looked like Jules wouldn't – couldn't – say anything, her entire body trembling so much. But then her jaw opened and words came out of her mouth, so soft at first, Trip couldn't hear them, but slowly becoming louder and louder.

"What she said?" Jules said, her voice coming as if from far away. "What she said! What she said!" Her voice became louder, more present, rising in hysteria as she repeated those three words over and over until suddenly, hands clutching her shaking head, her dark auburn hair lit from behind like some kind of wild halo, she shouted, "No. No. No! Take it back. TAKE IT BACK!"

Her yell rang through the room, followed by a horrible silence.

That silence was so thick, so heavy, that all any of them could do was stand there dumbly and stare between the two women.

The silence was finally broken by Korinna's sob. Then slowly rising to her feet, hands out, placating, she whispered harshly, "I-I can't. I'm so sorry, Jules. I wish I could. But, but it doesn't work like that. Y-you know it doesn't work like that."

Something cruel and hate-filled crossed Jule's face and she spat, "Since when do you have the Sight? How can I believe that this one, horrible thing you've just uttered is even a proper prophecy? How do we know it's not Perses getting to you – he has got to you before, right? Through your dad and then through you."

"He hasn't ... h-he didn't," Korinna stammered.

Trip moved to stand between the two women so Jules' gaze was now pinned on him. "He never got to us. I gave up my memory to ensure that never happened."

"But she said it did." Jules pointed an accusatory finger at Ilia.

"In the future. One possible future that Loki showed us," Ilia choked out, obviously as shocked as he was by

Jules' attack on Korinna, who she loved and cherished as a friend and member of her family.

"But it happens. It's going to happen. That's what all this worry is about, right? That Perses will use both of you to break into this Realm, destroy the pantheons and take over all the Realms. How do we know that this isn't the start of that? That he is trying to create strife between us by taking her over and giving her this prophecy?"

"Because he can't do that," Bas said, breaking out of the stupor his mate's words had sent him back into. "Forcing prophecy is not one of his powers."

"You can't know that," she snapped at her mate.

"But I do. His powers – all greater Beings powers: Gods, Goddesses, Titans, demi-Gods and -Goddesses – are recorded in the Eternal Well in the Hall of Records. The only ones whose powers haven't been recorded there are our daughter, our son and his mate."

The cupid was right. For if the truth of any of their powers had been inscribed there, some God or other would have come after them all soon after birth.

Bas continued. "Whether that's because Demeter did something as Trip thinks she did for him and Korinna – although, as far as I can tell, Demeter has never outright confirmed that?" He looked to Trip quickly, waiting long enough for his nod, then back to his wife. "Or because of something about their powers that makes them different from all other greater Beings and therefore not susceptible to the normal rules that keep the rest of us accountable in some way ..." He shrugged. "I cannot say. But that fact has boded well for us so far as it reveals things about Perses and the powers he controls. He is a God of Destruction. There is no nuance to his power. He doesn't and never has, controlled the power of prophecy."

"But his daughter, Hecate ... She's the mother of all witches and is said to have Sight as well. He could have manipulated her—"

"No. Hecate hates her father even more than Zeus and Hades and the other children of the Titans do. Her father killed her most beloved siblings. She would have nothing to do with Perses and his plans, no matter what enticements he offered. Besides, she went into hiding centuries ago – which is why the magics of many witches who worship her and rely on her power have been slowly on the decline. Their Goddess has withdrawn from them. Either because her power is waning or she is just going the way of many of their kind, becoming too other and separate from the world and the humans all the Gods and Goddesses once loved to rule over."

"I ... just ... but ... this can't be true." Jules' eyes – they'd been so dry and red it hurt to look at them – suddenly filled with tears that spilled down her face in a flood, wetting her pyjama top. "It can't be true. Not about our Dawn. They'll come for her. And we can't protect her. We don't have enough power to protect her. Not from all of them."

"I know. I know. Shh. Shh," Bas said, pulling his mate into his arms.

She sobbed into his chest, but they all heard her as she said, "But she's never told a prophecy before. Why now? Why this one?"

"I ... I have had them before," Korinna said in a quiet voice that nevertheless cut through Jules' sobs.

Jules turned her face at the same time Bas did, both of them saying, "What?" Then Bas looked around the rest of the room. "Did you any of you know about this?"

Tam shook his head. "She's had knowings but ... nothing like this."

Trip nodded gravely. "I knew it could happen when her powers manifested properly, but given it hadn't happened so far after I came back I thought ... I had hoped ..." He sighed as Bas pinned him with a stare. "This was the first one she's had that I know about."

"I heard Demeter and Persephone talk about it with each other – about how Korinna had the Sight," Ilia said. "When I was trapped in the HeartsBlood Gem."

"And you never said anything?" Jules said, her voice a whip.

Ilia shrugged but didn't drop Jules' accusing stare. "There was nothing to say. At least, I didn't think there was. They said that she could never be allowed to hone this talent and become a true Seer. That they were taking steps to stop her from using it again."

Korinna sucked in a breath, the sound a sharp gasp. "They always said that despite having some visions a half a dozen times over the years when my powers truly started to come in, that I was too weak to ever be a Seer and that my time was better spent honing the talents that were strong, not weak and haphazard at best." Her face bent into lines of anger. "They lied to me! If I'd known the truth, I could have prepared better, been able to do something, shape the vision more, get more answers."

Trip gently moved out of Ilia's hug and crossed to his daughter, hands going to her shoulders. "No, you couldn't. They couldn't let you. This was one of the reasons I had to leave before you were born. Without my power to activate yours, your true Sight would never come in. Not until you were old enough and strong enough to have full control of all your powers. So, they did not truly lie to you, because what you had back then was not anything like what you have now – it was weak. And they definitely needed to discourage it. Because your prophecies can be tracked, no matter how weak and insignificant, which means *you* can be tracked and monitored and classified. And that was the last thing we could have happen. Not only to stop Perses from finding you through his minions and using you as he once tried to do, but to stop the pantheons from coming after you."

"Like they'll now come after Dawn."

"Yes. I'm so sorry." His glance went around the room, meeting all the heated, pained gazes that were now pinned on him and his daughter – all except Ilia's, whose gaze was filled with empathy and love for him and Korinna. He took courage from that as he said, "And as they will now come after Korinna too because this has happened."

"But ..." Jules started, desperation in her eyes as she looked from one to the other, finally landing on Trip. "The Gods will take Dawn. Like they took Tamuel."

"Eros took Tamuel to save him," Bas said.

"He bound him with a curse and wouldn't set him free of his duties until recently for some unknown reason. For all intents and purposes, Tamuel was owned by Eros, cursed and tortured by being forced to be only half of who he was born to be. What part of that was saving him?"

She wrapped her arms around herself, fingers clenched at her sides as if she was trying to stop herself from falling apart. "And this is a thousand times worse. It won't only be Eros who is interested in our daughter. They will fight over her and then whoever wins will bind her to them. And I will never see her again. I can't ... I don't—"

"Jules," Korinna said as she stumbled forward to grasp her friend's hand. "It's not just ... They won't just ..." She broke down then, unable to speak.

Tam came up behind her and folded his mate into his

arms. He tried to talk, but all he could do was open his mouth and close it, nothing but a harsh wheezing sound coming out – because he obviously knew what Jules had not yet realised.

Trip was having problems talking too. He couldn't believe this was happening … that Jules and Bas had to go through what he'd gone through – and probably worse. Because he'd had Demeter and those working with her – including his other mothers, Persephone and Gaia – hiding the truth of him and his child from all the other greater Beings.

Except Perses. Somehow he had known. Trip wish he knew how, wished it because he didn't want Perses knowing this about Dawn as well because of the horrible consequences of that on Dawn and her family.

He wished he could hide all of this from Jules and Bas. To save them the grief he and Korinna had both suffered through. But he couldn't. They had to know. They had to be told. Hiding from the truth of what was coming would only hinder any plans they tried to make to save Dawn.

He was about to try to say something past the huge lump wedged in his throat, when Ilia said slowly and clearly, "Jules, I'm so sorry to have to tell you this, but you have to know the truth. The prophecy … it intimates Dawn is a God Killer, like my mate and his daughter are. And the pantheons, once they know, they won't simply try to take Dawn and find ways to manipulate her and use their powers for themselves, like Eros did to Tam, and was done to me and you. They will try to kill her. And failing that, they will banish her to the Void and into the Beyond where there is a place of nightmares called the Nowhere."

CHAPTER

SIX

"No," Jules said. "No. They can't do that. They can't kill my daughter or banish her. She's Goddess blessed. It's against the laws of the Eternal Well. They wouldn't. They couldn't."

Trip saved Ilia from responding, his voice kind even though the words were harsh. "I'm sorry, but they can. If she's a danger to them, they will."

"No. No." Jules' legs went from under her – Bas and Korinna caught her, holding her up as she wailed.

"Jules. My love. I'm here. I'm here." Bas enfolded her in his arms, hand stroking her hair and down her back, face exquisitely calm despite the terror shouting from his eyes.

Finally, after what seemed like forever, Jules stilled, took a deep, shuddering breath and shifted to look up at Bas. Her expression desolate, pleading, she said, "I can't lose her. I just can't lose her. We have to stop them. Stop them from knowing. There has to be a way." She turned to face Trip. "Please. There has to be a way. Oh they can't ... they can't kill my daughter. Or banish her. They can't. They can't."

As the rest of them rushed to help Bas comfort Jules, Ilia stayed in place, unable to move as a knowing shivered over her skin. The knowing sank in to her, filling her and everything she was until there was nothing else but the words that suddenly burst from her. "They don't know."

Nobody noticed she'd spoken. They were too busy ushering Jules across the kitchen, lowering her to a chair while she lost herself to uncharacteristic hysterics.

Ilia said the words again, louder this time, with an edge of her magic lighting them up – how or why, she didn't know – speaking the words again once, twice, thrice, turning her knowing into a spell that pushed all other sound from the room until her words were all there was.

The others were now staring at her – even Jules. For a moment, nobody said a word, then they began to talk at once. Unfortunately, because of the nature of the spell she'd inadvertently used alongside her knowing, the only voice that made it through was her soulmate's – not surprising given his power and the strange nature of it that could often undo other magics with nothing but the slightest of pushes.

"You mean the pantheons don't know yet because my shield is protecting us for now."

"No, it's more than that. They won't know even when your shield fails."

That information took one second to sink in before they started shouting questions at her again – their voices still silent.

Trip held his hand up and they all stopped. His brow furrowed into deep lines of confusion, he said, "But ... that's impossible. The prophecy ... all prophecies ... once uttered, get written down in the Hall of Prophecy, there to be read by any member of any pantheon whenever they wish. And any greater prophecy, like this one was, not only gets written there, but gets sent to them all by inter-dimensional dove. Which, along with my slowly disintegrating shield, is our only saving grace at this point – that they still use that outdated system of communication. It will take a few days at least, a week if we're lucky, for the news to get around and for them to band together and come for her."

Ilia shook her head – had been shaking her head from the moment he'd started speaking. "No. Not for this. Not with Korinna's prophecies."

Tam appeared before her, his mouth moving and no sound coming out.

"Oh, shit. Sorry." She closed her eyes and concentrated, saying, "I will my spell of silence to be undone," three times. There was a pop and she opened her eyes and said, "You should be able to talk now."

Tam nodded his thanks and said, "What you just said … it's … unheard of."

"Is it?" She tipped her head, gesturing at her mate and his daughter. "Demeter managed to hide Cassandra's prophecy about Trip and Korinna."

"But that's different," Trip said. "It's one of her gifts."

"Besides," Tam pointed out, "Demeter's not here and she's not answering any of our calls – and neither is Loki. And even if we found her now, it would be too late. Because one of us would have to leave to do so, which means Trip has to bring down his shield. The moment he does that, Rinna's prophecy will wing its way to the Hall of Prophecy."

"And once it's released," Trip said, "there is no way to intercept it unless it's blocked at its place of origin, within the space of a breath after it's uttered with a very particular spell only Demeter is capable of wielding."

"She acted that quickly for Cassandra's prophecy?" Korinna asked as she came to Tam's side.

Trip nodded. "She recognised as it was being spoken what it meant and acted without thinking."

"That's lucky," Tam said, his arm tightening around Korinna's shoulders.

Trip screwed his mouth to the side. "It's been both a blessing and a curse, because while her action saved us, without knowledge of that prophecy, the leaders of the pantheons refuse to believe her about the return of a Titan. Which leaves us at a big disadvantage in trying to stop Perses."

Silence greeted his words.

Silence that was broken by Jules' tearful whisper. "They can't take her."

Bas wrapped his arms around her, trying to be stoic, but his face gave him away. He was obviously moments away from falling apart like his soulmate.

"So, we can't do what Demeter did and block the prophecy from being inscribed into the Hall?" Tam asked.

"It's too late even if I knew how," Trip said sorrowfully.

"We don't need to know," Ilia said, the knowing growing inside her, giving her more knowledge as they spoke. "We don't need Demeter."

"But—"

"No." She put her hand over her soulmate's mouth. "You are not hearing me. The prophecy will not be inscribed in the Hall *because* Korinna spoke it."

Everyone shared a glance, the tension so tight between them Ilia was surprised it wasn't playing a tune. Eyes pools of aching hope, Korinna turned to her and asked, "Are you saying I already blocked the prophecy from going to the Hall?"

Ilia tipped her head to the side as she waited for the answer in the knowing that was whispers in her mind. "In a manner of speaking – although, you don't truly block anything. They just simply don't get written into the Hall and therefore aren't sent to the pantheons by dove or any other means. Your Sight … it's … shielded? … from the normal processes prophecies must adhere to. Because of your father's unique heritage. The only way one of the Gods or Goddesses from any of the pantheons could know about your prophecies is if they were in the room with us and heard it themselves."

"That's … incredible," Bas said as Jules lifted her head from his chest, eyes beginning to fill with hope. "Are you sure?"

"Yes." More whispers had her lifting her hand again to silence their questions until she'd got a sense of the words the knowing was trying to impart. Then slowly she said, "And even if they were in the room with us, I'm not sure they would be able to retain the information." She began to smile, the knowing giving them the first good news since Korinna had fallen into her Sight. Her gaze met Korinna's stunned one. "I always knew you were special. This is even more proof of that. Like father, like daughter, right?"

"I … I …" Korinna shook her head like a wet dog, letting go of Tam to press her knuckles into her temples. 'This is … my head hurts."

"Korinna? Are you okay?"

She looked up at her mate, eyes sparkling, then snorted – the sound a tad hysterical. "Am I okay? Am I okay? If Ilia is right, and I'm as extra special as she says, then Dawn is safe. Bloody right I'm okay. I'm better than okay. I'm ecstatic." She pumped her fist in the air and then burst into tears. "I haven't killed baby Dawn. I haven't killed her."

"You never killed her," Tam said gently, cupping her face and swiping at her tears with his thumbs. "The prophecies aren't your words."

"But I utter them. I uttered this. I doomed her." Her eyes moved in a way that indicated she wasn't seeing Tam even though she was looking up at him – that she was searching for answers in all this madness.

Ilia wasn't certain there were any to be had right now. Not beyond what she'd already said. The knowing had gone as fast as it had come and she had no more answers to give. "She isn't doomed," she said softly as she moved to Korinna's side. "Your uniqueness saved her. If you didn't speak the words of that prophecy, someone else would have. That's how prophecies work, right? The Eternal Well or whatever sends them through someone with the Sight. We're lucky that someone was you."

Korinna sniffed and managed a wobbly smile. "Freak-show for the win!"

"You are not a freak-show," Tam and Trip said together.

"Jinks," Korinna said, a giggle bubbling up in her.

"Jinks doesn't works unless you're one of the people who talked at the same time," Tam said, chuckling with her.

"You're right," she said, before losing herself in another burst of giggles.

"Rinna," Tam said, turning her towards him. "Are you okay?"

She scrubbed at her face, the giggles finally dying away, then took a deep breath. "I'm fine."

"You sure?" Tam and Trip asked together again.

She chuckled – they all chuckled, and then the chuckle became a laugh that went on and on and on until the insane pressure finally released.

It took a while, but finally the laughter died and they set to putting all the furniture in the kitchen back to where it belonged. Then, slumping into the chairs around the table, still wiping away laughter-tears and breathing deeply, they smiled at each other.

"I needed that," Jules said.

"I think we all needed that," Trip agreed.

All eyes moved to Ilia. She sat back in her seat and folded her arms as she met the stares. "What?"

"I've got questions," Korinna said softly.

"I've got questions too," Tam said, sitting forward, hands clasped on the table in front of him.

Of course they did. Ilia also had questions. Not that she was likely to get any answers right now – her powers and her knowings didn't seem to work like that. But she didn't admit it, not wanting to spoil the mood in the room after the horrible tension. "I'll answer if I can."

"Okay." Tam nodded his head, gaze darting to Korinna, then to his parents, over to Trip then back to Korinna. "So, I suppose the first one is – why are Korinna's prophecies different? What about Trip's heritage makes her powers work so differently? It's not dangerous, is it?"

Ilia smiled. She could answer that one – not because the knowing had left any specific information regarding that, but because ... she just felt it. "No. Not to her at least."

"Is it dangerous to us?" Jules asked, her gaze going to the ceiling towards where her daughter lay asleep.

"No. This difference will protect all of us from getting caught up in any God-related fall-out. They won't get a heads-up on things they might deem dangerous to them unless we choose to tell them. Which we won't. Because that would put Korinna in danger if they knew she was speaking prophecies they didn't know about."

"That's good." Jules reached across Tam to clutch Korinna's hand in hers. "I'm sorry for what I said before. I didn't mean it."

Korinna squeezed her hand back. "I know. It's fine."

"Thank you," Jules said.

"You never have to thank me. Especially when I am the one spouting what could put Dawn in danger."

Tam's eyes darted to Ilia. "But she's not in danger now, right?" Ilia nodded. "Great. Good. But ... going back to the prophecy and why it was different. I didn't realise until now but ... she uttered it like a spell. I'm not an expert on prophecies, but that's not usual."

Bas pointed a finger at him. "Good point. Maybe the Hall doesn't recognise it as a prophecy said in that way."

Ilia shrugged. "I think the reason it can't be shared or used in the way other powers can has more to do with the fact she's Trip's daughter."

"You're certain?" Tam asked.

"No." She raised her hands and dropped them. "My knowing didn't give me all the details, so I can't say for certain. All I know is, nobody else needs to know outside those of us who are in this room. It helped that Trip acted so quickly and threw a shield up so nobody could listen in, but I don't even think that's necessary. Because whatever difference is inside Korinna that makes her foretelling private, nobody aside from those she uttered the prophecy to can hear it. And right now, that's us."

"Are you sure about that?" Jules whispered, desperate hope threaded through the sound. "I mean, you're not sure about why her prophecies are different. What makes you so sure about this part?" She waved her hand. "I'm sorry, it's not that I don't trust you, it's just—"

Ilia grabbed her trembling hand, lowering it to the table. "I know. It's just ... hard to trust such an impossible thing. Especially when it comes from such an ... improbable source."

"You're not improbable," Trip said, leaning in kiss her temple. "We trust you. We all trust you."

"With our lives," Tam said.

The others nodded in agreement. She smiled, the glow of their trust sunshine in her heart. Blowing out a shaky breath, she said, "I can't tell you exactly how I know, only assure you that I do know it. The longer it sits with me, the more I am certain that what I have said is true. I am as certain of it as I am that Trip is my soulmate." A quick glance his way, a meeting of eyes, of hearts, of trust that filled her with a warmth she thought never to be hers. Then she returned her attention to Jules and said, "I promise, if we don't tell anyone else, nobody will know what Korinna just uttered."

"Thank the Well," Jules said on a rush of breath, tears of joy glistening in her eyes. "And thank you."

Ilia shrugged, uncomfortable with the rush of emotion inside her that came with Jules' words. "I did nothing but speak a truth."

"A truth that shows just how strange I am," Korinna said, then let out a laugh. "I don't think I've ever been so thankful to be different."

Ilia was aware just how much Korinna had struggled with her powers and their difference; what that had cost her and all the lives of those who'd once lived in Pompeii.

"Is there anyone in this room who can claim a relationship with normalcy," Bas asked, chuckling softly.

"Nope," Tam said, brow rising as he met his mate's gaze. "V*ive la différence*! We should celebrate!"

Ilia chuckled at Tam's nonsense. "Yes. Anything that keeps Dawn safe is to be celebrated."

"She's right," Jules said, shooting up from her seat to hug Korinna. "Thank the Eternal Well for you and your differences. Thank you. Thank you."

As they cried and laughed over this strange news – the first seriously good news they'd had for months – Ilia shifted in her seat.

She wished she could join them in their celebration – it truly was news worthy of celebration, that Dawn wasn't immediately in danger. But the fact was, the knowing only gave her so much ... and Dawn was still in danger. She was in danger from the coming menace of Perses. She was also in danger of the truth that she was a God Killer being exposed in some other way to the pantheons. And if that happened while they were trying to fight Perses, it would mean disaster and ruin. Because they couldn't fight against a Titan on one front and the pantheons on the other.

Without warning, her power surged inside her, rising to the surface like buzzing bees in her nerves and spitting snakes writhing just under her skin. She shoved her hands under the table and clenched them in her lap, fearful it might start to spark out of her fingertips. Her heart began to race. Her breath was hot in her lungs. She struggled to keep it even and calm, not wanting to alert anyone else to the problem.

Trip knew though. He always knew. He pushed back from his chair, stood, and held out his hand.

Without question, she took it and stood, then let him lead her to the back door that led to the patio. He closed the door quietly behind him as Ilia crossed the patio and walked down the three steps onto the lawn. Knowing her like he did, he didn't say anything, didn't move, just waited while she collected herself.

She'd learned in her past life, when she'd been a human witch, to close her eyes and sink into herself when she wanted to recentre the miniscule amount of power she'd had. But after trying over and over to use those calming techniques as she'd once done – to no avail – Trip had suggested something else.

He'd noticed she always calmed under the light of the moon. When they'd left the curtains open at night and the moonlight spilled across their bed, she never had one of her nightmares or an uncontrolled burst of power in her sleep. And the next day, her power was always more settled, more easily controlled so that she actually got something out of the lessons Violetta was giving to Jules and her.

The sky was heavy with clouds tonight – the tang in the air suggestive of a thunderstorm looming – but that didn't matter. There was always somewhere in the Stevens' garden she could find a patch of moonlight to stand in. It was almost like the moon loved this house a little bit more than others.

The whimsical thought made a smile hitch on her face. It wasn't like her to think such nonsense – life had taught her too well that fantasy was not reality, no matter how much you wished for it – but still, it felt true in some way. And maybe it was – because the moon had played a large role in every moment where the Stevens and their loved ones had won the day over some evil.

It had certainly played a major part in her resurrection, and was high and full in the sky when Trip and she came together.

Had its mysterious power helped them that night too more than she'd realised?

Could it help them again?

Hmm. A thought to put away to look at in more depth later. For now, she just needed to find the moonlight and stand in it; let it calm her and fill her with light, cleansing the darkness that still haunted her soul.

Just as she crossed the lawn to a patch she could see shining brightly at the back fence, a cloud moved and a shaft of moonlight lit the air around her.

She stilled, shivering delightfully in the silvery play of it across her face. She tipped her head, face to the sky, turning in a circle, arms wide.

But it wasn't enough. It only touched her face and neck. She needed more contact.

She peeled off her clothing until she stood sky-clad under the light of the moon. Then slowly, she turned, lifting her hands up in benediction as the moonlight played on her skin, lighting her up silvery-white in the dark.

SEVEN

Trip stood, still and quiet, as his love, his soulmate, filled herself with the moon's light. She glowed – and not just because her pale skin lit up in the silvery light, but because there was something about Ilia and moonlight that ... worked. In a way he'd never seen with other witches before. She belonged to the moonlight and it belonged to her. To the point where she almost disappeared within its glow when she communed like this with it.

It had frightened the crap out of him the first time he'd witnessed it, even though it had been his suggestion she try it. But he hadn't expected her to glow like that until she was as bright as the moon itself, her form appearing as translucent as the light. But after racing to her, he'd found her as corporeal as she always was – just cooler to touch and much calmer, yet very confused by his reaction.

For her, what had happened had been wonderful. Rejuvenating in a way nothing else was. Not even their blood sharing gave her the utter peace he'd felt in her, seen on her face, when he'd pulled her out of the moonlight that night.

After that, he'd never interrupted her communion with the moon again. He'd tried to encourage her to commune whenever she seemed stressed – strangely, even on overcast nights there always seemed to be moonlight when she walked into the garden. But she didn't like to do it too often because she didn't want to *need* it. Like she was afraid of becoming addicted to it.

Perhaps that was a thing – they were both addicted to their blood sharing after all. Although that had as much to do with love and connection and the sharing of their powers through their soul-bond as the fact it had saved both their lives and possibly was essential to Ilia continuing to be alive. Not that he would ever test that theory by denying her his blood. Hers nourished him in ways he couldn't explain either.

Given that need – that addiction – he could understand why she wouldn't want to rely on anything else to help her through difficulties with her emotions or powers.

She was stubbornly self-sufficient, so used to relying on herself and nothing else, that she didn't even want to trust that maybe the moonlight was not an addiction, but was like food or drink. That she needed it for the purest form of nourishment.

If he didn't know better, he would say she was a Moon Goddess – because no other being ever responded to the moon quite like a God or Goddess whose life-blood was attached to that orb in the sky. But to suggest she had somehow morphed into a new kind of Goddess ... he shook his head. To even suggest such a thing would upset her more than anything else ever could, so he didn't mention it. She was born of humans, gifted powers of healing by some whim of Hecate, probably when she was a child, then having lost her body to an evil that trapped her soul in a magical gem, she was brought back to life by Tam and Korinna and Dawn, and the beneficence of Ostara, in the light of the full moon on Oestra and had been gifted with powers they had no full understanding of yet.

His eyes widened as he realised the fact of her rebirth was possibly why she was more attuned to the moon than the dawn. Even though she'd been given corporeal form with the power of the Goddess of Dawn, it had been done under the power of a full moon.

She was a child of the moon!

Needing the moon's light to feed on as a babe fed on its mother's teat for nourishment.

Of course, like with his suspicions about her being a Moon Goddess, he wasn't about to say anything of the sort to Ilia. Anything that might put her hackles up – and she still had plenty. Not surprising after what had been done to her – was something to avoid as much as possible. And to suggest that she used moon-based power in a way that a normal witch or wiccan didn't and couldn't, would definitely make her hackles rise. It was fine to think she was gathering power or help like the Stevens witches might, but to think it was something more? Something different? Not a good idea. At least not now while they faced the problems they faced.

So he watched over her every time she 'communed with the moon' as she liked to call it and kept his mouth well and truly shut.

~

ONCE ILIA WAS sky-clad and standing in a full beam of the glorious silver light, it didn't take long for her power to settle and stop feeling like buzzing bees and spitting snakes inside her.

She sighed, glorying in the contentment and fulfilment that settled over her. It felt so good that she stood there longer than she needed and continued to soak it in even though Trip waited for her. It wasn't until a cool breeze rustled through the night, whispering across her skin, bringing goosebumps with it, that she finally moved to where she'd dropped her pyjamas and started to dress. Then turning to Trip, a smile on her face, she held out her hands to him.

He came to her as he always did, with such a look of adoration in his eyes that it warmed the chill from her skin.

"Feeling better?"

"You know I am," she said, slipping her arms around his waist, pressing her breasts against the hard muscle of him, and lifted her head for a kiss.

And boy, did he deliver. It began as a gentle caress over her lips as he brushed his mouth back and forth, teasing with a nip there, followed by a lick to take away the wonderful sting. Then when she could stand no more, her hands went to his arse, pulling him close so she could feel all of him against all of her, and whispered, "You're playing with fire."

"I love to be burned."

Then he opened to her as she opened to him and it was ... magic. Pure magic. His scent – like pine and a spring rain – wove around her, drugging her with warmth as his taste sank into her, making her endorphins fizz and her feel a little giddy, like she did after drinking a fine single malt scotch. Except better. Far better.

"What are you smiling about?" he asked against her

neck as he kissed his way down to suckle on the sensitive spot there that made her squirm – in all the right ways.

"You. Us. This."

"Good."

Then he proceeded to lick and kiss his way down between her breasts, somehow managing to undo the buttons of her pyjama top, one at a time, as he went.

"I've only just got dressed," she said, laughing in protest – a very weak protest, given her hands were in his hair, encouraging him in his endeavours.

His hands skimmed under the open fronts of her top, knuckles brushing over her nipples. She gasped.

He smiled up at her as he cupped her breasts, teasing them with his fingers, then bent to continue kissing and licking and nipping down her front. Finally, on his knees before her, he slipped her pyjama bottoms down and nuzzled his nose and mouth at the apex of her legs. 'Smells so sweet."

He breathed her in as he widened her with his fingers then licked.

Oh holy fucking Hells! She bucked and shuddered, her fingers curling in his hair tight. He licked again, his hands slipping around to cup the globes of her bottom, holding her tight against him – as if she could let him go.

"Trip," she managed to squeeze out of lungs that felt desperate for a breath.

He lifted his head, his eyes glittering in the moonlight – a sexy light green – his lips curved in satisfaction like he was the cat who'd just got the cream.

And he was. He most certainly was. Especially if he kept going. He'd have all the cream he could want.

As if he could read her thoughts, he waggled his eyebrows at her and said, "Okay," then proceeded to lick and suck and tease her until she was a quivering mass unable to stand under her own volition.

It was only after the waves of orgasm passed that she realised he'd lowered her to the grass, his shirt and jeans under her as protection.

She looked up at him as he hovered above her – all sculpted muscle and tousled hair – noting the way he trembled as he waited for her to come back to him. The moment their eyes locked, he moved, taking her in the way only Trip could ever take her – as if he needed her more than breath; as if she filled every part of him that had been empty until they'd met.

It wasn't a taking. It was a giving. And she gave back in equal measure.

She wrapped her legs around his hips, lifting so he could press deeper, pulling at his hips to make him go harder, faster, while lifting her head to give him a kiss full of tongue and teeth; of longing; of love.

And together, under the moonlight, they rose, driving each other to a pinnacle of release and relief.

Just before they fell over the edge, her fangs pressed into her mouth as they always did. She threw her head back, shouting as the orgasm took her – took him. Then she sank her teeth into his neck as he sank his into hers, and drank.

She drank until the stars collided in her head and all she could do was fall, fall, fall.

It was only much later when she came to, spent and more relaxed than she'd felt since he'd left with Bas and Tam to search for Loki, that she remembered the conversation she'd had with Jules and Korinna.

Slapping her head she moaned.

"What is it?" Trip said, moving back enough so he could look down at her face. "Was I too rough?"

"No. You were perfect – as always. Just beautiful. It's ..." She grimaced, relieved the moonlight had gone – clouds covering up the moon's glory – so that he couldn't see just how embarrassed she was. She wished she didn't have to tell him, but she did.

He needed to know.

So, taking a deep breath, she did.

It took Trip a while to get over his shock at what Ilia told him but when he did, he agreed with her that it was probably part of the power she'd got from Ostara when she was created. "You will be able to control it, but maybe until you do, we should find somewhere else to live."

She was relieved he thought that but at the same time ... "We can't go far."

He nodded. "We need to be close to work on the threat of Perses with everyone."

"And also because you have only just found your daughter. I will not be the cause of tearing you apart. Certainly not given how much you will both need each other in the coming fight."

"We also need to stay close to help protect Dawn." He brushed hair from her brow. "You are not the only one who loves that little girl with all of your heart."

She smiled up at him, struggling to hide her tears. He brushed wetness from the corner of her eye then kissed her softly. "Let's go to our room."

"Not to make love!" she said, holding up a stern finger as she pulled on her clothes.

"No. Not until we are truly alone."

They slipped inside and tiptoed up the stairs to their

room, placing pillows down the middle of the bed so they couldn't touch before hopping in to bed.

Ilia lay awake for the rest of the night, too energised – and embarrassed – to sleep. She was pretty certain Trip hadn't got a wink either – he never lay on his back like that, nor was he ever so still.

Finally, when the sun's rays began to light the bedroom, and the unmistakable noise of people in the kitchen rose through the house, they both rolled over to face each other.

"Morning," Trip said, leaning over the pillow-barrier to give her a brief kiss.

"None of that," she said, quickly pushing him back to his side before her hormones could get carried away.

"Of course."

She rolled onto her back and stared up at the ceiling. "I don't want to get out of bed and go down there."

"I'm not a huge fan of the idea either," he said, sighing heavily too. "But sticking our heads in the sand isn't going to help us face it later. Might as well rip the Band-Aid off."

"Good work with the mixed metaphors," she said. "I barely understood any of that."

He barked out a laugh then sighed again and flopped onto his back, his hand reaching for hers. She let him take it, even though the usual sparks and warmth fizzed through her at his touch. She could control herself. She *could*.

She rolled her head so she could see his profile. "We better just get up then."

"Yes."

She practically leapt out of the bed as he moved off his side, trying very hard not to look at the naked glory of him as he went about getting dressed.

Why-oh-why did he have to sleep in the nude? Normally she was a fan – a very big fan – but this morning

… it was just cruel. "Maybe," she said, turning to him as she tugged a t-shirt over her head, "when we feel the need coming on, we could teleport to the farm?" Her head popped out of the t-shirt and she was relieved to see he had dressed faster than her and had jeans and a t-shirt on and was ferreting around in his chest of draws. "Daphne and the boys are too far away from the farmhouse for it to affect them, right?"

Trip shrugged then turned, a roll of freshly washed socks in his hand. "I think so. I'm not sure what the range is of this Ostara gift of reproductive encouragement."

She snorted at his tame way of describing the 'gift'. 'Maybe we'll find out when we go down there."

"What do you mean?" He sat on the bed to pull on his socks and shoes as she did the same.

"Well, we've never made love outside like that before. They've always been in the same house as us. So … maybe they didn't feel anything at all."

"By the Well, I hope so," he groaned.

She turned to share a hopeful smile with him then stood and held out her hand. "Shall we?"

He rounded the bed and took her hand. "Let's beard the lion in its den."

She nodded approvingly. "Just one, simple metaphor. You're getting better at this."

He laughed and then bent to give her a quick, breath-stealing kiss before pulling back with a gasp and a horrified glance at the door. "Sorry."

"I don't think they can feel it when we kiss. Only when there's … you know …" Could her face be any redder?

"Are you sure?"

"As much as I can be given what Jules and Korinna told me. It's just the …" She wasn't a prude but saying the word out loud with just him in the room was intimate and likely to heat things up inside her even more. So she made a circle with the fingers of left hand and poked the middle finger of her other hand back and forth through it. Crude but effective and silly enough not to encourage those feelings just waiting under the surface to rampage through her and steal her of all control.

Trip nodded. "Right. Okay. Good."

This situation was none of those things, but she knew what he meant. Taking his hand in hers again, she pulled him to the door and said, "At least I can tell them if they did feel it that it was entirely your fault!"

"My fault? I'm not the one with the Ostara-gift."

"You're the one who sets it off in me."

"That's fair."

They opened the door and stepped into the hall.

Laughter rose from the kitchen below.

They grimaced at each other, and she knew Trip was hoping, as she was, that the happiness was a high from finding out Dawn was not going to be in danger from Korinna's prophecy, and not because of the other thing.

As they neared the kitchen, Tam's voice rang out. "I think Demeter and Persephone do know about this, Rinna."

"How can you say that?"

"Well, it's kind of been their raison d'être," Jules said evenly before her voice became sing-songy and she said, "Eat your toast, honey ... But you liked jam yesterday." Followed by the sound of a plate hitting the floor.

"Dawn! We do not throw food around in this house." Bas' voice was stern.

Then clear as day, Ilia heard a childish voice in her head say, "Vegemite. I want Vegemite."

"Did you hear that?"

Trip nodded. "Not with my ears though."

She shot Trip a worried glance. "She's getting stronger."

The sound of Dawn's voice in their heads increased as she flew into a full-on toddler tantrum. They could hear Jules and Bas, and Tam and Korinna, trying to placate her, but it seemed to be doing no good, even when Jules said, "I'm getting you Vegemite toast, honey. Just calm down. Please."

Ilia rushed in with Trip right behind her to see Dawn screwing her face up and banging her fists against her high-chair tray while her feet slammed against the foot rest. She was throwing herself around, fully lost in her tantrum. The screams in Ilia's head – full of Dawn's frustration and anger – were painful in their intensity.

As it seemed they were to the others in the room.

Jules was at the toaster, one hand to her head as she waited for the toast to pop up. "The toast is coming, honey. The toast is coming. Just calm down. Calm down for Mummy," she said, over and over. Korinna and Tam held hands, eyes closed, their other hands stretched out over Dawn, their magic a tingle in the air as they tried to weave a spell of calm over her.

They were having no luck. Dawn's tantrum seemed to repel their magic as if it was a shield.

Bas in the meantime was desperately trying to unstrap his daughter from the chair but was having no luck around the flailing arms and feet and the fact she was banging her body against the back of the chair over and over.

Not wanting to rush the baby and make her worse, Ilia drew close slowly.

"Do you see that?" Trip whispered in her ear.

She nodded. As she'd moved across the room and got a better look, it became clear that it wasn't the tantrum flailing that stopped Bas from unstrapping his child from her high-chair – it was the explosion of magic Dawn was generating with her tantrum. It seemed to be stopping all attempts to lay hands on her either magically or physically.

The chair tipped with the violence of Dawn's movements and Bas gave up trying to unstrap her and just held the chair steady as she threw herself about. At least she couldn't do any serious damage to herself given the high-chair was super cushioned.

Ilia took a second to take all this in, then rushed over to Dawn and clasped the child's red, tear-stained face in her hands. Unlike the others, she managed to get through the shield the tantrum had created without any problems.

At her cool touch, Dawn's eyes opened wide to meet hers.

Tear-stained and terrified.

CHAPTER

EIGHT

Of course she was terrified. It shouldn't be such a shock. The poor toddler had no idea what was happening to her. And she couldn't control it.

Dawn's screams in Ilia's mind no longer had words, but she was certain the baby was not in control. In the depths of her eyes, behind the layers of fear-laced anger, there was a plea: *Ilia, help me.*

Shit-fuck.

Ilia really had no idea what she was doing – she didn't have a clue why she was the one who could always calm Dawn down when she had one of her nightmares or one of the tantrums she'd been having more and more often of late – although, from the turmoil going on inside Dawn's head right now, she wondered if it was as simple as a tantrum. But that was a thought for another time.

And it didn't matter that she didn't know what she was doing or – truthfully – how to do it, she just closed her eyes, sank into her mind and pulled all the fear and frustration, anger and helplessness, from Dawn and into herself.

She sucked in a pained breath as it flooded into her –

there was so much more than there'd ever been before, even during one of the baby's worst night-terrors. It shuddered into Ilia, whipping at her mind, threatening to sink its claws into her and hold on.

Holy crapping fuck!

She wasn't sure she could do this.

Trip's hands were suddenly on her shoulders, his whisper in her ear, "Use me."

She shook her head. She didn't want to. Didn't want him to have to feel this. Nobody should ever have to feel this – especially not this beloved baby or the love of her life. So she held on, trying to make her mind as slippery as possible as the terrifying strength of Dawn's emotions tunnelled into her. Her jaw clamped together so hard under the onslaught she thought her teeth might crack.

"Ilia. Let me help."

She couldn't answer, there was too much inside her, too much to concentrate on if she was going to be able to swallow this whole and get through to the other side. But she felt like she was going to split open with the sheer force and violence of all that she was pulling into herself. Claws sliced deeper into her mind, no matter how slippery she made herself, and it wasn't going through her like it always had when she'd taken in Dawn's nightmares before this – the only way she'd discovered to help the baby.

Ilia had always thought of what she did as like eating then digesting, except it just disappeared rather than being expelled. Like she used up all the energy it gave her in her own cells. But each of those previous 'meals' had been small in comparison to what she was taking in now. This was a big meal. A feast. Something like the ancient Romans used to eat then purge so they could keep eating again. Yet, unlike them, there was no purging for her. It should just ...

go. But before it did, she had to take it in and she didn't think her body could digest all this as quickly as she needed to. If she had time, she might be able to take it in slowly. But there was no time. If she didn't take it all in now, the baby might not survive.

So she opened herself further, pulling more and more in, faster and faster. And as she did, it ripped and tore at her, making her bleed, making her see red ...

So much red.

So much anger. And violent rage. To be stuck in the body of this baby with no recourse other than to make her grow faster than usual but still too slow.

Too slow.

She wanted out. She wanted control. She wanted ...

Trip's fangs sank into her neck and he began to feed, meshing himself more deeply with her, taking on part of the burden. Ilia screamed her denial, tried to shut him out, to push him away with every ounce of power inside her — except, every bit of her power was being used to deal with what she was taking from Dawn. There was nothing else with which to fight him, to save him from this onslaught, this pain, these horrible emotions that only she knew were living inside of Dawn. Because she had never told any of the others that this is what she did to help Dawn. Never told them what the baby endured, what she endured. Had hidden the enormity of it from them because she didn't want them to stop her. Didn't want them to feel guilty for wanting her to continue either.

This was her choice. She did it willingly. But nobody was ever supposed to know, especially her soulmate.

Trip trembled against her with the enormity of what he was taking into himself — the oily, violent darkness of it, the otherness — but he held strong. For her, for Dawn. And through the blood-bond, he funnelled his astonishing power into her – power gained from his extraordinary birth. He was the Being brought forth by sheer love and need through the wills of three powerful Goddesses – Demeter, Persephone and Gaia. And with that singular power, he began to eat what she couldn't.

He pulled the clawing, terrifying emotions inside him, taking in some of the rabid beast that was part frustrated power, part Goddess energy – given to Dawn by Ostara during the baby's miraculous birth. He drank from Ilia and took in every bit that she couldn't handle until the baby fell still in her hands, her eyes shuddering closed as her body slumped in the high-chair.

Ilia pulled her hands back with a suddenness that made her stumble back against her mate – she didn't want to chance that any of the negative emotions might make their way back into the precious child.

Trip stopped feeding and his head snapped up the moment she let go.

"Dawn! Dawn, my poor baby." Jules almost knocked them aside in her panic to get to her unconscious child. "What happened? What did you do? Bas, is she all right?"

Before Ilia could reassure the worried mother, Trip grabbed her shoulders and spun her around to face him, eyes full of the dark horror of what they'd just taken into themselves.

"You shouldn't have done that," she said to him, her voice raw and edged with an echo of the horror writhing inside both of them.

"You do this every time?" She tried to break free of his grip, but he held her still. "Don't tell me this is how you calm her when she gets upset?"

"What? What is it?" Tamuel asked.

"What does she do?" Korinna asked at the same time.

"Ilia?" Tamuel's voice throbbed with questions, with worry.

She turned her head to see that Korinna and Tamuel had come up beside Trip and were staring at her. Out of the corner of her eye she could see Jules and Bas pulling their now sleeping daughter out of the high-chair to cradle the baby between them as they rocked and crooned.

"Ilia?" Trip's hands had slid from her shoulders and now he was pulling at her hands. "You don't do this every time?"

"What? What did she do?" Tamuel asked.

"She takes it in. She takes it all in."

"Takes what in?" Bas asked. "I saw something but I couldn't understand what it was."

Trip shook his head, but he didn't break her gaze. "That's because something like what she's been doing hasn't been done since ... well, since the war between the Gods and the Titans."

"By the Gods, what have you been doing?" Tam asked.

She shook her head, tearing her gaze from his. "I ... What I had to."

"Nobody expected this from you. Nobody here would have asked you to do this." Trip's hand tightened on hers and she couldn't look at him again, afraid of what she'd see there.

"But what has she been doing, Dad?"

Trip sighed, a sound filled with such pain and heaviness Ilia was surprised she was still standing with the weight of it in the room. "She takes in Dawn's darkest emotions. The rage and terror and frustration caused by the huge amount of power living inside a baby's body. But that—"

"The power Ostara gifted her?" Bas interrupted, frowning. "But why should that cause her any problems? Being gifted with Goddess powers never did any of that to Julianna when Vesta gifted them to her on her birth."

Trip shrugged. "I don't know why this is different, but the amount of power inside Dawn ... it is far more than I thought Ostara would ever give another being. This amount of power ... It was never meant to be held in something so small. It's has to be why she's growing fast to try to enable her to encompass it. But it's not fast enough for the enormity of it. This is why she's been having the night-terrors and increasing tantrums. The power is growing too fast inside her for her little body to handle. I should have recognised this was happening – something similar happened to me, forcing me to be born from the Earth almost as you see me now. But this ... she only has the power of one Goddess, not three, and I just didn't think that ... Maybe I would have if I had all my memories back. I would have seen—"

"Dad, you can't hold yourself accountable for the memories that haven't returned to you yet. You've been doing your best to get them all back."

"My best isn't good enough. Not when I miss something this ..." He shook his head.

"This what?" Bas asked.

"Horrific. You see, all of what is inside Dawn, all of what is trying to become more, thousands upon thousands of years of longing and grief and pain and everything else ... Ilia has been siphoning it out of her and taking it into herself."

Ilia blinked. It sounded so ... wrong ... when explained like that. "There's nothing wr—" Why was everyone staring at her like that? As if she was crazy? "I-I had to take it from her. To help her. To save her. It's not right that a baby or toddler should feel any of that. I'm an adult. I can take it."

"That's horrible," Jules said, her expression grateful as she met Ilia's gaze. "But thank you for doing it. For taking that from my precious baby. I don't know how to—"

Bas put his hand on Jules' arm, stopping her from going to Ilia. "No, don't touch her."

"Why not?"

"Because she didn't say anything about expelling it," Trip said, the heaviness in his voice becoming even heavier, more full of horror and pain. "By the Well, please tell me you've been expelling it, my love?"

"Expel it? What are you talking about? I'm taking nightmares. Images that frighten her. It's nothing ... nebulous. It's like eating something. I kind of just take it in and use it up but there's no roughage. Nothing to expel."

"Nothing to expel?" Korinna said, the horror she heard in Trip's voice dawning on her face.

What were they so horrified about? "I ... That's right."

"So ... you haven't been expelling it?" Tamuel asked.

"I just said, there's nothing to expel."

"Oh Hells. Ilia!" Korinna's voice was filled with a world of concern. "Dad – she has to expel it. Now. Or it will eat her alive. If Dawn can't take the power of the Goddess that was meant for her, then Ilia can't take it either."

"I know. I know."

"How has she survived this long if that's what she's been doing all these months?" Tam asked.

"I don't know. But I'm bloody-well going to find out."

"After we make her expel it. And you too, Dad. You can't keep it inside you either."

"I know."

"Stop talking around me as if I'm not here."

"But you don't understand."

"No, it's you who doesn't understand. I know it can be necessary to expel or purge when you've taken something inside you that isn't good for you, but this isn't that. It's caused me no problems so far. I'm sure it will be fine. As it's been fine before."

"It won't be fine." He fisted his hand against his chest. "All I know is what I feel. And what I feel is that this needs to be purged. And it needs to be purged now!"

"I'm sure you're wrong."

He shook his head. "I took some of it in so I know it does. Quite urgently. You have to be feeling it."

Yeah. She was feeling it. She always did. And it always went away. Except ... except this time, it wasn't. This time it was becoming more. Like the horrible feelings and images she'd taken from Dawn were multiplying inside her.

But surely that was just because they were all making such a fuss over nothing and scaring her? Images and feelings couldn't hurt you.

Could they?

Trip gripped her hands again and started pulling her towards the door. "Come on. We have to get down there. You have to purge this now."

"Purge what?" She had no idea why they were so panicked – she wasn't feeling great by any means, but it wasn't like she was about to fly apart either.

"The thing you took in. You have to feel it growing. I can feel it inside me and will have to purge it soon too."

"I still don't understand how she's managed it this long without purging," Tam said again, following along beside them.

"Maybe it wasn't the same thing as what she took in today," Korinna said hopefully.

Trip glanced at his daughter and shook his head, his features graver than she'd ever seen them. "It was. You know it was. She did exactly the same thing today that she's done every time. I was just too stupid to realise it. She seemed okay. She seemed …"

"Stable?"

"Yes."

"You don't have to talk about me like I'm not here." She stopped abruptly and pulled her hand from Trips, folding her arms over her chest. Tipping her head stubbornly she said, "I tell you, I'm fine." Except there was a crack in her voice as she said it, the thing inside her pushing and roiling and making her feel … wrong.

Trip's gaze flickered to her then away, like he couldn't risk looking at her. "No you're not. You can't be. Not with what you've been taking in all this time."

"Are you certain?" Tam asked. "She does seem fine."

"Look at her eyes."

Tam swung to peer into her face. His eyes flared wide. "Holy shit! They're completely black. We have to get her down there now!" Korinna nodded and took off, Tam right behind her.

Trip's arms went around her and scooped her up then he took off after them.

"What? Hey." Her eyes weren't black. It had to be the shadows or something. "Put me down."

"I can't. You have to get it out. Now!" Trip grated between tight lips as he ran.

She looked up at him, at the tightness of his features, the mix of pain and fear playing there. At that moment, Tam glanced back at them and she saw the same expression on his face.

What the fuck had they seen in her eyes? She was about

to ask but realised exactly where they were taking her – the library. "Surely we can do this later," she said, starting to struggle against Trip's hold – a useless gesture given he was not only much bigger than her, but was something more than a God.

"No. We have to go now," Korinna said as she stopped at the head of the stairs that led down into the depths of the earth under the house where the library lay. The Melbourne Coven's library that was owned and overseen by the Stevens witches as it had been for centuries. The largest library of its kind in the Southern hemisphere. A place full of knowledge, mystery, magic – good and evil.

The place in the house she hated the most.

It wasn't that she didn't enjoy reading, researching and learning – she did.

It wasn't that she didn't love a library – she did. Especially an old one with astonishing architectural features that smelled so deliciously of wood polish, leather, parchment and paper.

It wasn't that she didn't enjoy the buzz of magic in the air that took a person's breath and made you feel alive – she did.

It wasn't that she hadn't been down there many times before today – she had.

It was the ghosts. The family ghosts. They wouldn't leave her alone. She thought she'd got it sorted last year before Christmas when she'd used her powers to keep them away and stop them from using her like some obscene meat puppet. They'd run from her in fear and she thought she'd won a victory.

She should have known better.

They came for her each time she went down there, forcing her to put up strong shields that were tiring to maintain, especially with bloody ghosts pummelling at them. So she barely went down to the library and had to rely on the others to bring up the books she needed to continue her research into people who were corporealised like she had been.

But it seemed she had no choice now as Trip careened down the stairs with her cradled in his arms. If they were right about this thing inside her — and she had to admit they were, given it felt like the thing inside her was growing and her skin was stretching to encompass it, causing increasing pain — then there was only one place she could purge that kind of energy safely.

She sighed, and tried to raise her shields.

Her magic slipped through her fingers and flew away before she could wrangle it.

What the fuck?

She tried again. But her magic wriggled and slithered away from her grasp, refusing to be moulded into anything useful.

Hells.

As their footsteps echoed in the stone stairwell, drawing her ever closer to the library and the ghosts, the panic that had reared up when she realised they were taking her to the library rose up again, but this time it wouldn't be pushed back down.

She couldn't go down there. Not now. Not without her shields. Especially not with this inside her. She might not have thought it was much of anything before, but it most definitely was something — and not a good something. A bad, bad something. And in her experience, that combined with the already bad, bad things that had happened to her in the library in the past was not a good mix. Too much could go wrong.

Knowing her luck, too much *would* go wrong. Especially given there were bad things in the place in the library where she knew they had to take her.

Bad things that could be affected by the horror writhing inside her. She couldn't go in there without her shields.

It would be a disaster.

Surely Trip knew that? Surely he would stop when he realised she hadn't put up her shields?

But he kept running down the stairs, carrying her towards catastrophe.

"Stop. You have to stop. You can't take me down there."

"I have to. There's no time to take you anywhere else."

"But the ghosts. My shields!"

"Put them up now."

CHAPTER

NINE

Fuck. Trip hadn't realised her shields weren't up or taken time to wonder why she hadn't put them up. Neither had Korinna or Tam. They obviously weren't thinking of anything but getting her to where she needed to purge what was inside her.

"I tried to put them up," she said, her voice tight with the growing pain inside her. "But I can't."

"What?" His eyes flared wide. "Why?"

"I can't get a hold of my magic."

"Fuck."

She sighed in relief as he gathered his magic but then the something inside her that had been roiling and slithering ever since she'd taken it from Dawn spat and growled. The slithering quickly turned to slicing, the pain bright and sharp. "Holy fuck!" Burning was added to the slicing as claws dug into her mind and threatened to shred her apart. She screamed and jerked so hard, she almost pulled from Trip's grip.

"Ilia!" Trip yelled, firming his hold on her.

"What the ever-loving fuck!" Tam shouted as he scrambled to try to help Trip hold onto her.

She spasmed, her back bowing so hard she thought her spine was about to snap. Her screams echoed in the stairwell, so loud she could barely hear as Trip yelled, "Ilia. Ilia hold on!" His voice was desperate and full of fear. "Hold on. Please hold on until we're there. Just hold on!"

"Do something, Dad," Korinna shouted.

"I'm trying."

And he was. Ilia could feel that he was. He was doing something with his power, trying to make it wrap around her, push inside her, take some of this from her ...

"No!" she screamed.

She couldn't let him do that. He'd already taken enough. If he took more this would only be happening to him – and while he was a God-like being, what little he had in him was obviously already hurting him, so what would this do to him? Could it put him out of commission? Could it kill him?

The thought of either sent horrifying chills through her. Not only was she not strong enough to deal with losing him for even a short time – let alone in a forever kind of way – she was afraid none of them were strong enough to deal with that. He was not only essential to them as a family member and friend, but was also essential to the coming battle against Perses. And the simple truth was, she wasn't important like him. They could afford to lose her in ways they couldn't afford to lose him.

But even if him taking this on wouldn't kill him or sideline him, it would cause him terrible pain. And she couldn't deal with that. Couldn't deal with him feeling what she was feeling. It was bad enough to know that he too would need to purge the small amount he had in him once they got to the Black Magic and Dangerous Books room.

She shuddered, and not just at the thought of the pain he'd be in as the purge happened. The room itself terrified her – full of evil spirits and entities that had been embedded into the books and manuscripts and magical items that were in there. It made her feel unwashed on the inside the one time she'd gone in there with Tam when she'd been inside the HeartsBlood Gem – and she'd had the protection of the gem's lattice then. It had to be so much worse now she was out of that cage and its protection.

And given she felt that way even with the darkness that marked her soul because of what had been done to her, she couldn't imagine what it would do to Trip given he was so good.

She wished they didn't have to go in there, but they had no choice. According to Trip, it was the only place close enough to safely expel what they'd both taken from Dawn.

There was a reason the Stevens kept all the most dangerous things in that cavern of a room. It was because they could create impregnable shields powered by the Vortex of lay lines that ran under the heart of the library. It was also the reason the library and Stevens House had been built here. That well of power had been what Tam had tapped into for his trip into the Hell Realms over eighteen months ago because its potency was that great.

That amount of raw power in itself wasn't comfortable to be around; that added to the fact so much evil was contained in that room was why she'd never ventured in there after she became corporeal. She'd like to avoid going back in there for the rest of her life if possible.

But it wasn't possible because ... holy crapping Hells! If

they didn't get this thing out of her soon, she wouldn't have any insides left that hadn't been turned to mush.

She gritted her teeth through the pain and held herself together because if she didn't, Trip wouldn't stop trying to take more of the negative energy from her. She pushed against him even though it took every reserve she had left that wasn't already fighting off the pain that made her body spasm. But fear of him going through this lent her strength, enabling her to refuse the help he offered.

"Ilia. Let me help!"

He pushed harder, but she couldn't let him. "I'm fine," she managed to gasp before her jaw clamped shut. She bore down on the eviscerating pain, pushing it down, down, wrapping her claws around it as it had done to her. And by some miracle, it worked, because the pain let up enough that she stopped writhing and jerking against her mate.

Thank the Gods.

Yes, she had just thanked the Gods – something she'd sworn never to do. But right now she really needed help to stop Trip from taking more than he had, more than he should.

"Ilia. Please, let me help."

"No. Just get me there. I can hold it until then."

They came to the bottom of the stairs and the lights flickered on. And she remembered.

Her shields!

She still didn't have any. In the panic and fear of what was happening inside her and trying to stop Trip from making things worse, she had forgotten all about them.

And so had the others.

But the ghosts hadn't. They knew she was here – they always knew she was here. Could feel her just like she could feel them. And they were coming – rushing through the library towards her – and nobody had managed to put shields around her yet.

She tried to raise them again herself but couldn't get a hold of her magic.

Crap! Whatever this was inside her was obviously doing something to stop her from accessing her powers. Which meant she wouldn't have access to them until she'd purged it from her. And she couldn't do that until they'd made their way through the library to the room where the oculus to the Vortex lay.

Holy crapping Hells!

The ghosts were almost here. They were almost here! "Shields," she screamed as Trip, Korinna and Tam leading the way, rushed her towards the stacks where the ghosts were now exiting, arrowing towards her like heat-seeking missiles.

"Shields, shields, SHIELDS!"

As the word burst from Ilia, so did her powers – a giant wave shimmering like moonlight on a rainbow that pulsed out in front of them.

Trip skidded to a halt, curling over his love as if he could protect her – which was ridiculous given the wave of power came from her.

Korinna and Tam had stopped running as well, turning to raise their shields, but before they could, it hit them.

It passed over them – through them – leaving them standing there blinking in shock as it continued along the stacks and hit the ghosts like a giant wave smashing into hapless swimmers, dumping down on them before catching them up and carrying them back down the stacks in a tumbling – and wailing – wall of flickering light.

"Holy shit!" Korinna said, gaping at Ilia.

"Did that feel warm to everyone?" Tam said, brushing

down his arms then made a sucking sound with his mouth and tongue. "And why do I suddenly taste mint and lemon?"

"I can taste that too!" Korinna said, gesturing at her mouth.

As did Trip. He'd also felt the same warmth as Tam had when the wave of power had exploded out of Ilia and over him. He glanced down at Ilia – she seemed no different than she'd been before. And Korinna and Tam seemed fine too.

Huh.

"How did you only affect the ghosts? That was incredible!" Korinna exclaimed.

"Hang on. Was that the purge?" Tam asked, now looking more baffled than Trip had ever seen him as his gaze flickered between Ilia and the rainbow wave disappearing into the dark depths of the library.

"I don't know," Ilia said on a gasp. "It didn't feel—" Her jaw clamped shut with violent force and her eyes – the blackness in them that had told Trip exactly what she'd done and what was happening to her – flared wide before they rolled into the back of her head, only the whites now showing.

"Ilia!" Trip's grip on his mate tightened as she bowed backwards, her entire body going rigid. Then she began to spasm, more violently than before, and all ability to think and hear flew away in a swirl of grey and sparking white.

"What's happening?" Tam asked as he leapt to Trip's side once again to help hold on to Ilia.

"No time for questions now," Trip said as he pulled her tighter against him and began to run. "Tam. Get down there and open up the bloody door. Now!"

To his credit, Tam didn't hesitate. He waved his hand, opened a portal and disappeared.

"Shouldn't we have done that to take her straight from the kitchen to the Vortex?" Korinna asked as she ran after them.

"Can't," Trip shouted back over his shoulder. "Her power's reacting to what she took from Dawn. It's too unstable for portal travel. Or teleporting. Which I don't think I could do right now anyway given I'm not feeling exactly stable myself. It's why I didn't suggest it when I realised what she'd done. On foot is the only way."

So much for all his vaunted, God-like powers! They barely worked on Ilia at the best of times, something about the way she'd been reborn made magics of all kind react strangely around her. So far he'd thought that was a positive thing until he'd realised what she'd been doing for Dawn. It shouldn't have been possible – not in the way she'd been doing it and certainly not for the length of time in which she'd been doing it. She'd thought she'd only been taking bad nightmares away from the little girl, but given what he felt inside himself now, he realised it was nothing so simple – and Ilia being as extraordinary as she was, didn't realise just how big a thing it was.

It wasn't images and feelings or even bad energy – or too much energy from the Goddess. There was something inside Dawn … a living something that had nothing to do with what the Goddess had gifted her … and that's what had been causing her problems. It was dark and malignant and Ilia had been taking it from Dawn all these months.

She had been taking the thoughts, emotions and negative energies of something that was most definitely not Ostara inside her. Some kind of … Being? God-like but not quite.

Whatever it was, it wasn't good. The strength of it would cause even a strong higher Being problems if they'd done it a couple of times over a few months. And she'd been doing it nearly every night, and sometimes during the day, for four months.

Nightmares from the greater Beings weren't nebulous things. They became reality. The God of Nightmares had been born from a bad dream one of the ancient greater Beings had had.

Was that what was happening now?

No. No. It couldn't be. It would have sprung from Dawn as an entire entity by now if it was a God coming into reality. So, it wasn't that. But it wasn't much better than that. Because, if they didn't get it out of the toddler, it could become that.

Shit.

How Ilia hadn't been swallowed whole by the darkness she'd been taking in long before now he didn't know. She said she'd been using it up like the body did food. But he'd never heard of anything like that before.

The only thing he *was* certain of was that she was remarkable.

Not just because she had done it, but because despite what she'd said and how she acted, it had to have been causing her pain. And yet, she'd kept doing it.

He would be in awe of her if not for the fact that he was angry with her for not sharing this with him. That she'd made sure he didn't know because she'd shielded him from it and kept it to herself.

And also angry with himself that he hadn't known.

If she wasn't having some kind of seizure, vibrating with power ready to explode, he'd yell at her. Probably would yell later when they were safely past this.

Please Gods, let them get past this. Because he couldn't

live without her. Couldn't live without her smile, her acerbic wit, her slightly husky alto voice that wove magic in the air every time she spoke. He couldn't do without the lightness he experienced every time she walked into a room, or the way her gaze sought his and lit up no matter her mood. And he certainly couldn't do without her touch and the way even the most casual brush of her hand sparked a fire of desire inside him that couldn't be assuaged by anyone else but her.

Ever.

He also couldn't do without drinking her blood.

Having her drink from him was astonishingly erotic and fulfilling too, but for him drinking her blood went so much deeper than that.

He'd never realised that the ache he'd lived with all his life had been hunger. But since drinking from her regularly, that gnawing ache had gone. Until this last week when he'd spent more time away from her than he had ever before since they'd mated. That hungry gnawing ache had increased over that time to the point that both Tam and Bas had commented on his 'hangryness' . He hadn't put two and two together until then – had thought he just missed her. Which he did. With everything in him. But that was a different ache.

He knew, given he'd lived perfectly fine for so long without her blood that he didn't need it to live, but he certainly needed it to fill the hungriness that had always been a part of his existence.

A hungriness that seemed bigger now it was getting fed regularly.

Maybe he couldn't do without it. He shook that thought away – he didn't have time to wonder about that now. It was getting harder to hold onto Ilia, she was shaking so violently in his arms, her body spasming every few steps so hard it was a wonder she wasn't tearing ligaments, breaking bones.

They hit the mid-point of the library where a large corridor bisected the stacks, and turned left.

Almost there. Almost there.

He could feel the room they were heading towards looming ahead of them, even though he couldn't see it yet. The entry was at the end of this long corridor and off to the right. A big ominous door of steel and iron and so many magic spells to hide and shield it that he shouldn't be able to feel what was inside it at all.

And yet, he could.

He could feel it when he was in the house upstairs.

He could feel it when he was in the garden outside.

He could feel it when he was streets away in the next suburb.

He knew the exact place in Thompson Street where he stopped feeling this ... evil nothingness. This ... anti-life. That wasn't exactly the right description, because the things trapped in this room were living and were desperate for that to continue, but it was the closest thing he could come to explaining what it was he felt. The things inside that room were furiously angry and hateful. They didn't respect life, just wanted to use it so they could gain more power; to rule over everything in a way that would mean misery and destruction.

They were the antithesis of everything he was. He'd been made with the spark of creation from three different creation Goddesses. His energy was the energy of all living things. And those things in that room would try to use him – as Perses wanted to use him – to free themselves and get everything they wanted and more.

Because he couldn't die.

A fact he'd still not fully shared with any of them because he feared they'd look at and treat him differently. And because it just simply couldn't be known that he wasn't immortal like other Gods: he was immutable.

His lifeforce could never change from what it was now. He had long realised he would still be a living being much like he was now through eternity and beyond.

Which, he assumed, was why Loki hadn't shown him and Ilia at Christmas the rest of those terrible futures where she was sucking the life from everything to try to save Dawn. Those possible futures only went so far, never showing his inevitable rising and the fact that, if Ilia was so far gone as to suck life from this Earth, she would have used him like a battery – she couldn't have stopped herself – until she'd sucked the life from all the Realms and every universe, and left only her and him in a nothingness so huge and terrible she would never have lived through a second of it.

It was why he stayed away from dark magic users and creatures like wraiths – because his lifeforce was eternal, and they could feed on it for eternity.

So it was only natural to have avoided going anywhere near this room until now. He hadn't planned to go in there now – he was going to let Tam and Korinna take Ilia in there and help her. He wasn't as badly affected as she was – had only a small percentage inside him in comparison to what she still had in her – so he didn't need to purge now. He had time to get himself to another Vortex, one that didn't have all that evil around it, and purge there.

But now he had no choice. Ilia needed it. She would die if she didn't get in there immediately. There was no time to hand her over or explain why he couldn't go in. He just had to.

Shit. This thing she'd taken inside her from Dawn was right out of his nightmares. Something huge and powerful and too big to be held within a human shell. Or any shell. It didn't want to be contained. No wonder it was causing little Dawn so many problems. What the Hells something like this was doing inside a little girl, he had no idea. Ostara couldn't have given it to her alongside her Goddess gift, surely? She wouldn't be that stupid. Or cruel. Ostara was one of the good ones. She didn't play with people like other Gods and Goddesses did.

So what was this? Where did it come from?

And did it have something to do with the prophecy Korinna had spoken only last night?

Ilia spasmed more violently in his arms, making him stumble and almost drop her. Fuck. He needed to stop the panic and fear from forcing his mind to go off on tangents.

He had to concentrate. Concentrate on taking the next step.

And figure out how he was going to stop the dark things from getting inside him when he was in that room and had to open himself up to purge.

But he couldn't think beyond his panic and fear. Ilia was being destroyed from the inside. He could feel the powerful thing inside her, tearing at her, ripping her to shreds. He could feel it because she was his soulmate, but also because it was tearing at him as well.

Then there was no more time.

They were at the door and it was opening – Tam had disarmed the magic and shields in record time – and he had no choice but to carry Ilia in.

Everything in him screamed 'Run the other way!', but

he couldn't because … Ilia was dying. She was dying. And this was all he could do to stop that horror from occurring. He couldn't do this living-thing without her. Couldn't fight Perses without her. Couldn't do anything without her.

"Come on. What are you waiting for?" Tam said, waving wildly.

Trip realised he'd come to a stop. He hadn't meant to. Didn't want to. But his entire body vibrated in protest, his muscles locking up, stopping him from walking forward. From doing anything more than just standing there unable to budge.

No, no, no, no, no, no, NO!

"Trip! What are you doing? Move."

"Dad? Dad? What's wrong?"

He couldn't move. Couldn't move. And Ilia was going to die and it would be all his fault. Because he wasn't strong enough to fight this feeling of fear that was fast becoming everything he was.

"Trip. My love."

He looked down to see Ilia staring up at him, and despite the blackness swirling in her eyes – eyes that were usually the colour of darkest purple lit by sunlight – they were filled with such trust, such love. And it tore him apart because he was letting her down. "Ilia. I can't."

"It's okay."

No. No it wasn't. It was so far from okay. Okay was in a different universe; in a different Realm.

"Save yourself. Let me go."

Gods – the thought of that. It energised him in a way that nothing ever could or ever would.

Gathering every single bit of willpower he had inside him, he forced it into his muscles and bones and nerves and said, "Never."

Then he forced himself to move.

His teeth ground together as he crossed over the threshold, his entire body aching and shuddering in protest. His hands clenched tighter on Ilia – she groaned and shook harder. Hells – was he hurting her? It took everything in him to loosen his grip a little, but then he had to tighten it again when she spasmed so hard she almost flipped out of his arms.

"I've got you," Tam said, jumping in front of him and helping Trip to hold on to Ilia as he edged into the room.

Ilia groaned but then the sound was lost in the cacophony of noise that started up in the room as they entered.

It was like everything in there had suddenly come to life the moment he'd stepped inside. Things that were trapped inside books and scrolls, gems and statuary, started moaning and groaning and shouting. And every single item – whether a trapped soul or just an item full of black magic – shook and shuddered and strained against the chains, shields and spells that kept them contained.

They were excruciatingly loud. So loud, it made it hard to think. Not that he particularly wanted to think because those thoughts were suddenly full of horrors. Every bad thought, every bad dream, every bad thing that had ever happened to him or could happen to him now lived large in his mind. It was all he could do to keep standing, and if it wasn't for Tam helping to hold Ilia steady while walking backwards in front of him, forcing him to keep moving or risk dropping his mate, he would probably be in the foetal position on the floor, sucking his thumb and whimpering.

"Rinna – can you open the oculus?" Tam shouted over the noise. "Rinna?" The ex-cupid peered over Trip's shoulder when there was no answer, his eyes going wide. "Rinna! Are you okay?"

"What's going on?" Trip asked, wanting to turn to look, except he couldn't – if he got sight of the door, he'd probably bolt for it and run far from here.

However, he could go nowhere but towards the oculus in the floor on the far side of the room. An oculus that was still closed because Korinna hadn't moved past them to open it. "Korinna?" Why hadn't she answered Tam? It wasn't anything good going by the look on his face. "Tam! What is going on?"

"Korinna has stopped just inside the doorway."

"Why?"

"I don't know. But she's looking around her as if she can see something."

Holy shit. "Tam!" The other male's gaze snapped back to him. "Is she having a vision?"

"No. I don't think so. At least, she doesn't look like she did back in the kitchen. Her eyes are wide but they're *her* eyes. She just looks ... terrified."

"Gods." He was so stupid. "She can feel it too."

"What?"

"The evil things in here. Pushing into her, trying to take over her mind."

"What?" Tam glanced around. "But ... she's strong enough to keep her shields up like the rest of us. She shouldn't feel them at all."

Trip shook his head. "Shields won't help her." Not now she had her full powers at her fingertips because he was back in her life. "And what you feel ... it's not what happens to us."

"What are you talking about?"

He hadn't wanted to explain this, hadn't thought they

had time … but strangely enough, thinking about this and explaining it was enabling him to keep moving. Slowly, but surely. "It's not just an uneasy feeling. It's …" It wasn't easy to talk. His throat wanted to close up and his teeth kept chattering, but while he was talking, he was walking one slow step at a time towards the oculus. "They want us. Want to use us … b-be us … t-take over us and everyth-thing w-we are … a-and t-twist us unt-til we are o-one."

"Possession? But they want to possess all of us?"

Trip took another step forward – they were halfway across the room towards the oculus and couldn't stop now. "Not j-just p-possession. We w-wouldn't just be along f-for the ride – it w-would be our r-ride. We would b-bec-come them as much as they bec-come us. Everything w-we are, would be l-lost. Only evil w-would be left, w-worse than anyth-thing that came b-before …" Fuck, it was getting so much harder to talk, his jaw was starting to clench shut, but he forced the words out, forced himself to keep talking to keep taking one painful step after another. "A-and th-there would b-be no end to it. It's wh-why P-Perses wants us. Wh-why we are s-such a th-threat."

"Then why the fuck are you in here?"

Trip glanced down at the woman in his arms then back up at Tam, his brow raising.

Tam nodded then yelled, "Rinna. Don't come in. Just stand outside and make sure nothing gets out."

"I'm sorry."

"D-don't be s-sorry," Trip shouted through clenched teeth, hoping Korinna could hear him. "J-just b-be s-safe."

"How can you stand it?" He could barely hear her now – she must have already moved back outside the door.

"F-for Ilia. F-for you." He wanted to say so much more, but could barely get the words out.

"I love you, Dad."

Her words gave him strength just as it had been faltering. He firmed his grip on Ilia and shouted, "L-love y-you." Then he firmed his gaze on Tam. "O-open … oc-cul-lus."

"But I can't let go."

He couldn't answer because his jaw was now locked shut. So he did what he had promised himself never to do just because he could – he forced his voice into Tam's mind. *"You can. I've got her. Open it so we can purge the moment we get there. She's not going to last for much longer. And neither am I."*

Tam nodded, his eyes bright with trust. "You've got this."

"I hope so. Go."

Tam let go and ran to the covered opening in the floor, the one that gave them access to the lay-lines that ran under the house and created a special Vortex of power that they could use now to safely expel what was inside Ilia and him. Because the best way to get an excess of power and negative energy out was to give it some place it would want to go. And the power of the Vortex was a place it most definitely would want to go. Even though the power of the earth was not something it could use – that energy in this form was, in its own way, immutable too. But the amount of energy would be too enticing for a power-hungry thing not to want to grasp at it.

The groan of metal over concrete told him the door to the oculus was opening. Ilia immediately screamed as the power from the Vortex flooded into the room.

Everything else in the room screamed as well. Her scream was one of near release, but the evil things screamed in terror because the Vortex was a threat to them. Its power was the antithesis of everything they were, dampening their magics and suppressing their energies. They'd been here long enough to realise that.

The thing inside him and Ilia ... it didn't share that realisation. It lurched forward, as if suddenly wanting to get out of him.

It gave him exactly what he needed – a little bit of relief from the darkness that had been riding him ever since he'd stepped into the room.

He stood straighter and doubled his pace, and seconds later he stood over the oculus. With Tam's help, they maneuvered Ilia upright and dangled her forward over the opening. Then Tam said the words of release.

Ilia's mouth opened and the thing inside her came flying out.

He expected the same to happen to him, felt the part of it that was inside him begin to move up and out.

But nothing came out.

He began to choke. The world tipped on its side and began to spin away.

CHAPTER

TEN

There was so much. Too much.

Ilia thought she might split apart with what was roaring and spitting and pushing inside of her. She screamed except there was nowhere for the scream to go. It rattled around in her head, made the thing scream too. It didn't want to be inside her. She wasn't big enough for it. It wanted more. It needed more. It needed ...

Metal groaned against concrete. Light spilled out into the darkness that had become her life. A voice she knew intoned some words. And the thing inside her lunged, forcing her mouth open on a scream, spilling out of her. It flew towards the light, wanting it, drawn by it, forced by it to escape from her.

The purge!

Trip had got her there. Into that room and over to the oculus. Which was now open. She was hanging over it. The Vortex was below her – bright, so bright. And the thing was spewing out of her mouth. Not dark like she thought it might be. It was orange and pink and purple with a sickly green-hue tinging it – almost like the colour of the dawn

99

but wrong somehow. And it lit up with something like … happiness … as it was pulled into the Vortex, joining it, becoming one with it in a way it couldn't with her.

It was such a relief, the release of it. Her entire body vibrated, almost like she was orgasming. Although no orgasm hurt like this did. It had dug its claws in, slicing and cutting as it had tried to fill her, and become one with her; and now it was leaving her, those claws were being torn from her.

She screamed. She couldn't help it. The sound going on and on as the thing kept pouring out of her.

Hells – when would it end?

It was exiting from her mouth and nose and ears and eyes. It poured out of her skin. It was blazing hot and ice-burn cold; it felt like her insides were becoming her outsides. She couldn't breathe. All she could do was hang there and scream as it tore out of her.

Holy crap, she hoped Trip wasn't experiencing the same thing. She hoped, given he only had a small amount inside him, that it was already out and he had barely experienced more than an uncomfortable sensation. It was the only thought in her head, the hope that he was okay and done with the purge.

That and the screaming plea for this to be over.

She couldn't take much more. Her heart beat so fast and hard, it might explode any moment from the effort. Her lungs burned with the need to breathe but she couldn't and …

Hang on. If she couldn't breathe then how was she screaming?

Because the sound was no longer coming from her.

And it wasn't the evil things in the room either – they'd shut up the moment the purge began.

It was a female voice screaming.

Korinna.

But she wasn't simply screaming. She was saying a word over and over.

Ilia wasn't able to make it out at first but as the purge came to an end and the pain, and everything that came with it, receded, she began to make it out.

"Dad! Dad! Dad!"

Korinna was screaming out for Trip.

"Dad! No! Dad! Tam – help him! Gods help him!"

Ilia wanted to turn to see what was happening but could do no more than hang over the pit as the thing inside her finished coming out in spurts like water from a rusty tap.

"Tam! You have to help him!" Korinna screamed again.

"I can't. I can't let go of Ilia. She'll fall in."

She wanted to scream at him to let go, that it didn't matter about her, that he had to help Trip, to save him. Because Korinna was not one to panic and if she was screaming and begging like that, whatever was happening had to be bad.

She wanted to do something, anything, but she could do nothing until the purge was finished.

When would it be finished? Hurry up! Just go. Go. GO!

The word was a shout in her mind and as it left her, so did the last of the thing in one great burst.

Stars filled her eyes as she sucked in a breath. Then with that breath she croaked, "Help Trip!"

"Ilia. Are you okay?" He pulled her back so she was no longer hanging precariously over the pit in the floor.

She sucked in another breath – fuck that hurt – and said hoarsely, "Fine! Just help Trip."

She wanted to ask what was wrong with him but quite

frankly didn't have the energy or the breath, so just stuck with the most important bit. Besides, once Tam let go of her, she'd be able to turn and see what was happening – after these stars and bits of hazy fog in her eyes fucked off.

Tam pulled her away from the oculus and went to let go, but her legs did a great impression of cooked spaghetti and she would have slumped to the floor if he hadn't held on.

"Whoa! I think fine doesn't mean what you think it means."

She didn't even have a 'ha-ha' in her, so she just said, "Floor. Me. Now."

As he lowered her, propping her against the wall, she tried to look past him to see what was happening to her beloved.

Her eyesight was still a little funky but it wasn't hard to miss him, outlined as he was by the bright light coming from the pit.

At first it seemed there was nothing wrong with him. His face was turned away from her, what she could see lit up too brightly by the light from the oculus. He stood straight, one arm reaching towards the light, the other at his throat.

Hells. Was he clawing at his throat? Couldn't he breathe?

He staggered, as if pushed from behind, then his body snapped back and forward in a way that would have broken any normal man's back.

"Trip!"

Her scream – his name – came out more of a gurgle given she still couldn't breathe properly – but he heard it. He turned his head in her direction, eyes bugging as he gasped for breath. His veins pulsed under his skin; his lips were blue – holy shit! – which was totally wrong. He was a God-like being with their capabilities and more, and while he needed breath, he didn't need it like she did.

What the fuck was happening? "Tam! Help him!"

Her yell joined Korinna's. The other woman was stuck at the doorway, her face a portrait in suffering as she watched her father struggle to breathe while it looked like his body was being torn apart.

"What's happening?" she asked Tam, who was now by Trip's side, trying to hold him steady.

"He hasn't purged," Korinna yelled. "He went to do it with you but nothing happened then he went rigid and started clawing at his throat and spasming so hard he almost toppled you both in. Tam shoved him away with his power and took over holding you and I tried to go in there to help but I couldn't. I couldn't."

"Don't blame yourself, Rinna," Tam said, voice and face tortured by the need to go to her versus the need to help Trip.

The other woman obviously felt something through their mating bond because she yelled, "Don't worry about me! Just help my dad."

Ilia shared her sentiment, and was glad when Tam turned his full attention back to helping Trip. But it soon became apparent that whatever Tam was doing wasn't working because her mate continued to look like he was choking and that something was doing its best to tear him apart.

It was the thing he'd taken in from Dawn to help Ilia so she didn't break apart or burn up or whatever would have happened if she'd taken it all in. It was trying to get out of him but for some reason, couldn't manage it.

"Get him away. From the oculus!" she yelled to Tam. Or

tried to yell – but her voice was working about as well as her legs. Stupid jelly. Stupid huskiness. Stupid thing that made her feel so Gods-damned weak just from getting rid of it! She needed to get to her mate; her lover; the other part of her soul that made her whole.

But she was about as useless as Korinna, who couldn't come into the room. Not that she'd know what to do even if she could move.

She screamed again for Tam to move Trip away from the oculus and by some miracle this time he heard her – or maybe he'd just realised the same.

He put his arms around Trip's large form and tried to wrestle him away from the opening. But as they moved awkwardly back – a staggering shuffle – things just got worse.

Trip clawed at his throat with both hands, jerking so violently Tam was thrown back. Her mate staggered closer to the pit, but it didn't seem to help either. He gaped like a fish out of water, eyes bulging, veins standing out in his neck and hands as he jerked and spasmed. "Trip!" she cried out. "Trip!"

He was suffering more from lack of air than he should. Whatever was going on, whatever was stopping the thing from coming out was affecting him in some fundamental level she didn't understand because it just didn't make sense. This shouldn't be happening to him. But things had gone wrong from the moment he'd entered the room, becoming even worse when the oculus was opened.

Her eyes flared wide as realisation hit.

It was the power in here.

Not only the dark magics but the raw power from the lay lines that met under this place and created a Vortex of incredible power. They were oil to the water of his power for some reason. She didn't know how she knew that, she just did. He probably could cope with one but both – it was too much. They had to get him out of here but he couldn't leave until he'd purged – the thing inside wanted to get to the Vortex and wasn't about to be taken away, by the look of what was happening to him as he spasmed closer to the oculus.

She had to help him! She couldn't just sit here. She was his mate. If anyone could help it should be her. Her hands fisted and she thumped them against her stupid jelly legs. "Work you fuckers. Work!"

It hurt. You'd think that because they were made of jelly they'd be numb too. But they weren't numb. They'd already been aching. She'd held so much of that thing inside her, so much alien power, that it had come out of her from everywhere, including her legs. The muscles and ligaments felt like she'd run a major marathon. They hurt. And punching just made them hurt more.

Tears sprang to her eyes, a sob so large caught in her chest it made it difficult to draw breath. Gods, why was this happening? Why didn't they stop fucking with her and those she loved? Why give her so much love she thought she might burst from it, then threaten to take it away like this.

But what could she do if she couldn't even get over to him? Not that she knew what to do if she did get over there. Moving him away from the oculus seemed to make the thing inside him want out even more violently, threatening to tear him apart. But whatever was stopping the purge wanted him away from the oculus, so every time he took a step closer, it fought against that motion by crushing his throat and chest and lungs.

Fucking Hells. Despite him being a God-like Being, she

was certain he was about to die right in front of her and there was nothing she could do to stop it or help him.

She wasn't the only one thinking that. Korinna was screaming her father's name over and over, begging Tam to help him, but there was nothing Tam could do either. She could see it on his face as he stood there, lit by the light of the Vortex. The hopelessness. The helplessness. For all his double power – cupid and warlock – he could do nothing but watch as Trip died.

Oh. She sucked in a ragged breath. Her mate was dying. *"He can't die."*

ELEVEN

"What?" She looked around her, but Tam and Korinna had definitely not spoken and there was no-one else here. "Who said that?"

"He *can't die,*" the voice repeated.

At least, she thought it was a voice, although neither Korinna nor Tam seemed to have heard it. Maybe it was something on her side of the room talking.

She didn't want to take any notice of it – it was distracting her from her efforts to get to Trip, from trying to think of some way of saving him.

"For my's sake! I said he can't die. What part of that don't you understand?"

Despite herself, she glanced around looking for the source of that voice, staring into the darkness in the corners near her, then at the shelves above her head where the things kept there had begun to moan and groan and rattle their chains in fear of the light from the Vortex. It had to have been one of them that had spoken. Except, she thought the magic chains, shields and spells placed on everything in here made it impossible for them to say anything intelligible.

So who had spoken? Had someone else crept into the room when they weren't looking? It wouldn't have been very hard given what had been going on. They would have had to make it past Korinna though, and despite her frantic and upset state, Ilia really didn't think she'd let anything or anyone past her.

So it did have to be something in the room with them already. But what?

"I'm not out there. I'm in here. In your head."

"What?" She touched her head. Had she hit her head somewhere along the way? It certainly ached like a son of a bitch. Or perhaps she was going insane – a definite possibility given what was going on.

"Not at all. You're as sane as I am."

"Well, that's not saying much given I now think I'm suffering an hallucination."

Laughter in her head. *"Not an hallucination. I'm real and I'm here and helping in the only way I can."*

"Who are you?"

"Can't tell you that. It might get out. Especially given you're a bit chatty at the moment. You know you don't need to speak out loud for me to hear you? I'm in your head. I can hear anything but your most secretest of secret thoughts."

There was something familiar about the voice – something annoyingly familiar – but she didn't have time to figure that out right now. Because it had said something she needed to pay attention to. *"What do you mean he can't die?"* she asked in her mind, deciding it best to play along with whatever this was – an actual presence of something in her cracked subconscious.

"I mean he can't die."

She rolled her eyes. *"That's no more information than I had when you first said that."*

"Well, there's not much more to say."

"Oh, I think there's a lot to say. Especially if it has bearing on what's going on now."

"Well, the fact he can't die doesn't have much bearing on what needs to happen next other than he's not about to kark it before you manage to move your arse and do what you're supposed to do."

"Kark it?"

"You know. Bite the dust. Pay the ferryman. Pushing up daisies. Playing Russian Roulette with the Grim Reaper."

"I know what 'kark it' means. I just can't believe a bodiless voice said it to me right now in this dire situation." She shook her head. That more than anything else told her the voice was not insanity descending but was in fact what it said it was – someone real and alive talking to her in her head. Because there was no way in this life or any other she would have said 'kark it'.

"Oh. Well ... good. Didn't think you were that plebian, but never hurts to check."

"It hurts. It hurts very much when your carry on is taking us from the subject at hand which is ... why the fuck are you talking to me and telling me my mate can't die? And how is that going to help him?"

"That would seem like two subjects to me, not one."

"Oh, for fuck's sake! Help him. Please, stop talking and just help him."

"But I can't help him."

"Then what's the point of you? Why are you wasting my time?"

"Because you're going to help him."

"How? How can I help him when I can't even stand?" She

burst into tears – she couldn't help it. They just exploded out of her on a sob. Because the love of her life was currently being torn inside out and choked to death – well, if the voice was to be believed, not to death, but he was in excruciating pain. She could feel it through their bond. Even though he was trying to mask it – and oh, the strength in him to be able to protect her in that way given what he was going through – she could feel his pain burning in her veins.

"Now, now. Don't cry. Please don't cry. I really can't stand it when they cry." The latter was said sotto voce, as if he thought she couldn't hear him. Then louder, *"I thought you were made of tougher stuff than that."*

"You try being almost torn apart by some entity thing and having all your energy taken from you and your muscles turned to jelly and your head pounding like someone's using it for hammer and anvil practice and also be forced to sit and watch the love of your life tortured in front of you and keep your composure."

"Huh ... well ... I still wouldn't cry."

"Oh, for fuck's sake!" she screamed. "If you know how to help him just help him!"

"He *is* trying to help Trip!" Korinna yelled back.

She then realised her friends were staring at her as if she was going insane. But she didn't care. Because if this annoying arsehole in her head could help Trip somehow, then she was happy to pay the price. Whatever that price was. She would give her sanity, her life, her very breath and heart and soul for her love. *"Just help him."*

"As I said, I can't help him. But you can. Just go to him and be the conduit you were meant to be."

"Conduit? What conduit?"

"The conduit. That's what you are. Surely you've figured that out already."

"What the fuck are you talking about?"

"Who the Hells are you talking to, Ilia?" Tam asked as he did his best just to hold onto Trip and keep him stationary – the only thing that seemed to, if not help, not make things worse.

Crap. She hadn't realised she'd reverted to responding out loud to the thing in her head. Too late now. "Shh," she said and waved her hand at him. "A voice is talking to me in my head." His eyes widened – not surprising given she sounded insane. "It's telling me how to help Trip."

"Really? Who is it?" Korinna asked, seemingly ready to believe, whereas Tam was still giving her the side-eye. But then, she was about as desperate as Ilia was to save Trip.

"I have no idea."

"You shouldn't listen to it," Tam said, gaze roving around at the shelves surrounding them. "It could be anything in here."

"No. No it's not."

"How do you know? Because it told you so?"

Well, actually, yes. But she wasn't about to say that. "I recognise the voice, I just can't place it. And even though he's bloody annoying and a bit of an arsehole—"

"Hey!"

"I trust him."

"Then what's he saying?"

"That I'm a conduit and—"

Korinna suddenly went ramrod straight, her eyes swirling darkly with sparks of gold in the black.

"Rinna!" Tam looked like he was on the verge of letting go of Trip to race to his mate, but Trip convulsed violently at the very second and he was forced to stay to keep holding him upright. "Rinna! Are you okay?"

"She's having a vision."

"Duh," she said to it, but then repeated what it had said.

"What? How? Seers of *grande-visions* don't ever have them so close together."

The panic in his voice made her gaze snap to Korinna. Tam was right. She shouldn't be able to have a vision so close to last night's one. Visions like that took too much out of the Seer. She shouldn't have enough Seeing power to even allow her to have a knowing, let alone another full-blown vision.

"She's not like other Seers. And this one is different from last night. See?"

Ilia had to admit the voice was right. Korinna didn't rise into the air as she had in the kitchen – good thing given she stood in the doorway and there was only a few feet between her head and the door jam. Her head dropped back though, the skin of her throat glowing pearlescent in the light coming from the Vortex, and then she moaned, a great shuddering sound that seemed to come through her from the depths of the earth. The sound became a hoarse keening cry as her mouth opened wider and wider – so wide it seemed her jaw might break.

Tam made a sound – possibly words but she couldn't hear what over the horrible, nails-down-a-blackboard noise Korinna was making. Ilia put her hands over her ears, but it didn't help – the noise vibrated through her entire body.

Suddenly, when she thought she couldn't take anymore, Korinna's mouth slammed shut with a jarring snap of teeth. Her head fell forward and her eyes stopped swirling black and gold. The gold became a splatter that grew and grew until it filled the entire orb of Korinna's eyes, glowing brightly in the light of the Vortex.

Her lips began to move.

At first there was no sound but very soon a whisper filled the room, soft but harsh and grating, and perfectly clear:

> *"The spirit made of moonlight and dawn*
> *Turned corporeal in a holy storm*
> *Is the conduit between known and unknown*
> *A power to compliment that which is grown*
> *From Heaven and Earth and Spirit and Well*
> *She spans time and space and all the Hells*
> *The pantheons will shudder before her might*
> *But none will be jealous of her terrible plight*
> *For she stands between us and the fall of all*
> *Of everything from the beginning to eternity's call.*
> *So saeth the Well three times three times three*
> *From my lips to your ears so mote it be."*

KORINNA GASPED and shuddered as the last of the prophecy left her lips, then started to crumple.

"Rinna!" Tam cried, one hand stretched out, the other still holding Trip. A streak of his power – brilliant amethyst – flew across the room to Korinna, surrounding her in a bubble, cradling her inside before she hit the floor. It was a remarkable thing Ilia had seen him use on their journey to Tartarus when she was still locked in the HeartsBlood Gem – but not since. He obviously had a handle on his warlock power now in a way he never had before – a remarkable feat given, since he got his cupid magic back, he'd had trouble using one without it being affected by the other.

But if he could do what he just did, why not use it to help Trip? She was about to ask when the voice said, *"Were you not listening? Only the conduit can help him. And you are the conduit."*

"But he could put up that bubble shield he used on his journey to Tartarus to protect him and Korinna. He could wrap it around Trip and protect him from the influence of this place and the Vortex. If those things are cut off, he'll be okay."

"Sure. If okay includes being ripped apart by the thing still growing inside him and wants out."

"But you said he couldn't die."

"He wouldn't die when it rips him apart. He would live through the entire excruciating experience, as he would through the agonising process of reforming, as the shreds of him came back together and unrepairable bits regrew. What Prometheus goes through is nothing to this. It's pretty bloody horrific."

She blanched at his words. *"Gods, no."*

"They won't help him. And stop worrying about that. You need to concentrate on being the conduit, as Korinna just told you."

"I have no clue what being a conduit means or how that's even supposed to help Trip now. The bubble shield is a better idea. It would give us time to get him out of here and to somewhere else that doesn't affect him like this place does."

"Oh, if only that were a possibility now," the voice drawled. *"But I'm afraid the thing has tasted the Vortex and wants to go to it. All it can see is the endless power before it and not the fact there is no escaping that power once melded with it. Which is why it's the perfect place to purge such evil things because once there, they can't affect anything. But as I said, it doesn't know that. So it won't want to leave with him. And it*

won't be contained by Tam's pretty bubble-shield. If it thinks he's leaving this place, it will redouble its efforts to tear him apart to get out."

"That's ... I can't ... I don't know what to do."

"Do? All you have to do is get up and go to him."

"What a brilliant idea. Why didn't I think of that? Oh I know ... because my legs won't work!" She thumped them and felt nothing more than the aching pain of before; her legs still didn't move in response.

"Such passion! Trip's a lucky God-thing."

"You call that luck!" She jabbed her finger towards where Trip was jerking around violently like some tortured marionette. *"It's killing him!"*

"Don't be so dramatic. As I've already told you multiple times, he can't die. Even if he's torn apart, he'll live. It will be bloody painful for him reattaching and growing his body again from what's left, but it will happen."

"Then why bother coming to me if it's no problem for you? Why not let it tear him apart and let him ... grow back? It can't be because his pain bothers you. Maybe you just don't like blood and gore," she said, inner voice dripping in sarcasm even as it shook with emotion – her gaze was glued to her love who really looked like he was about to be torn apart. She had never seen such agony on anyone's face. She wished she could take away his pain.

"But you can. That's my point. It's why I'm here – okay, the idea of all the blood and gore if he got torn apart is a turn off; it's so hard to wash out of all those hard-to-reach places!"

"You are an arsehole."

"So I have often been told. But that's neither here nor there. You can stop it from happening. All you have to do is stop feeling sorry for yourself and giving in to your pain and just go over to him. Once you're there, you'll figure out the rest."

"But how do I do that when my legs won't move?"

"Being locked in a gem for thousands of years and thinking you had no particular power of your own never stopped you from learning how to make things happen outside of your prison. How is this different?"

All arguments she was going to throw at the voice disappeared. He was right. Sheer bloody-mindedness had worked for her for all those years – so why couldn't it work for her now? Especially for Trip?

She could do this for him – even though she still wasn't quite certain what 'this' was. But maybe the voice was right and all she needed to do was get over to Trip and it would all fall into place.

Whatever she was going to do, she had to do it quickly because Trip was now being pulled and pushed more violently by the two opposing forces inside him and he wasn't going to last for much longer. Even if what the voice said to her was true and he would survive whatever happened, she didn't want him to go through that kind of pain.

So, if she was going to stop him from being torn apart, she had to move now!

TWELVE

Ilia smacked at her legs, willing sensation back into them. It hurt – a lot – but the pain helped because suddenly they stopped feeling like they were made of jelly and started feeling like bone and muscle and ligament.

"Harder," the voice inside her mind said.

She just grunted. She was already punching her flesh as hard as she could and at this stage she was going to be black and blue tomorrow. None of that mattered though – only getting to Trip and using this conduit-thing to save him mattered.

So she kept hitting and shouting at herself until she had enough feeling in her legs to move, pulling herself up and onto her knees. She didn't try to stand. That was a feat beyond her at the moment. But crawling was do-able.

She hoped.

She moved her leg forward and almost collapsed. Holding herself up with her arms, she tried again, moving more slowly, taking note of when the sensation in the moving leg changed and stopped there.

It wasn't much movement, but it was something. So she

did that. Moving half an inch at a time, waiting in between while she panted and punched at her other leg so she could feel it enough to get the muscles moving forward another half inch. It was slow ... so slow ... but she could do it. She had to. She had to get to her soulmate, the love of her very long life.

"That's it. I knew you weren't a weakling."

She grunted again but couldn't answer. Sweat was pouring down her face and her t-shirt was already plastered to her skin. Every movement forward was an agony, but she gritted her teeth through the pain and kept her gaze on her love.

He was jerking and vibrating so violently now, Tam could do nothing but stand there with his hands out, ready to catch him if he fell.

"Tam should push him over here with his powers."

"Yes," she gritted out through clenched teeth. She tried to open her mouth, to call out to Tam, but her jaw wouldn't move, her vocal chords frozen.

There was an expectant pause and then, *"Why aren't you telling him that?"*

"Because I can't talk, you idiot!"

"If you can talk to me, you can talk to him!"

"I can only do that because you're in my mind."

"You used to talk to many people when you were in the HeartsBlood Gem."

"That was different."

"Not different at all. The talent was always yours, you just thought it wasn't. In fact, you prescribed a lot of your power to other things. You really don't have much self-esteem at all, do you?"

"Arsehole!"

"That's excellent. I think Tam heard that. He's looking over here. Do that again, but directed at him."

"It's not me he can hear. It's you."

"Sorry, no way, nuh-uh. Bags not it. Non possiblo."

She was beginning to realise who it was in her head, so decided to use his name to see if that would stop him being this annoyingly cryptic. *"Loki! Stop being unreasonable. Just bloody well talk to him and get him to bring Trip over here. I'm not sure I'm going to make it in time."*

"I'm not being unreasonable. And I most definitely am not this Loki person you think I am. Although, handsome and charming devil that he is, I wish I was him. But I most definitely am not. Him. Not at all. Nope. You got that wrong, sister."

Despite the direness of the situation, she couldn't help but snort. *"You give yourself away with every sentence. So stop fucking around, Loki, and just be honest for a change."*

"I am not ... agh! Fine. It's exhausting trying to pretend I am not the magnificent me. You saw through me. Three cheers and big congratulations on your smarts and all that. But as I was saying, I'm not being unreasonable. I cannot talk to Tam right now."

"Why the fuck not?"

There was a long pause – she managed to move a whole foot forward during that pause – before he responded.

"It's too dangerous. Others might know if I speak to another God or Godling in that way. I can speak to you because your mind is so different – locked against leaks so to speak. Nobody can know I am here and helping, and nobody will as long as I speak only to your mind. You, however, can speak to whomever you choose and nobody will know. I have no idea why – so don't question me about it – but it's true."

"I have no idea how to do it!"

"You are speaking to me and you can't even see me and

didn't know who I was to begin with. Just focus on Tam and speak to him with your mind."

"I can't!"

"Of course you can. You've been doing it with Dawn since she was born. And talking to babies is the hardest thing to do — their thought processes are nonsensical."

She rolled her eyes. *"That's because we were linked."*

"No. It was because you are strong enough to do it. You just supposed it was because you were linked. But you have also spoken to Trip with your mind and—"

"We're soulmates."

"And me," he continued. *"You're not linked with me in any way. How do you explain that?"*

"Because you're a God and made it so with your belief and magics."

He made a snorting sound. *"If that was all it took to make things happen, my life would be a far different thing from how it is now."*

She was surprised at how bitter he sounded, but she didn't have the time or energy to wonder why or ask him about it. Maybe later if they actually lived through this.

Which she wouldn't if Trip died. She knew Loki said her mate couldn't die but the way it seemed like he would be pulled apart any moment ... how could anyone survive that?

She moved another few inches forward – so slow!

"Oh for fucks sake! Just focus on Tam and tell him to move Trip to you."

She wanted to scream at the annoying God but even if she could it wouldn't shut him up. Only proving him wrong would do that. So she stopped moving so she could focus on Tam, then as she'd done with Loki, she formed the words in her mind, *"Tam. Move Trip with your powers. Towards me,"* and shoved them at him.

Tam's head snapped up and he looked straight at her. "What?"

He'd heard her. He'd heard her!

Ignoring Loki's 'I told you so' crowing, she repeated what she'd sent to Tam.

His brow furrowed, but he answered her in the same way, *"I might hurt him if I move him away from where he is."*

"He'll hurt more if this goes on. Just push with your powers so I can get to him faster. I need to touch him. If I am what Korinna's prophecy stated, then I should be able to channel the thing inside him into the Vortex."

"How can you be sure?"

She looked around, wishing Loki would show himself so Tam knew for certain she wasn't just making wild guesses. But of course he wouldn't be that helpful. So she just said, *"Korinna said this is what I am and if I don't try ... we have to do something!"*

Tam paused then nodded and lifted his hand. But instead of summoning his magic to move Trip, he pointed it at Ilia. It wrapped around her, lifted her in cushioned air and pulled her across the room in less than a second. Then, he held her cradled in his power so she could put her hand on Trip's chest.

She slipped her hand under her mate's shirt collar – not an easy feat with how he was jerking around – and placed her palm over Trip's heart. The beat of it was a wild vibration of rolling thunder against her hand – how it hadn't already exploded from the trauma of that she didn't know. Then without letting herself think, she gave in to instinct.

Her other arm thrust out, hand pointed at the brightest part of the oculus, and saying in her mind to the thing inside him, *"Use me to leave,"* she imagined herself a conduit – like copper wire was for electricity – and just opened herself to it. The brightest flames licked to life inside her mind then exploded out of her in a brilliant wave.

TRIP DIDN'T THINK he could take much more of this. The thing wanted out and yet some part of it wanted to stay inside him and both were fighting to win – with him as the weapon and the muddied and bloodied ground they battled on.

It wouldn't kill him if they tore him apart but fuck it hurt. It was taking everything in him to stay conscious and not pass out from the torture of it.

And he had to stay conscious. Because the force of his conscious will was the only thing stopping the part that didn't want out from winning the battle.

Because it was strong. As strong as him and the part that wanted out combined – which said something. A terrible something. Something he didn't want to think about right now, because to do so might actually give it more strength.

A thoroughly terrifying thought.

So he fought – against it. And he fought not to succumb to the pain and let blissful unconsciousness take over. Because he couldn't let this thing win. Not just for himself but for the others here with him. Especially Ilia.

He could let nothing bad happen to her. Ever. She'd already suffered far too much. He couldn't stand that she had; he couldn't bear the thought of her suffering more. And she would because he knew if this thing won and stayed where it was, they'd all suffer worse than those tortured in Tartarus.

So he held. For his daughter. For his new family he had through her. But mostly, for Ilia.

As if just the thought of her had conjured her, she appeared before him, reaching out to touch him.

He wanted to warn her – he was shaking so violently, he might hurt her with his movements. But he had no words – no access to his vocal chords or to his mouth or jaw to open them and make any sound that wasn't screaming.

But she shoved her hand under his shirt and pressed her hand against his chest.

Such warmth. Always when she touched him, such warmth. It radiated out and filled every corner of him, taking away the pain and—

Ilia flung out her other hand towards the Vortex. Power shot through him like an electric bolt. And that electric bolt gathered all of the thing inside him – the bit that wanted to stay and the bit that wanted to go – and sent it flying out of him.

And in to her.

She was taking all of it back into herself.

No!

He tried to shout at her, to stop her, but even though he was far more powerful than her, he could do nothing.

He'd never felt more useless. This was what he'd tried to avoid and now he could do absolutely nothing to save her.

He was going to lose her. It would tear her apart, fracture her, consume her, kill her.

She was going to die and in her death he would find endless torture. To live without his mate ... He wanted to die with her and yet, he never could.

No. No. No. N—

Light and darkness streamed out of the hand she was pointing towards the oculus, flying into the Vortex to disappear inside it.

What? How the—

She wasn't keeping what she had taken into her. She was getting rid of it. Not like the purge. This was controlled, purposeful. A beautiful use of power; an exquisite show of magic. She wasn't consuming or being consumed – she was channelling. Like she was a magical, wonderful, powerful conduit.

By the Well, he loved her. She was magnificent. Just magnificent. He had no idea what or how she was doing this, but doing it she was.

She was saving them both.

The last part of the thing left him with a final, painful tearing whoosh. It flew through her, out her hand and disappeared into the oculus.

"Close it up, Tam. Close it now!" she yelled, then collapsed in front of him.

He reached out to catch her just as unconsciousness claimed him and he fell too.

CHAPTER
THIRTEEN

V oices.

Flickering light.

Nausea.

Ugh! Was she going to throw up?

Yep. She was going to throw up.

Ilia rolled quickly, hanging over the side of the bed to vomit – no, not a bed; it was far too soft for her bed.

"Ugh ... here."

Magic sizzled in the air around her and the vomit hit the bottom of a bucket with a splatter.

Hands stroked her back and held her hair while she evacuated the contents of her stomach – although what she had to evacuate she didn't know because she was pretty sure she hadn't eaten since last night.

Was last night even last night? She had no idea how much time had passed after she'd done the conduit thing to save Trip and then passed out.

Trip!

She wanted to sit upright to ask about him or see if he was there too – the hands were most definitely not his, nor were the voices she'd heard before – but her body was not finished with the vomiting.

So she clung to the edge of whatever she was lying on, and just let what needed to happen, happen.

Finally, the vomiting stopped and, groaning, she rolled over to her back, her eyes slitting enough to register she was lying on the lounge room couch – the ceiling there was a lovely calming eggshell blue with beautifully patterned cornices.

"Here. Drink this. It will settle your stomach and give you some energy."

Hands helped to lift her up and positioned cushions behind her so she could sit upright – in a very lounging-Pharaoh kind of way – and sipped at the warm tisane she'd been handed. It was slightly minty, with chamomile and ginger, and helped rid her mouth of the horrible vomit-aftertaste. Also, it did seem to settle her stomach right away. Which it shouldn't be able to do if it was just a tisane. There must be a magical spell in it – but it was very subtle because she couldn't sense it like she usually could most magic.

Jules must be getting much better at making healing potions.

Except, the voice hadn't been Jules' . It had been Violetta's.

Ah, now that explained it. She stopped sipping and managed to say, "You're back."

The older witch sat on the arm at the end of the couch. Her silver hair hung in a neat bob around her jaw and she wore a lilac twin-set with one of her dark purple pencil skirts. As she shifted to get a more comfortable seat on the arm of the couch, the strands of beads she always wore clattered together as they shifted across her surprisingly perky breasts. Her dark eyes sparkled in a relatively unlined face – for someone going on eighty, she was remarkably well-preserved in a loving-her-age kind of way – and a smile warmed her intelligent face.

"Yes," she said, answering Ilia's question. "I got back last night when all the commotion was going on downstairs. My arrival at that time was actually quite fortuitous as it turned out because whatever you did caused a backlash and knocked Tamuel and Korinna unconscious as well as you and Trip, and poor Bastien was beside himself trying to manage looking after all of you but really wanting to stay with Jules and Dawn."

Hells. She'd had no idea. "Where is Trip? Is he okay? Did I get all of that thing out of him?"

The older witch patted her leg gently. "You did. And he's fine. Bas got him to your bed upstairs and he's sleeping soundly."

She looked around her – she was most definitely in the lounge room. "Why am I here and not with him?" Didn't they know that as soulmates they'd heal faster if they were together?

Violetta heaved a sigh. "We had to separate you, my dear. We couldn't stop you from touching him and every time you did, something began to happen we were uncertain of, so we brought you down here."

She managed to edge up on the cushions without spilling the tisane, her brow furrowing over Violetta's words. "What do you mean 'something began to happen'?"

Violetta waved her hand. "You were … channelling from him and then to him. I wasn't worried so much about that, given whatever you were taking you gave back, but it was using up your energy and we were concerned you might slip from restful sleep and into a coma. You didn't seem able to stop no matter the shields and barriers we put up. So we had to separate you to keep you safe."

Heart banging in her chest she asked, "Did I hurt Trip?"

"No dear, you didn't." Relief rushed through her as Violette shifted. The older witch sat down on the lounge and lifted Ilia's legs up to put in her lap – a curious action that somehow comforted her. "As I said, what you took from him, you gave back and actually seemed to help him. No, my concern was for you and the fact it was uncontrolled and such a curious magic that neither Bas nor I had seen anything like it before. When Tam woke up though, he told us it was because you are a conduit, which made sense, because you were probably still locked into a cycle of doing what you were doing before you lost consciousness. We moved you into the room on the other side of Dawn's which was the furthest one upstairs from your room. But then you started doing the same thing for Dawn even though you were in the room next door. Every time she had a night-mare, your magic flared and she calmed down moments later but you became agitated and unsettled again. It took us a while to figure out what was going on and nothing we did stopped it. So we decided to see if distance would work and brought you down here. Given it's at the front of the house and not under either of those bedrooms it was the furthest place we could bring you without moving you down to the library. But thankfully it seemed that here was far enough away that you couldn't easily ... conduit, or whatever it is you want to call it. Plus, there is also the matter that you wouldn't heal if you were using all your energy to do your conduit thing."

"Conduit thing?"

"I'm not sure what else to call it. Because, as I said, we haven't seen anything like it before."

"It's a kind of channelling."

"Yes, dear, in a way it is. But it's also very different. Channelling is taking something and using it, but that's not what you're doing if I have it right. As a conduit, what you take should pass through you, not stay in you. With Trip it was passing from him to you and back again – so not such a big issue except for the use of all that energy. But with Dawn, it was just staying in you as far as we could see. Which Tam said is what caused the issue in the first place, so we couldn't let you continue to do it."

"But ... Dawn needs me to do it."

Violetta tipped her head on the side, her straight bob swooshing silkily over her ears, exposing the angle of her jaw. "If it hurts you dear, that can't be true."

"Better me than Dawn."

An eyebrow quirked up. "I don't want my great-grand-daughter to hurt or be upset like she is by these nightmares either, but swapping the pain to somebody else isn't the answer. Surely you see that?"

Ilia edged up a little more on the cushions so she was better able to look Violetta in the eye. "If I am a conduit, surely that's my role. And now I know that's what I am," she hurried on to stop Violetta's response – which from her expression was one of instant denial – "it's my responsibili-ty." She frowned. "No, not even my responsibility. It's my need. I need to do it. I need to take the badness from her and pass it through me."

"But you're not passing it through you."

"I feel fine."

Violetta's frown deepened. "Hmm. Maybe you can take in a fair amount before you need to purge it. Even so—"

"She's wrong there. Oh so wrong. Very, very wrong. The wrongest that wrong can be!"

Loki's voice sing-songed in her head, so she didn't hear what Violetta had to say on the subject. She tried to concentrate on Violetta's words, but it seemed Loki wasn't going to be put off because he said more loudly, *"I said. She's wrong there."*

"I heard you."

"You didn't respond."

"I'm responding now."

"You should have responded when I said it."

"Loki!"

"Don't Loki me. You're the one whose being rude. All I want is a response."

"Fine. Then what do you mean that she's wrong?"

"You don't feel like you did before, do you?"

"No."

"Which means you are conduiting properly."

"That's not a word."

"It is if I make it a word. Besides, it's better than 'conduit-thing'!"

She had to stop herself from rolling her eyes because Violetta was already looking at her curiously. She felt like she should tell her she was talking to Loki so she wouldn't be more concerned than she obviously already was, but Loki said, *"You can't tell her I'm talking to you. You can't tell any of them I'm talking to you."*

"Why not?"

"We went over this before. Nobody can know I'm here. It's too dangerous. The only reason I can talk to you is because your mind is a vault."

"What do you mean my mind is a vault?"

"Unless you let someone in, they cannot read your mind or mind-speak to you. It's a peculiar little thing gifted to you by the

HeartsBlood Gem to protect you when you were trapped in there – and when you were let out, it didn't go away."

Ilia took a moment to take that in, closing her eyes so that Violetta would think she was resting and wouldn't question her silence. *"Right. Well, if that's true and my mind is a vault, how can you get into it to talk to me."*

"Ahh, that is a little trick I have up my sleeve, gifted to me at birth – I can pretty much break into anywhere I want. It has come rather in handy over the years of mischief making. And is what made me perfect for my role in Demeter's plans."

"Which are?"

"Ah-ah-ah. That would be giving far too much away. Which would not be a good thing right at this point, because while your mind is a vault, if someone powerful enough wanted to get in and didn't care if they turned your brain to mush, they could smash their way in and read your thoughts. So until there are further protections, I can tell you no more at this time about that."

"Then what can you tell me."

"Well, we were talking about your conduiting before you so rudely interrupted me with your questions about vaults and my interesting little quirks – which I don't blame you for because I certainly am interesting."

"Loki!"

"Why do people keep saying my name like that?"

"Because you are frustrating and annoying."

"Really." A pause. *"Good for me."* He cleared his throat. *"So, as I was saying, you held onto what you took in before because you didn't realise what you were doing or what you were. But now you've realised you can purge, you're doing it naturally without the need to use something as powerful as the Vortex to send it to."*

Her eyes snapped open. *"What are you talking about? How can I possibly be doing that?"*

"You are live-streaming, to use a modern term. Putting it out as it comes in so it can't hurt you and it can't form enough structure to attach to someone else and become a problem. You're being a good conduiteur."

She didn't bother telling him that wasn't a word either, instead asking, *"But how am I doing it?"*

"Do I look like a conduiteur encyclopaedia?"

"Umm, you don't look like anything at the moment, given I can't see you. But besides that, you are the one who told me about this, so excuse me for thinking you're an expert."

"I'm not. So stop asking. I only know what I know and nothing more."

"How can I know what you know if I don't ask you?"

There was a pause and then, *"Fair point. Fine. You can ask me. But accept that I might not be able to answer."*

"Fine."

"I think you need to answer Violetta. She's giving you that look you don't like."

"Oh. Yes." She'd been so caught up in talking to Loki that she'd forgotten she wasn't actually saying anything out loud. It truly was a strange thing to get used to.

"Try communicating like this when you're non-corporeal."

"I did. For 3000 years. When I was in the gem."

"Oh, right. So you know."

"I know. Now shut up so I can talk to Violetta. I can't listen to you and have a conversation with her at the same time."

A big sigh. *"Humans are so basic in the most annoying ways."*

"I'm not human, I'm a witch and ... Shut up!"

She met Violetta's gaze. She had no idea what the other witch had been saying to her. "I'm sorry. I'm having a little problem concentrating fully. I think I'm still half asleep." She sipped at the tisane again – her throat was still bone dry and felt very strained – probably from the screaming she'd done before the purge and then the effort after that, which hadn't been at all helped by the vomiting session on waking. "What were you saying?"

"I was asking if you were okay. You had such a strange look on your face."

"Oh, umm ..." She couldn't admit she was talking to Loki given he had forbidden it. And her brain truly was working sluggishly, so it took her a moment to think of something. "I ... umm ... I was worrying about Trip. And Tam and Korinna. And of course Dawn. And wondering how long I was unconscious. And if Trip had woken up yet? And how long I've been unconscious? And I was also thinking about how this conduiting thing is supposed to help. I mean, it has to have been given to me for a reason, and if I can help take bad things from other people, or things that overwhelm them, then that can't be a bad thing, so I should learn more about it, right? Figure out how to use it so it doesn't hurt me or others. And also if somehow it could be useful in the fight to come against Perses. I mean, maybe I can suck his powers from him or something?"

Violetta's expression turned thoughtful. "Maybe. It's worth looking into. As is whatever happened that knocked Tamuel and Korinna out. That could come in handy too if you can knock such powerful beings unconscious."

Eyes flaring, she realised she'd completely forgotten Violetta had mentioned she'd done that. "Oh H-Hells. I'm so sorry I did something to knock Tam and Korinna unconscious too. Are they okay? I really want to see them."

"They're fine. They'll be down soon I'm sure."

"Oh, good." She took another sip of tisane. "And

perhaps I should see Dawn to make sure she's okay. And I wouldn't mind seeing Trip and talking this all through with everyone as well because we've already lost this time I've been unconscious ... How long was I unconscious for and—"

Violetta began to laugh as she held her hands up. "Okay, okay. Your mind truly is spinning with all sorts of questions and thoughts, isn't it? I'm happy to answer your questions and talk through your thoughts, but one at a time. So, first things first, you've been out of it for two days."

"Two days!"

"Yes. Trip did wake, and just wanted to get to you, but he was so exhausted and needed to heal – his insides were virtually mush. I'm not sure how he survived that."

She didn't know if others were supposed to know he couldn't die, so she kept her mouth shut on that one until she could ask him.

"Anyway, Bas put him into a healing sleep to stop him from getting up. This soulmate thing is a blessing but it's also a worry when none of you seem able to do what's good for you when you need to help your mate."

Ilia wasn't in the mood to argue with that ridiculous statement – a mate-bond was a blessing and nothing else. But then, Violetta had never experienced one, and before she had mated with Trip, Ilia hadn't understood either. But she did think differently now and because of that, there was only one thing she wanted to do.

"I need to see Trip."

FOURTEEN

Ilia swung her legs off the couch while trying to juggle her mug of tisane – and managed to spill it on herself, the couch and the floor when dizziness struck and the room spun.

"Whoa!" Violetta leapt up and grabbed the mug in one hand while using her other to steady Ilia. "You are not going anywhere right now."

"I need to see Trip. I'll feel better if I see my mate is okay."

"Is my word not good enough?"

Ilia looked at her sideways. "Normally, yes – but seeing is truly believing and I don't just need to see him, I need to touch him. I need to be with him, to lie beside him, to hold him."

"I'm not sure that's a good idea."

"Call Bas or Tam. They can portal me up to the room."

"No they can't."

"Why not? You can't keep me away from my mate. Especially when he's being kept unconscious." How could she have been out of it for two days? How could she have left her mate to suffer like he had for days without her there to comfort and help like only she could. What kind of mate was she? Now her hand wasn't encumbered by the mug, she used it and the other one to push up from the couch in an effort to try to get to her feet again.

"Ow!" She collapsed back onto the couch the moment she put pressure on her legs. "What the fuck is wrong with my legs?" She had long compression tights on so she couldn't see. But she could feel – and they were so stiff and sore she could barely stand it.

"Tam said you bashed your legs black and blue in an effort to crawl across the floor to Trip. And this after you'd already damaged the muscles when the purge occurred – it came out of your entire body he said. Tam thought it was going to tear you apart."

She remembered. It had been one of the worst things she'd ever experienced – and she'd experienced some terrible things. But ... "Why hasn't Bas healed me?"

"He's tried, but it hasn't worked like it should. Not even after we brought you down here. Hence the tisane." Violetta handed the mug back to her with an expression that said 'drink – or else' and under the elegant older witch's stare, Ilia had no choice but to lift it to her lips and take a sip.

Swallowing it down, she asked, "Why wouldn't Bas' healing have worked on me?" It had the few times he'd used it on her.

Violetta sighed again then screwed her mouth to the side. "I'm only guessing because I'm still so uncertain about this new power of yours and how it works, but I think you conduited the healing magic out of you and into the closest person in need of healing."

"Who?" If it had been Trip, then she wouldn't feel so bad about not being with him. Or Dawn. If it had helped the toddler with the nightmares, then that would be good too. She looked hopefully at the other witch.

Violetta smoothed her hair, sat next to Ilia, then held her hands out.

Ilia stared at them. Not sure what she was looking at or why, she raised a questioning brow.

Violetta tapped her knuckles. "My arthritis is gone. In my knees and hips too. They're healed."

"Gone?" Bas had been using his healing to help Violetta with the pain and lack of movement her arthritis caused her – one of the only true indications of her age. But no healing magic, no matter how strong, could permanently heal certain ailments and life-threatening conditions – things like arthritis or cancer, spinal injuries or things people were born with. Healing magic could alleviate symptoms and help with pain and mobility for a while, they could keep people alive for longer while other healing measures were explored, but there wasn't a single spell or powerful enough healer who could cure those things in the long term. A God or Goddess probably could, but Bas was a demi-God, so didn't have their power.

So it seemed unlikely Violetta actually meant what it sounded like.

But the other witch was nodding. "Bas says all signs of my arthritis have disappeared. If I'm right about what happened – and I think I am – it seems like you not only acted as a conduit for Bas' healing powers, you strength- ened them and shaped them so that they did what they couldn't do by themselves: they helped rid me of my greatest pain."

"That's wonderful." She was so glad she'd been able to help this witch she admired so much. Yet ... "How come I've not done it before now?"

Violetta gave an elegant shrug. "I don't know that I can answer that with any certainty other than to say it is possible that by using the power purposefully like you did in the Vortex room, you opened yourself up to it."

It was similar to what Loki had said about her channelling the badness away. "Huh. That makes sense."

"Yes." The other witch's brow furrowed as she looked down at her hands.

"What's wrong? Does it not feel good?"

Violetta clenched her fists then flexed them out again. "You have no idea the gift you've given me. It's so wonderful but ..." She tipped her head from side to side. "It also frightens me."

Ilia jerked back a little. "You're frightened of me? Why?"

Violetta reached out and smoothed her thumb over Ilia's furrowed brow. "Not frightened *of* you, my dear. Frightened *for* you and *with* you. We have no idea what this means, what dangers it brings, or what you could do – or be made to do – with such a power."

Oh. She hadn't thought of that. "Could I hurt someone?" she asked Violetta at the same time she posed the question to Loki with her mind, hoping he was still there. "I mean, I know I already did given I knocked Tam and Korinna unconscious without realising it."

"I don't know," he said at the same time Violetta said the same. *"This is not a power we've seen before."*

"It's a new power?"

"Sure is."

Violetta pursed her lips as if thinking something through. Then she said slowly, "I think what happened to Tamuel and Korinna was a backlash thing because of how much energy you released, which given you seem to be releasing constantly now is unlikely to happen again." She tapped her finger against her chin. "But whether you could hurt someone with the conduiting power itself ... I do think it's unlikely, but I suppose it could be possible. If you took something they were not prepared to give."

"Is that true?"

"As I said, new power, so no idea. But wouldn't it be a bit fun if that was true."

"No. It wouldn't!" Her heartbeat speeding up, Ilia opened her mouth to question Violetta further, given Loki was not only being completely unhelpful but was spitting out his usual brand of crazed nonsense.

The other witch held her hand up, halting the words on Ilia's lips. "That is something we can definitely look into," she said, "however unlikely I think it is. Magics are governed by the heart of the person who holds them, and I know you are not a person who goes around wishing people ill, so your magic is unlikely to do so either."

Ilia let out a heavy breath at Violetta's words as Loki said, *"Pooh! She's probably right. Spoilsport. I could think of a bunch of my fellow Gods it would have been fun to try it out on."*

"Your idea of fun and mine are very different."

"And this from the witch who has always wished all sorts of ills on the Gods. Will wonders never cease."

"I—"

"Shh. Violetta is talking. You need to learn to respect your elders."

In her mind she narrowed her eyes at the annoying mischief God, but focused back in on what Violetta was saying.

"Pursuing the angle that you could use it as a weapon against our enemy is something we should look into — although not until we are more certain about what is going on."

"Why? If it could help?"

She took Ilia's hand in hers. "Well, my dear, I'm worried about what it's doing to *you,*" she said, index finger winding around one of the strands of beads hanging around her neck. "The fact Bas has struggled to heal you is not a good sign." She paused, pressed her lips together in a line, her face creased with worry.

"It isn't, is it?" Ilia's chest squeezed as her heartbeat pounded in her ears.

"No." Violetta reached over to take Ilia's free hand. "Bas and I have been discussing what the best thing to do is at this point."

"What have you come up with?"

"We would like to try and suppress it. To stop you from using it like you're doing – unknowingly and wholly untrained. Until we know more about it."

"You want to trap my power?"

Another pause then a slow nod. "Yes. I think it's necessary."

"No! You can't let her do that!" Loki shouted just as another voice – a voice that made her heart sing – said, "You are not trapping my beloved's power!"

She looked up to see Trip standing in the doorway. Korinna and Tam had their arms around him. "Trip."

He was awake. Not only that. He was coming towards her. Obviously weak and still in pain, but he had made it down the stairs to her and was limping across the room with Tam and Korinna's help.

She tried to stand but her legs just wouldn't support her, so she held out her hand and had to wait as he moved slowly towards her. But finally – finally! – he grasped her hand and it was bliss. Just his touch made her forget how much she ached. Then he took Violetta's place beside her after the other witch hastily rose from the couch, and carefully pulled Ilia into his arms. She sighed in contentment as comfort and joy and passion filled her and all the worry slipped away.

She lifted her face to his and welcomed his gentle, longing-filled kiss, giving herself over to the joy that sang a song of life and harmony between them.

But finally, all the questions and worries in her head intruded and she pulled back. "Are you okay?" she asked softly.

"Getting there." He glanced down at her legs then cupped her face. "I think I'm better than you. You're still so pale."

"You should look at yourself." She let her gaze rake over him. He was so thin, like that thing had consumed parts of him before she'd managed to get it out of him. She turned her head to find Tam, who stood just behind Violetta, his arm around Korinna as he watched them carefully. He was obviously worried too. "Where's Bas?"

"Why?"

"You need to get him," she said to him.

He tipped his head, glanced at Violetta then Trip before asking again, "Why?"

"I need him to heal Trip so I can do my conduit-thing."

"No!" Three voices shouted all at once.

But the only voice she took note of was Loki's – a strange fact to her – because he said, *"That's the smartest thing I've heard in days!"*

Trip gasped and gripped her face to turn her to him. "What was that? Did someone speak to you?"

"You heard that?"

"He heard that?" Loki said at the same time.

"Yes. Kind of."

"Fuck. He's not supposed to. How is he hearing that?"

"Through our soulbond?"

"Yes! Possibly. Maybe. Except, not really. It's probably got more to do with how he was created and who created him. I really need Demeter to tell me the full story around that so I'm not caught out like this. How am I supposed to do what she commands of me if I don't have all the information. I swear, that Goddess is made of secrets and shadows and I'm thoroughly sick of being kept half in the dark most of the ti—"

"Would you shut up!" Ilia and Trip barked at the same time.

"No need to be rude about it." Loki said grumpily. Then he sighed. *"So, Trip, you can hear me?"* Loki asked Trip.

Ilia waited for Trip's answer, but Trip was looking at her as intensely as if waiting for her to say something. "Exactly what can you hear?"

Trip tipped his head on the side as if listening. "Not words exactly – although sometimes I can gather the gist through your reactions and our mating bond. It's like an echo heard in the distance."

"Well, that's not as bad as I thought," Loki said. *"Demeter won't be quite so angry. Although why she would be angry when my failure to do as she commands isn't due to any failure of my talents but rather a lack of proper information to safeguard against certain oddities."*

"You'll be an oddity if you don't shut up and let me talk to my mate," Ilia snapped.

"Feisty. You know I love it when you show your true colours."

"I swear to Gods—"

"You swear to me? How sweet. I didn't know you cared that much."

"Argh!"

"Who are you talking to?" Tam asked. "Is it the same

person you were talking to in the Black Magics and Dangerous Books room?"

"Yes. Unfortunately."

Tam's eyes narrowed as he tipped his head to the side. "It's Loki, isn't it?"

"*What?*" Loki shouted at the same time she and Trip said the same thing, their heads snapping to Tam.

Tam snorted. "There's only one Being I know of who could put that look on your face ... Loki."

"*Hey! I can hear you.*"

"*Yes, but he can't hear you,*" Ilia crowed to him with her mind-voice. "*Now you're relying on me to be the go-between. Gotta hope I don't make things up.*"

"*That's not nice.*"

"*Who said I had to be nice?*"

"*Well I—*"

"Loki's talking to you?" Korinna asked over the top of Loki's tirade.

There was an aggravated sigh and then, "*Would you please tell them to stop saying my name! Someone might hear — and that won't be a good thing. And shields. There need to be shields. Right now.*"

"What?" Ilia said, trying to concentrate on Korinna's question while Loki was rambling. She held up her hand to Korinna. The other witch stopped talking and waited, giving Ilia the chance to say, "There are shields around the house all the time but they were strengthened after Korinna spoke her prophecy to ensure there were no prying eyes or ears. Although, we didn't know about you. For that matter, how did you get through the shields?"

"*I established a link with your mind last Christmas as you know, but I also inserted a piece of my consciousness then as well.*"

It gives me a back door so to speak into your mind regardless of shields."

"What?! So you've been in my mind all this time? Seeing everything?"

"Well, not everything. There are certain things one can never wash out once seen so I set an alarm to tell me when you might be doing the horizontal mamba, but other than that, yes, I have used it to pop in and out fairly often."

She was only slightly relieved that he hadn't seen her and Trip making love, because the thought that he had been there all this time ... "Hang on. So you know we've been looking for you?"

"Of course."

"Then why haven't you contacted us? There's things we need to ask you."

"I know. And those are things I'm not able to share with you right now. But I have been keeping an eye on you all to see how far along you were in figuring everything out and of course to ensure none of you are getting into too much trouble."

"Comforting."

"Yes, isn't it. Mostly you're all boring, and a bit slow in figuring things out if truth be told, but sometimes the show has been very entertaining listening to all your suppositions."

"What's he saying? What's going on?" Tam asked, looking between her and her love.

She held up her hand because Loki was still talking.

"... better things to do. You're not my only priority, you know."

"And I'm supposed to be happy about all this?"

"Well ... I didn't really give much thought to your happiness, but honestly, I would expect you would be happy to have a Fairy Godfather type – emphasis on the God part – keeping an eye on you."

"Right. So having no choice in this is supposed to get my stamp of approval?"

"Please don't let us sink into one of your whinge sessions about how you've been done wrong. Not when there's more important things to focus on."

"Like what, you insufferable arsehole?"

"What is Loki saying?" Korinna asked.

"Like them not using my name and giving me away. Tell them to stop using my name."

She blinked and realised everyone was staring at her. "Sorry. He goes on. And on."

"Yes, well that's Loki for you," Korinna said.

Ilia gestured at all of them. "He doesn't want you using his name out loud. Apparently he's worried someone in the Godly Realm," she waved at the ceiling, "might hear it and that would be bad for some reason he's not sharing with me."

"Well, if we can't use his name, then how should we refer to him?"

"How about Mr Amazing?"

Ilia's mouth split into a grin. "He wants us to refer to him as Mr Crap-tastick."

The others laughed as Loki shouted, *"That's not what I said at all."*

She shrugged, mouth twitching. "It fits better."

He growled in her mind and she laughed.

Once the laughter had died down, Korinna said, "So, Lo... I mean Mr Crap-tastick—"

"Oh for me's sake! That's not what I want to be called."

Ilia ignored him. "Yes?"

"He's been in your mind?" Korinna repeated her question from earlier. "For how long?"

"Apparently Mr Crap-tastick's—"

"Stop that! It's not funny."

"... been using a link he established in my mind at Christmas. He's been watching on and off since then."

"What?" Trip said. "That bloody little arsehole." Her mate looked like he wanted to strangle something – namely Loki if he were here.

"I'm not the one who needs to be strangled."

"You sure?"

He grunted. *"Even if I was, it wouldn't work. I'm unstrangleable. Besides, you kind of need me."*

She returned her attention to Trip, who had thunder in his eyes. She cupped his face. "I'm not particularly happy about him being in my mind either, but I have to say, I'm glad he was there when we opened the Vortex, because he was the one who helped me help you."

"Ah, so you do acknowledge I'm indispensable."

"That might be taking it too far."

"How?" Trip asked, and she didn't have to think back to what they were talking about – she was starting to get good at this having two conversations at once thing.

"He spoke to me after I purged at the oculus. He came to me so I would know how to help you. Although, being Mr Crap-tastick, he was only partly helpful. He keeps telling me he can't tell me too much."

"What can you tell us?" Trip asked frowning hard as if trying to hear what was being said.

"Hey! Tell him to stop that. And you ... you need to stop talking out loud to me. Use your mind. And don't tell them what I'm saying until there are steel-clad shields in place."

"There are steel-clad shields in place. Besides, if we call you by your code name, Mr Crap-tastick, what's the harm?"

He growled but didn't correct the name again as he said, *"Not good enough. They need to be titanium strength shields. More than what was used to keep prying eyes from knowing Korinna is speaking prophecy."*

"I think you're being a bit dramatic."

"I'm not. You might find this hard to believe given I'm me, but I'm serious. We don't want my name or my words or thoughts bandied about too much outside your vault of a mind. People who shouldn't hear certain things might hear them and then we'd be in trouble."

"You mean you'd be in trouble."

"No. We'd be in trouble. All of us. I'm not simply hiding for my sake, but for yours. I know things that can't be known yet, because once they are, you'll all have to make your move against Perses and you're not ready yet."

"But that doesn't make sense as a reason to hide. You could simply not tell us the things that are dangerous for us to know now."

"I could. But that still wouldn't safeguard me against the things certain Beings think Demeter has told me and would want to get out of me. Which would distinctly not be good for me."

"But who knows you're working for her?"

He snorted. *"After the events of Christmas, you think certain entities haven't figured out I'm involved somehow with what is going on?"*

FIFTEEN

Her mind spun as she tried to process his words and the extreme level of his worry, because what he was inferring ... it didn't seem possible.

The evil they were fighting shouldn't be able to see anything they were doing, given he was still locked away in the prison of the Void. But, there didn't seem to be any other reason for Loki to be so ... panicked about being heard or found out. If he was normal – and he was far from that – he might be concerned about how his father and brother would react to discover he was working so closely with Demeter. But she was certain he really wouldn't give a shit if they did find out. So, that left only one entity he would be worried about. *"You mean Perses?"*

"Don't say his name – not even in your steel trap of a mind!"

"You just said it."

"I'm different. I'm in your mind using shields and layers of other protection so others can't hear what I'm saying. Which is why it's not a little annoying that your mate can feel me here and—"

"Loki! Get back to the topic at hand. Why can't I say you-

know-who's name? We've been saying it since we learned who was behind what's going on. What's different now?"

"You should never have said his name."

"Then why didn't you tell us?"

"I didn't realise you were saying it so freely without the appropriate shields being in place."

"I still don't understand why it's a problem. Because his minions are out and about once again. They are sensitive to it and will zero in on anyone saying or thinking it."

"Minions? But Clodia is his only follower," she said, touching the HeartsBlood Gem embedded in her chest where that evil witch now resided.

"If you think that, you're not as smart as I thought. Do you truly think someone as powerful as he would rely on only one follower? He's had people working for him since he lived in this Realm and that hasn't changed since he was trapped. He has minions everywhere. In fact, they've touched all of the lives here, some since they were children."

"Children? Who?"

"I can't tell you that."

"Why?"

"Because it's dangerous. Dangerous for me to tell you; dangerous for those affected to remember in case it calls his attention to them once again more than it already is — and believe me, you don't want that. Not if you want the time you need to plan and strengthen as you will need to if you are to win against him. So don't ask me about it, okay?"

She rolled her eyes because now all she wanted to do was ask him about it, wondering who he was alluding to — all of them had been fucked over by a God or Goddess in their lives, so it could be any one of them — except Violetta.

"Oh, she's been touched too. By Clodia in Roma."

That's right. At the time, she hadn't known Clodia

was being influenced and used by Perses, so she hadn't really woven those threads together to create a picture. Her gaze slid to the older witch. *"She's okay now though, right?"*

"She will always be damaged by that possession; however, she is free of any influence ... for now. But she won't be if you all know things too early, because it will be far easier for Him or one of his minions to find her and slip inside her again to use her. Knowledge is power and not always in a good way. So if you feel anything for her at all, you will keep your mouth shut about what I'm saying."

"You know you're not saying much at all."

"I do. But I can't say more than I am. And I can't show myself to any of you. Not until you have all figured out some things and got past certain ... informational blocks on your own."

Trip shook her hands to get her attention. "I know he's talking to you. What's he saying? Does he know we've been looking for him all this time?"

"Yes he does. But he has to hide because—"

"Ilia! What part of don't tell them did you not understand?"

Her brows rose. *"So I can't tell them anything? They've got questions!"* Her eyes flared as she thought of something and she reached for the pen and pad of paper that was always kept on the side table behind the couch where the phone was. *"Can I write down what you're telling me?"*

"No. Not even that will work. The written word is as powerful as the spoken word – sometimes more so." She dropped the pad and pen and pouted a little. *"You're a party-pooper, you know. I should change your name from Mr Crap-tastick to Debbie Downer."*

"Ha-ha. Very funny. But this isn't a joking matter. You can't tell them without stronger shields than you're capable of creat-

ing. Not through speaking, writing, thought projection or anything else you might think of.”

“My shields are strong.”

“Not strong enough. And stop talking out loud, for fuck’s sake!”

“What’s he saying to you?” Trip asked.

“He can’t say much of anything – and he’s not letting me say much of anything – until there are stronger shields than what we are currently using to protect the house from outside spies.”

Trip’s brows rose. “If he needs stronger shields, he’ll get stronger shields. Tam, Korinna, Violetta, link hands. I’m still not at full power, but can utilise the strength of others to boost myself to create the most impregnable shields there are: The shields that hid me for all those years and kept my memories from me.”

“I thought that was a spell.”

“The original magic was a spell, but it alone couldn’t have kept my memories from me for all those centuries. Things of such emotion have a habit of seeping through. No, shields were used inside my mind and around me to hide me and keep the knowledge from me.”

“Demeter’s shields?” Tam asked, eyes going wide. “But how will that help us? We can’t use the shields of a Goddess like her. Not even Jules or Dawn could create shields that strong even though they are Goddess-touched.”

“We don’t need a Goddess. Demeter used my shields. She used my magic against me because it’s the strongest magic of all.”

“Show off. But actually, yes, his shields are what we need!”

“He’s already shielded the house.”

“Not with the magic that’s at the heart of him – his most powerful and enduring magic. I will feel safer if he uses that.”

Tam was pointing out the same thing she had to Loki, so she quickly told them what he had said about Trip's magic.

"It will be stronger if I can put it around one room rather than the entire house. So where do we want to be when I put the shield up?"

"Any objections to the kitchen?" Tam asked. "There's food and water in there in case we're in the shield for some time."

"Sounds good," Korinna said. "But first we need to get Bas, Jules and Dawn so they're not shut outside the shield."

Trip nodded at Korinna's suggestion. "Good idea. And they can help. We'll need all the power we can get, given I don't want Ilia to be a part of this in case we start up her conduit magics by accident."

"Do we have to have Jules and Dawn here? I'm not sure that's wise after what happened before," Violetta said, nodding towards Ilia.

Bristling a little at what she considered too much mother-henning worry over her, she said briskly, "Wouldn't it be better to simply get Bas to do a healing on Trip so I can use my channelling to make it stronger and actually heal him? Then he'd be able to form the shield himself and Jules and Dawn can stay out of it if you wish."

"No!" they all said again.

"Why not?"

"Because it hurts you," Trip said, gripping her hands and pulling her attention back to him. "Look at you. Look at what happened to you after you channelled that thing out of me."

"I was already hurt from the purge. I actually think using my conduit powers helped a bit. At least, I felt super energised while using them."

"But you passed out for two days afterwards."

"That was from not *using your powers and keeping that thing inside you for too long. And of course what you went through to get to Trip when they removed the two of you. If they'd kept you closer, you would have woken up yesterday. It's been kinda boring waiting around for you to open your peepers. You know you make funny noises when you're unconscious. Oh, you can tell them that if you want to. It's not particularly important or relevant to my personal safety."*

"Thank you for your generosity," she said wryly.

"You're welcome," he said superciliously.

She rolled her eyes and told them what Loki had said — everything except him being bored and her making funny noises.

Looking reticent but willing to believe her, Trip asked, "I'm finding it hard to believe that's true. I mean, using power usually saps energy from a practitioner. It doesn't energise them."

"I know. But why would Loki lie about this?" Tam asked. "I know he's a trickster, but he's also my friend and it does seem like he has always been helping us in his own way. I think we can believe him right now."

"Yes," Ilia drawled. "As far as anything from Loki's lips is true — I think Tam's right that we can believe him this time."

"Thank you for your generosity."

"You're welcome," she said, mimicking him in tone.

Chuckling in her head made her smile, but she wiped the smile off her face as she looked at all of them. "Seriously. I'm certain I will be okay."

"Is that a knowing? Not just Loki saying it, but a true knowing?" Korinna asked.

Ilia tipped her head to the side and thought about

Korinna's question for a moment before answering. "You know, I actually think it is. I feel it here." She rubbed over her chest then touched the side of her head, "And here. Just like with my knowings. It feels true. If I become a conduit for Bas' powers to fully heal Trip, I will be fine. More than fine. It will help to heal me too. I think part of the reason I've had so much trouble with everything since what happened at Christmas is I have been treating my magic like it's normal magic – which it isn't – and I've been fighting the non-normality of it; I've not used it as it was meant to be used because I didn't understand that it was okay for it not to be normal. I didn't understand it at all."

"And you understand it now?" Tam asked softly.

"Yes. Not all of it, but enough to do this. And the more I use it, the more I will come to know."

"But none of us can help you with this, dear," Violetta said gravely, hands clasped tightly in front of her. 'As you said – it's not like normal magic."

"Neither is Tam's mix of warlock and cupid magic. Or Bas' cupid and healer magic. Or Jules' and Dawn's Goddess-gifted magic. Or Trip's and Korinna's nature-and-the-universe magic."

"Good point," Trip said, his mouth curling at the corner.

Violetta made a small hissing sound and waved her hand at each of them. "Which is my point exactly. You've each struggled with the different nature of your powers and how they don't comply to what magic normally is and how it works. For each of you, it has made things so much more dangerous. And in some ways, Ilia's power is more ... " She waved her hand as if trying to conjure the word from the air.

"Disparate," Korinna offered.

"Mismatched," Tam said.

"Unique," Trip whispered, kissing her temple.

"Fuckingly awesomely wrong and yet so right," Loki said joyfully.

Ilia shared his words with the others and they all laughed – except Violetta. She made a clicking sound with her tongue and waved their laughter down. "Your magic is dysfunctional in the sphere of normal magic. It's divergent. Which is not a good thing because we don't know how to train it or capture it if it gets out of control."

"Korinna's magic, and mine for that matter, was treated as divergent when we were in the training camp together," Tam said. "But being afraid of it, trying to make it work like regular magic, just made things worse. It cut off half of who I was meant to be and it was mostly behind the reason Korinna lost all those souls in Pompeii." His gaze fixed on Korinna his expression solemn, pained, as if apologising for bringing up such a memory.

"It's okay," Korinna said solemnly. "You are right. Not understanding the differences in my magic is why I screwed up with Pompeii; why it was destroyed. I was trying desperately to use my magic in the way my mother had, but it was never meant to be manipulated into behaving like normal magic."

Tam pulled her into his side and hugged her close. "We both made mistakes because of how we were trained *not* to embrace our differences, but to be more homogenous with everyone else." She looked up at him and he kissed her gently on the lips before saying, "I think Ilia's right. I think she needs to learn how to use her extraordinary power – and the only way she can do that is to use it. Like how Korinna and I have been getting a grip on our singular powers."

"Thanks." Ilia smiled at him. "What Tam said."

"This is foolish until we have looked into it further," Violetta said, but her protest sounded weaker than before.

Ilia gripped Trip's hand. "You're forgetting I also have Trip. He will know when I go too far and will pull me out."

"Yes. I will." He lifted her hand and kissed her palm.

She instantly heated but forced the sensation aside as she pulled her gaze from his to look from one to the other of her friends. "All of you will be there too, watching over me, watching the magic, talking it over with me afterwards so we can learn more about it together."

"Can Loki point to any texts that might help us understand a bit more before you go do something this reckless?" Violetta asked, her hands clenched tightly in front of her neat purple pencil skirt.

"Can they please stop using my name out loud like that before this great shield is in place?"

She snorted. *"Fine."* Then she said out loud, "Remember not to use his name until Trip's shield is up in case it pulls unwanted attention. He's Mr Crap-tastick until then."

"For fuck's sake! I don't like that name."

The corners of her mouth ticked as she suppressed a smile and tried to school her features into the serious expression the occasion warranted. *"Stop complaining and answer Violetta's question."*

He let loose a long-suffering sigh and then said, *"Fine. Tell her this: There are no texts because there's not been anything quite like you before. Violetta is right in that your magic is divergent. It's like your brain and your entire body work differently — even before you were made into a spirit, you were different because you were moon-touched."*

"Moon-touched?"

"Don't interrupt with inconsequential side-topics especially given I can't answer the why, only the is. You were moon-

touched at both of your births, as well as being dawn-touched at your second birth. But it is the moon-touched thing that's the most important now. It was what called the she-wolf to your babes when they were taken from you. It was a big part of why Tiberinus used you to power the HeartsBlood Gem. And it was one of the reasons Demeter worked so hard to get that gem into her possession – not simply because of Cassandra's prophecies, but because no normal soul could have been meshed in a gem's crystal in the way you had been and, rather than get weaker, became stronger as the years passed."

"I was supposed to get weaker?"

"Of course. Tiberinus was using your soul like a battery when he meshed you into the gem. And all batteries lose their power over time and eventually die. You did the opposite. So, when the gem came into Demeter's control, she wasn't surprised to discover you are a natural magical conduit like the moon is. But when you were pulled out of it by Tam and Korinna and made corporeal with Ostara's gift to the newborn, it melded something else into the mix ... and that singular combination makes you more than any moon-touched conduit has been before. We're not exactly certain how it all works – just that it does and that it's not dangerous ... to you."

Her mouth popped open a little. *"What do you mean by that?"* She glanced around at these people who she loved more than her own life despite everything she'd tried to do to make certain she never got so close to anyone ever again – you couldn't feel loss if you weren't close to people.

Of course, Trip had changed all that and now here she was, terrified of losing these people who had become such an essential part of her life. Terrified of causing that loss. *"Are my powers dangerous to others?"*

"Only if you mean them harm."

"Oh." Well, she would never mean any of the Stevens

family harm. Or Trip's found family in Tasmania. Or most other people for that matter. Just the Evil Ones. And perhaps the Gods and Goddesses who fucked with people for the fun of it. They deserved a bit of hurting.

"I'm sure you don't mean me or Demeter or Persephone in that group of my kind you'd like to hurt."

"Not unless you do something to hurt me or mine."

A cartoon-style gulping sound echoed in her head and she choked on a laugh, amused despite herself at Loki's ridiculousness. But she still wanted to make certain Loki wasn't just making light of something that was a deal breaker for her. *"So if I act as a conduit to help Bas heal Trip right now, I can't hurt Trip? Or Bas?"*

"No. You will only help them and make them stronger. You can tell them that too. Right now until certain other things occur, your ability to do that will not alter the shape of what lies ahead with the fucker of an Old One we will war against."

"Umm, that's good?"

"Yes it is. So tell them what I said."

She did so to a mix of relief – Trip, Tam and Korinna – and remaining uncertainty – Violetta.

"Okay. I'll call my dad," Tam said, then closed his eyes.

Magic prickled the air – enough to tell her Bas was not in the house. "Where is he?" Why would he go elsewhere when his skills were needed by all the injured people in the house?

"You know what I was telling you before about moving you down here to be away from Dawn as well as Trip?" Violetta asked. Ilia nodded. "Well, while it stopped you from trying to do your conduit-thing, you still seemed to be able to sense her distress and were disturbed by it, which made Trip worse. So it was decided it was best to remove the baby from the equation."

"Dad and Mum took Dawn down to Trip's farm in Tasmania to stay with Daphne and the boys for a few days," Tam said as he opened his eyes, having apparently sent his message to his father. "She was always calmer around Daphne and Gideon when we were down there for Christmas, so we thought it might help her now."

"Daphne? She's okay? And Gideon?"

Something in Loki's voice caught Ilia's attention. "Why do you care? Do you know them or something?"

"No. Not now."

Her chest ached with the utter sadness that threaded through his tone and she was about to ask about it when a portal opened near the doorway and Bas stepped through.

CHAPTER

SIXTEEN

Bas' gaze landed on Trip and Ilia as the portal snapped closed behind him. "You're both awake!"

Ilia waved at him. "And in need of your talents."

"Oh?" He turned to Violetta. "What's changed?"

"Everything apparently."

"You didn't bring Dawn and Jules?" Tam asked.

Bas shrugged. "Through the portal?" His faced filled with an 'are you kidding' expression.

"Yeah. Right," Tam said, looking sheepish.

"They need to be here," Korinna said, voice full of worry.

Bas sighed and ran his hand over the stubble on his jaw. "I know Tam said something about bringing them back to be under Trip's shield, but it took us a day to get there and I don't really want them to have to turn around and travel back without a few days' rest. Both Jules and Dawn need it. Besides, they're already shielded at Trip's farm – Jules and I re-secured all the shields we put in place to make sure

Daphne and the boys stay off the pantheons' radars in case they were drawn to them after the events of Christmas."

"But didn't you have to take the shields down to create your portal?" Violetta asked.

Bas waved his hand. "Jules is capable of putting them back up. Her shield work has become stronger than mine."

Korinna shook her head slowly. "I don't think you should have left them there."

"I actually agree," Loki said. *"It's not a good idea given—"*

Ilia interrupted Loki, saying to him, *"Dawn doesn't do well with travel, especially portal travel."* Then to Bas she said, "I think you did the right thing in giving her time to get over the trip down there – and I'm sorry it was necessary to do so."

"Not your fault." He waved his hand then rubbed his eyes – they were bloodshot and full of exhaustion and worry.

"It must have been hard to leave them," she said, trying to show him the sympathy Korinna and Violetta were suddenly lacking for the ex-cupid who looked like he could do with a week of good sleep. He'd been using too much of his power healing them all recently.

He nodded, glancing at Violetta and Korinna. "I don't like leaving them, believe me. But Dawn was asleep for the first time in over twenty-four hours, and Jules didn't want to disturb her."

"Oh, poor baby."

"Yes." Bas wiped his hand over his face, blinking hazily. "Being with Gideon and the others has helped to keep her calm, but she hasn't slept since we left here – the bloody nightmares keep waking her up."

"I can help with that—" Ilia began.

"No!" Violetta said sharply. "At least not until after you are stronger."

"They need to come back," Korinna said again, more doggedly this time.

Ilia frowned at her – what was wrong with her? She wasn't usually so clueless. She glanced at Trip to see him looking worriedly at his daughter too.

Bas made an irritated sound. "Okay. If it's that important, I'll let Jules know they need to get back here. And in the meantime, you can tell me what I can do here and we can get on with that while we're waiting for them to arrive. It could take Jules a day to organise a flight for her and Dawn."

"Not by plane. They need to get here now," Korinna insisted.

Tam frowned at his mate. "You know Dawn can't do portal travel."

"Teleport her."

Bas jerked his hand, obviously irritated. "Don't you think I would if I could? I had to portal here myself because I've used too much magic lately to teleport easily or accurately. Not to mention the use of teleport magic affects Dawn almost as badly as portal travel. I can't even open a portal near her without upsetting her. As it was, I had to drive to the far end of the property to open the portal to make sure the magics of that didn't disturb her sleep. That's why I didn't appear immediately after Tam's ca—"

"No. Jules and Dawn need to be here," Korinna intoned stubbornly. "Right now."

They all looked at Korinna as Tam asked, "Why? If Dawn is being so disturbed by all the magic and she's safe behind the shields on the farm with Mum and Trip's adopted family, isn't it better we keep her out of this?"

"No. No. No. No. NO!" Korinna's eyes went wide and turned black and swirling gold as the last 'no' exploded from her mouth.

"Shit! Not again." Tam leapt forward to hold onto his mate as she began to shake. "Bas. Help me hang onto her."

Bas raced forward, his hands grasping onto Korinna's other side as she shook back and forth.

But her shaking didn't progress like it had before when she'd fallen into prophecy and she didn't rise into the air.

Her eyes stayed black with swirls of gold and a voice came out of her that was a harsh echo of her own voice:

"The one we are fighting, part has broken free
A threat to this Realm and yet we don't see
For two beings came to life the night of eternal birth
Both born to fight the evil that threatens beautiful Earth
But the evil did not escape like we thought it did
It used the birth energy, its power, and it hid
Inside the only one who could hold it and not break
But now it tries to shape her into something filled with hate
The only one who can save her is the one reborn that night
Only she can split the powers and light darkness into moon's
light
For she is the true conduit, born to light like moon and sun
It is her destiny to split the powers and burn out the Evil One
For he cannot be allowed to control the Being of Light and Day
If he does we lose all and the Realms fall into decay
The conduit must do, the conduit must be
Three times three times three times three,
So saeth the Well, so mote it be."

SHE SHUDDERED as the last words left her then slumped into Tam's arms, but rather than falling into unconsciousness like the other times she'd spoken a prophecy, her eyes stayed open as she stared up at Tam.

And they were filled with horror and knowing.

In a voice harsh with emotion, she said, "Dawn. It's Dawn. It's in Dawn."

Silence followed her statement as her words, added to her prophecy, fully registered.

Trip broke the silence. "A piece of the Evil One is inside Dawn?"

"What?"

"No!"

"That's impossible."

Their voices, their denials, tumbled over each other as Korinna, tears pouring down her face said, "It's true. I didn't know until now, but it's true. I'm so sorry."

Trip cupped Ilia's face, meeting her eyes, his reflecting her terror, and whispered, "You knew. You were trying to help her right from the start because you somehow knew."

She shook her head in sharp, rapid movements. "I didn't know … I just did what felt right." She pulled away from his gentle grip so she could face Korinna. "But you can't be right. Maybe it's in me? That would make more sense. It disappeared just after I came out of the Void, corporeal. The bit of the Evil One that escaped before we could stop it had to have gone into me then. It had to have been me. Not a baby. What could it want with a baby? She can't talk or walk or do anything for herself. Not for years."

Violetta gasped. "Oh Gods no! That's why."

"That's why what?" Bas asked, striding across the room to Violetta who had begun to shake. He gripped her shoulders gently, even though he looked like he wanted to tear things apart, and held her steady. "What have you seen that we haven't?"

"Dawn's fast growth. It's not because of the powers Ostara gifted her – I should have realised a Goddess of light and birth and nature would not distort the natural course of things in that way."

"Then what's making her grow so fast?" Tam asked.

"Him," Korinna said, her voice tortured. "The piece of him that escaped. It was held at bay by the link between Ilia and Dawn, probably because Ilia acted as a conduit even then, taking from it the power it was using towards its evil ends. But when it was broken ..." She shook her head.

"You mean, I started this?" Ilia asked, horrified.

"No. No." Korinna looked up at her, her eyes pools of empathy and grief. "The link was killing you both; you had to dismantle it. The fact it was there for so long is possibly what enabled you to naturally continue helping to purge Dawn of what the Evil One was doing to her."

"Which was?" Bas asked, his voice choked.

"The part of it that's in her ... it's somehow using her birth gift from Ostara, warping it to make her grow to maturity in preparation for the time the rest of it is ready to come into this world. It intends to use her, to turn her into nothing but a shell of power that can hold it and let it do as it wills."

"But ... but ..." Bas looked around desperately at all of them, his fear a punch in the guts. "I thought it wanted to use Trip and Korinna."

"It does," Trip said slowly, as if something was just dawning on him. "It needs our powers to fully escape its prison. But it also needs a body to come into as it no longer has one." His gaze went to his daughter where she stood cradled in her mate's arms.

She nodded. "But it can't use our bodies to help come into this world can it?"

"No. We are not compatible with its kind of evil."

"That's why you couldn't go into the Black Magic and Dangerous Books vault," Tam exclaimed. "Because your power is the absolute opposite of the evil that exists in there. And the evil that exists in what is left of this Titan." He jerked as if hit, his gaze snapping to Trip. "That's what the problem was in there with you ... what was tearing you apart. You took some of what Ilia took from Dawn – so you took some of it into you, right?"

"Yes. I didn't fully realise it until now, but my power was fighting with it, trying to destroy it rather than let it out and all the time, it was trying to go into the Vortex – despite the fact it couldn't exist there; because there was always the chance it would survive and be sent back into the Void to join with the rest of it. Whereas in me, it would have been destroyed. I am too formed. My power, my magics, are too much a part of every cell in my body. That piece of it could never exist in me despite the fact I am everything it wants and needs."

"Why didn't it try to take over Ilia then? Bits of it have been in her for months."

"I'm the conduit," she said as a knowing shivered through her again. "There's nothing inside me it can hold onto. It tried as you were taking me to the oculus, but it couldn't hold on. I'm too ... slippery. It doesn't know what I am so it can't use me."

"Lucky for you," Loki said. *"And lucky for us."*

"But why Dawn?" Bas asked. "Why does it want her?"

"It needs a body used to enormous power that won't break when it enters it fully. There's only a handful of beings I know of with the right combination of heritage, genetics and power that a Titan like it could use – some of the older Gods, us," he waved his hand between him and his daughter, "and Dawn."

Bas was still shaking his head as he obviously struggled to accept what he was hearing. He turned to Korinna, his eyes desperate, pleading. "But, the prophecy … I thought the prophecy you spoke about Dawn the other day said she was the one who would help to destroy the bastard."

"And so she could," Trip said softly. "Which is why it wants to control her. Why it tore itself apart so a piece could go inside her and work at taking her over slowly so nobody noticed until it was too late." He clenched Ilia's hand and looked down at her with eyes filled with wonder and pride. "But somehow you naturally knew her fits and nightmares weren't normal for a being like her. That she needed the thing behind them taken from her. You've been doing it from the start, taking bits of it in, making it weaker so it couldn't do what it planned in the time it meant to do it."

"What do you mean?" Bas asked.

"She not only took much of the evil from Dawn, she slowed the speed of growth it truly needs."

"Of course!" Violetta exclaimed. "It would want her close to adult size as soon as possible."

"And at the rate she's growing that would still be years away," Korinna said. "It wouldn't want to wait that long, not when everything else is falling into place."

"What is falling into place?" Tam asked. "It's no closer to escaping than it was the night we sent Clodia into the Void."

Korinna's eyes darkened again, but this time they didn't swirl as she said in that same echoing voice,

"The day is ordained, the day is near.
The time when the veil thins is when the Titan will be here."

Her head jerked up then back and her eyes cleared. "All Hallows Eve. That's when it will try again."

"But when? How many years away?" Tam asked her.

She looked up at him. "Not years. Months. The time is this year."

"Holy fucking crap!"

"Which is why you need to get that fucking thing out of Dawn now!" Loki said.

CHAPTER

SEVENTEEN

Ilia jerked at his words.

"What is it?" Trip asked. "What did he say?"

She turned to him slowly. "He says that we must get it out of Dawn now."

"Ah-ah-ah. Don't misquote me. I said you. Not we. You."

"I do not like the look on your face. What is that fucker saying?"

"Oy! Rude!"

She ignored Loki and repeated what he'd said about her ridding Dawn of the darkness even though she wasn't sure he was right – or if she could. Taking small parts of it from the toddler was one thing, but getting rid of it all?

Getting it out of herself and then the small bit out of Trip had almost killed her. How could she survive more?

Perhaps I'm not supposed to.

The errant thought hit her hard, so hard she was worried she'd moved or made a noise. She glanced at Trip, hoping he hadn't felt the enormity of that thought, but he was frowning over what she'd said, too lost in his own thoughts to register hers.

Thank the Gods for that mercy. Because if it came down to a choice between saving Dawn and her own life, she would always save Dawn. She wasn't certain Trip would agree – not that he wouldn't want to save the baby, but he would never agree that Ilia must give her life for that purpose – or any purpose.

And maybe now she had so much to lose, she'd agree except …

It was Dawn. And she would do anything for that baby. Anything.

Still, it made her furious to think this was the price she must pay. And she was pretty certain it was the price. Her life.

The Gods were fucking with her again obviously. To gift her with life and a mate and family and then tear it away from her before she'd had much of a chance to explore such happiness.

Fucking arsehole misogynistic egotistical sadists.

"Not all of us are like that!" Loki said, sounding obscenely hurt.

"I'll believe that when you do something to actually help. When you *sacrifice* your *heart like Trip and I are being asked to do."*

"You have no idea of the sacrifices I've made or continue to make," he said, his voice harsher than she'd ever heard it and full of a deep hurt. But right now she didn't care about his sacrifice or pain.

All she could feel was what loomed ahead of her: her death. And the never-ending ache of loss her death would bring. Trip wouldn't want to live without her but he wouldn't have a choice because he couldn't die.

She gasped – she still hadn't asked him about that. But now wasn't the time.

Her gasp pulled Trip out of his deep thought and he gripped her hands tightly as he met her gaze. "Are you okay?" he whispered.

She nodded, unable to speak for fear of what might come out of her mouth if she did.

He gave her a soft kiss. She leaned into it, needing to savour it, to feel everything she could right now because who knew how many more she'd have. She wished they could go up to their room and make love from now until the time when Dawn arrived. But she couldn't. Not only was Trip still in need of healing, she needed to be part of the discussion about what she was going to do with the bit of Perses that she was going to have to take out of the precious toddler. And it wasn't like she could just let it go into the air – it would find someone else to take over or wreak some other havoc. She would need to put it somewhere where it could do no harm. Perhaps they could open the oculus again – although maybe even the power in the lay lines wouldn't be enough to contain more of the Titan. They could open the Void and thrust it in there with the rest of him – but would that make him whole and more powerful? Not to mention once the Void was open he could slip more of himself out or even fully break free.

So that wasn't really an option either.

Maybe a crystal such as the HeartsBlood Gem with a lattice structure strong enough to trap him like they were trapping the evil witch Clodia. She touched her chest, finger running over the slight coolness of the gem that she was keeping safe there.

The gem had always been warm when Ilia had been trapped inside and used to power it. Strange that it was now nearly always so cool. Maybe it had something to do with the soul that powered it. Hers had been full of love and hope and the need to help and do good – okay, it had been soured by all the centuries she'd been trapped and used and abused inside the gem, but deep inside she was still a good person who wanted to do good. Clodia was the opposite. She'd been seduced by power – the offer of it, the having of it, the abuse of it to gain more. She hadn't cared who she used or tortured or killed to get it. Her soul was damaged and evil and incapable of love and giving. So maybe that's why the gem was cold with her inside it.

"Yes of course. That's the purpose of it," Violetta said softly, grabbing her attention from her spinning thoughts.

What had she missed? She looked around to see everyone else equally puzzled.

"What is the purpose of what?" Tam asked.

"Ilia's conduit powers. She was remade on the night that Dawn was born – just after it. After the bit of the Evil One slipped from the Void and into Dawn apparently. Under the full light of the moon." She gasped and glanced up. "She was made with Ostara's power *and* Luna's power. She is doubly Goddess-blessed."

"But ... those Goddesses don't usually play well together, given the coming of the dawn is when the moon must wain, losing its power," Tam said. "So why would they both bless the same person?"

Violetta's gaze settled on Ilia. "She was already blessed by Luna if my reading of her past is correct. Those powers protected her all the years she was in the HeartsBlood Gem. The Moon Goddess' powers are beneficent and loving. She would look after one of her own as far as she could. Even so far as to add itself to the dawn's power so that Ilia lived."

"Wouldn't adding moon power to dawn power cancel each other out? As Tam just said, the moon's light wanes in the light of the dawn," Bas said.

"True. But they had to have felt that piece of the Evil One escape the Void and enter Dawn. Desperation makes strange bedfellows. I'm thinking, given the prevalence of both powers within Ilia, the two must have struck a bargain. I mean, it's the only thing that makes sense. It's why I didn't see this because conduit powers are traditionally gifted by Luna and I didn't think they could exist in Ilia because she was gifted powers by Ostara when she was made corporeal and one would cancel out the other, making her powers very weak. But Ilia isn't weak. She's incredibly strong. Far stronger than she should be if she was a normal witch. So the two Goddesses *had* to have allowed their powers to mingle within her so she could live and be the conduit we need her to be to help, and safeguard, Dawn. For that is her true role – now and in the battle ahead. As Guardian to Dawn and her God Killer powers." She turned her gaze to Ilia. "You were wondering your purpose and this is it. Not necessarily to hurt or damage the Evil One yourself, but to ensure others can." She looked up at the ceiling. "Luna and Ostara must believe Demeter for them to have worked together like this." Her gaze returned to Ilia. "My dear, you are as the Goddesses intended you to be."

"But, if you are right," Bas said. "And both Goddesses knew Dawn was in danger from the Evil One, why wouldn't they have taken care of it themselves right then and there? I mean, if they could subvert the very nature of their powers so they could blend together within Ilia, allowing her to be a powerful conduit—"

"*The* most powerful conduit," Korinna said, her voice still husky with the power of her vision.

Bas waved his hand. "Yes. If they could do that, why not take care of the evil themselves then and there?"

"What the Gods and Goddesses do doesn't always make sense," Korinna said, her voice sounding more normal with every word spoken.

"It rarely makes sense," Ilia said bitterly.

"*That's unfair. Luna and Ostara's hands are as tied as Demeter's,*" Loki said softly. "*Violetta is right – they do believe Demeter. And both of them helped in the only way they could but could do no more for fear of bringing more danger down on all of our heads. And no, you can't tell them that.*"

"*You know you're very annoying,*" Ilia said, glowering at him inside her mind.

"*So you keep telling me. Most people wax lyrical about my charm though, so I think you're wrong.*"

"*You obviously have selective deafness.*"

"*And you have an extraordinary tendency to overlook the important things I say.*"

"*Like what?*"

"*Like the fact you need to get Dawn here. Now!*" The last was shouted, followed by a, "*Holy fuck!*"

"*What? What's happened?*"

"*One of the Evil One's minions knows where Dawn is and they're almost there now. Bas needs to help you fix Trip so he can raise his special shields while Tam goes and gets Jules and Dawn and brings them back here. Right now! Trip can keep them safe in his shield while you get that thing out of that baby girl.*"

Hells – she had less time than she thought. But she swallowed down that terrifying thought and concentrated on the task ahead – one she wasn't quite sure how to do because—

"*Tell them! Tell them now!*"

She did as he said.

Before she'd finished saying who needed to do what, Bas was opening a portal. "I'll get my girls."

"No! None of it works unless we've healed Trip and he can use his shields to hold us all safe. We need you to stay here to do that, Bas," Ilia said.

"I'll keep them safe, Dad. I promi—" Tam's words were lost as he stepped through the portal he'd already opened.

"I know," Bas replied even though the portal had closed. He stood there chaffing his hands together, worry written in his eyes.

"They'll be back in a few moments," Violetta said, squeezing his shoulder.

He glanced at her, nodded then turned to Ilia. "So what do we have to do?"

Ilia glanced at Trip then back at Bas, her lip catching between her teeth as she frowned. She still wasn't sure how to do what she did, only that her knowing – and the prophecy Korinna spoke, and Loki's assurances – said she could do it. That this was the thing she could do. That she was the only one who could do it.

They were all looking to her though as if she was suddenly some great expert. If accidentally discovering you could do something, and then doing it uncontrollably, made you an expert, she was a bloody amazing expert!

"Loki? Any help?"

"What?"

He sounded distracted. What would he have to distract him when he was obviously supposed to be concentrating wholly on what was going on with all of them? *"I said, any advice on how to do this?"*

"Fuck! Tam – no. Take them too."

"Loki?"

"Sorry. Got to go."

"Loki! Don't you dare leave me to deal with this myself, you—"

"You've got this. Just go with your gut." There was a pop and then the distinct feeling of an emptiness in her head where there'd been an annoying – and aggravatingly comforting – presence before.

"Fucker!"

"What?" Everyone in the room asked her as the swear word exploded out of her.

Fuming, fists clenched in her lap, she said, "Loki's left. Rather than staying to help, he left. I swear, if he shows his face again I'm going to kick him in the nuts repeatedly until my toes hurt and then keep going with my other foot."

There was a snort at her side and her head snapped around to glare at Trip. "I expect you to hold him still for me."

"Of course." He kissed her pouting lips then the angry furrows on her brow before leaning back. "But you know, you don't need him. You've figured out exactly what to do every time and you'll do so again now."

"You have a lot of faith in me."

"Justified faith," he said.

She wasn't certain but Violetta said, "He's right. Trust your instincts. Open yourself to your knowings. You are a strong and powerful woman and witch, doubly Goddess-blessed. Nothing anyone has ever done to you has overcome you or taken you down – you have always risen. Trust yourself and rise now."

Korinna came to her side and put her hand on her shoulder. "Violetta's right. You have everything you need. And you have us here to support you and catch you if you fall. You are not alone."

Ilia's chest was suddenly tight and burning as she sucked in a breath, tears prickling her eyes. But for the first time ever, she realised her emotions, her tears, weren't a weakness – they were a strength. Because they were proof of all she'd fought to have, all she did have, and who she'd become. She was indeed a strong woman and witch, fully capable of taking on anything. She was smart and resourceful and someone capable of great love and being loved. She deserved everything good, always, and she was going to get it – not just for herself but for those she loved with every crazy, dark, joyful, hopeful and needy part of her heart and soul.

She did not need any selfish God or Goddess to tell her what she could or couldn't do or how to do any of it. She just needed to trust these wonderful people – her family – and the trust they had in her.

She needed to trust herself.

Taking a deep breath, she turned her attention to Bas and said, "We need to hurry. Stand there and start a healing like you normally would on Trip. I'll put my hands on both of you and do my thing."

Bas nodded, taking his place, immediately trusting her. His power buzzed in the air a moment later, zipping over her skin, a scent like the honeyed warmth of honeysuckles opening in the sun wafted around her, sinking into her senses, making her feel calm and strong.

She put one hand on Bas' chest, gasping as his power fired into her, filling her, growing in her. She put her hand on Trip's chest to complete the circuit.

"Oh my. Feel that!" Violetta's voice was filled with awe and resonated with shared power.

"Extraordinary," Korinna said on a gasp.

"You can feel that? You shouldn't be able to feel any of it where you're standing," Bas said, his voice vibrating with power.

"Oh but we do," they both said on a sigh.

"Yes. It's extraordinary," Trip said. "What does it feel like for you, Bas?"

Bas' face shone as he said reverently, "I've never felt anything like it. Not even when she was doing it before when she was unconscious."

"Yes," Korinna said. "This is so. Much. More."

"Like Godly power," Bas whispered. "Like when Eros worked through me in the past when I was his."

"No, it's more than that," Trip said, beginning to glow with that golden-green power Ilia had always seen shining from him. He was smiling at her in a way that was awe and pride combined, but before she could return the smile he said, "It's as if she's channelling directly from the Well. Like she is its child, not Ostara's. Not Luna's. But a true child of the Well."

She snorted. "As if."

Korinna stiffened at her side and Violetta said worriedly, "Korinna?"

"I'm fine." Her voice echoed strangely again and when Ilia glanced up at her it was to see her eyes, black and swirling gold, staring down at her.

"She is the Well's child. And she's going to help us save it all."

EIGHTEEN

Her words landed like lead weights in the room, stunning everyone into stillness and silence.

Except for Trip.

He knew. He'd always known. He'd known before they mated, from the first moment he'd seen her in those visions last year. But even if he hadn't known then that there was something more than part of a Goddess in her, he would have known when they mated and every time they shared blood. He couldn't miss it.

Her blood ... it fed him like it shouldn't. Powered him like it shouldn't. And yet it did.

She did.

So yes, he'd known she was special, that she was something extraordinary, something beyond all of them, something more, something ... unknown.

If Korinna's words were right – and he knew they were – Ilia was nothing they'd ever come across before.

The Eternal Well made the Gods and Goddesses of all pantheons – it was the source of their power, the place their eternal life-source sprang from. But none of them could ever be termed a 'child' of the Well. They were from it, part of it, but not of it in the way a child was of its parent. He knew this to be true through his connection with Korinna. It was unlike any other connection. It was stronger, more constant than even his connection to his magic.

He had no true idea what it all meant for ilia – just like nobody had known what his unique beginning would mean – but what he did know was what he'd always known.

She was a saviour.

She'd saved Tam and Korinna. She'd saved Bas and Jules. She'd saved baby Dawn.

And she'd saved him.

Over and over she'd saved him. Not his life – he couldn't be killed. But his soul. His heart. His sense of self and what he was meant to be. So it didn't surprise him that she was as essential to the coming fight as he or Korinna or Dawn.

He knew she'd been fighting feelings of uselessness for months. The burden of being surrounded by extraordinary, gifted powerful warriors who were essential in the fight to come when she didn't feel she had a purpose ... it had weighed her down. He'd tried to help her see she was extraordinary and essential too, but she hadn't been able to see it because her powers never worked properly and it just made her feel like her purpose was done. That it had ended the night she'd helped Tam and Korinna return Jules' powers.

But the role she'd had then ... it was only the beginning. And the realisation of that was just now blooming in her eyes – a sight that took his breath and filled him with pride.

He wanted to catch her into his arms, shout his jubilation at the joy coming through the bond from her; the sense that finally she had a purpose that was hers.

He could do that now because the healing had worked and he was so full of power and energy, he could do anything.

He turned, but stopped as a gust of wind spiralled from the space in front of the doorway just as a portal opened – purple and swirling blue and more erratic than it should be.

Tam came stumbling through, a screaming Dawn in his arms, Jules at his side. They were both covered in blood and brought with them the smell of burnt flesh, their hair was in disarray, their clothing torn.

Tam yelled something as he waved his arm to collapse his portal, which was spitting and hissing behind them, but Dawn was screaming so loudly that Trip couldn't hear what he said. Her screams, incredible waves of power, pushed against him, making his nerves and muscles vibrate painfully.

What had happened to make Tam bring her back through the portal like that? By the looks of him and Jules, it was something pretty dire. But before he could address that, he had to address Dawn's distress because the room wouldn't survive if she kept up her screaming.

Just as he was rising from the couch, the portal snapped shut with a screeching roar of primal power being cut off in a way it never should. It caused a whump of air to shove through the lounge room, the impact tossing the lighter furniture into the air and across the room, forcing Bas, Korinna and Violetta to dive to the floor so they didn't get hit. The heavy couch he and Ilia were on was shoved backwards a few feet before hitting a fallen piece of furniture and tipping over.

"What the fuck!" He reached for Ilia to protect her from the fall.

But Ilia wasn't there. She was floating in the air, arms outstretched, power, like the lick of flames, in the air around her as she sucked in all the extra energy in the room, including the waves of power created by Dawn's screams that were flinging more things around the room, turning it into a disaster zone.

Ilia pulled it all towards her like a black hole sucking in light.

Then it was gone.

And he finally heard what Tam was yelling.

"Shields, Trip! Now! Before it gets through!"

He registered then that the panic on Tam's face, the pale-faced terror on Jules', wasn't about Dawn's reaction to portal travel. Their eyes were fixed, horrified, on the place they'd come through.

What the fuck had happened?

"Trip!"

Responding to Tam's urgency, he lifted his hands to summon the full force of the different aspects of his powers – earth and wind and water and fire; flora and fauna; life and death and spirit. They came to him faster and stronger than ever before thanks to what Ilia had given to him through Bas' healing – nothing would get through this shield once he was done.

Before he could cast it, there was a violent tearing sound and suddenly Loki fell into the room through a shimmering light in the air that looked like paper unfolding. He had a body in his arms covered in blood and three boys clinging to his arms and back – Charlie, Harry and Gideon.

Trip's gaze snapped to the bloodied body in Loki's arms.

"Daphne!" No! They should have been safe on the farm – he'd made certain of it before he'd left. They each wore his personal shield and he'd put shields over every part of the farm, keying them to his bloodline and the Stevens bloodline and their mates so that they could visit without him having to take the shields down.

Nothing should have been able to get to them.

Something obviously had.

And it was his fault.

It was his fault for leaving those who meant so much to him vulnerable and alone down there without him.

"Daphne!" Gods – she looked dead. "Is she——" He couldn't say the word.

Instead of answering, Loki yelled, "Put the bloody shield up now, you stupid arse. He's right behind me!"

His urgency made Trip jump to do as bid. He gathered the power that had fallen away in his shock – which meant it would take a few more seconds before he could loose the shield spell.

"Bas – help Daphne," he yelled then shouted to Loki, "Close your transportation fold."

Loki was already closing it.

Not that it mattered. A tear in the air began to open just behind the God alongside a swirl of black sparking power that heralded a portal being opened by something else – something that should be impossible given the strength of the shields they'd raised when Korinna began to have her prophecies.

"Where the fuck is that shield?" Loki screamed, backing away from whatever was trying to come through while endeavouring to stop it with his own magic. But his power snapped around him in a way that suggested it wasn't working properly – Trip didn't want to think about what could do that to a God of Loki's experience and power.

The room shook as a massive roar shattered the air, a huge, clawed hand coming through the fold as a portal beside it began to solidify.

Fuck! That couldn't be ... it was impossible!

He shook his head, shoving the terror deep down – it would do none of them any good. The only thing that would protect them now was his shield. Except, he still had another few seconds before he could raise enough power to release the spell. He couldn't hurry it or the shield wouldn't be strong enough.

And those things were coming through now.

Ilia put her hand on his shoulder. Power shot through him, stronger and with more of a sense of control over it than he'd ever felt in his long life. It shot into the air with an electrified sizzle followed by a loud snap as his impregnable shields burst into life, obliterating all the shields that were already there with a loud pop before settling over and around the house and the library beneath it, sinking into the ground and slicing through the layers of earth deep under them – the magics clever enough not to disturb the ley-lines but rather use them to further strengthen his creation: an impregnable bubble of protection around them.

There was no way those things could get entry through something that strong.

As the bubble's edges came together with a satisfying smack, the black portal disappeared and the transportation fold snapped shut, slicing the claw from the thing it belonged to so that it thunked, smoking, to the floor.

Its roar of pain echoed in the silence and quickly faded away.

Trip glanced at everyone – the suddenness of his spell, the power of it, had quite literally set everyone's hair on end like they'd been electrified.

Korinna looked ill as she pushed upright, eyes glued to Tam. Tam was covered in cuts and burns and blood but his attention was on his mother and sister even though he was obviously straining to catch his breath. Jules didn't seem to be listening to her son, her gaze on Dawn who lay limp in her arms. The witch seemed unhurt even though he could now see through the blood that covered her, that she had a burn on her face and her arms were covered in cuts and burns. Violetta was sitting on the floor, shaking, a cut on her brow bleeding – a piece of flying furniture had obviously hit her.

He worried for each of them, but his worry for Daphne and the boys was greater as his attention returned to them.

Ilia's hand was still on his shoulder, which was the only thing that stopped him from racing across the room. She still hung precariously in the air beside him. Perhaps she'd move with him. But when he tried to walk forward, he found that she couldn't be budged. Shit. Fuck. He needed to check on Daphne and the boys – who looked terrified if uninjured. Unlike their mum.

Bas was the first to break the silence as he pushed to his feet. "Jules? Are you and Dawn okay?"

"Don't worry about them!" Loki shouted harshly, his voice curiously close to a sob. "Help Daphne."

Bas didn't seem to hear him as he rushed to his mate and daughter – only natural his concern would be there, but Trip wished it otherwise because ... Hells. Daphne didn't look good at all. She needed Bas' help now.

Thankfully Jules waved Bas away before taking Dawn from Tam's arms. "Loki's right. Daphne needs you more.

Tam, help him please. The boys will need you after ..." She swallowed hard. "What they saw."

"What they saw?" Holy fucking Hells. How traumatised were they?

Jule's gaze snapped to him. "Are you okay?"

He blinked at her. "I'm fine. I just can't move." He nodded towards Ilia who still clasped his shoulder as she floated by his side. "I want to help but ..." He had to stand there and watch while others took care of his family for him. It was excruciating.

"You did enough getting the shields up."

But was it too little too late?

"Are you sure you don't need any healing?" Bas asked Jules.

"Yes. I will be fine – just scrapes, a few small burns and bruises. I can wait. But Daphne needs your help right now. Look at her."

Loki snapped, "Thank fuck someone here's got some sense."

Bas quickly wove his way through the wreck of splintered furniture that lay scattered across the once immaculately kept room. "Boys, you okay?" he asked as he got there. They stared blankly at him. "Tam – move them away. I need to make room on the floor for Loki to put Daphne down."

Tam managed to quickly pull the boys from where they clung to Loki and their mum with Korinna's help – she'd followed Bas across the room – while Bas cleared the floor of debris with a wave of his hand, his spell pushing it in one sweep against the far wall. "Put her down here," he said to Loki.

Shaking badly, Loki managed to gently lower Daphne to

the floor. "Help her," he whispered harshly. "I can't lose her again."

Again? What in all the Hells was the God talking about?

"Loki, you're hurt!" Jules said on a gasp.

The God of Mischief glanced down at his chest and stomach. "Well damn! The bastard got me. Sneaky fucker." Then he collapsed on the floor.

CHAPTER

NINETEEN

S hit hit the fan.

At least, that's what Ilia saw when she came down from her conduit-high – literally. She floated down into Trip's arms.

"Ilia."

"I'm fine, my love. In fact, feeling so much better. Which can't be said for them." She gestured at the new arrivals. "I can help."

"No. You must be exhausted."

She loved his caring for her, but it was unnecessary. "I'm not. I'm ... the opposite." She couldn't stop the beaming smile that lit her face at how she felt despite what had just happened and the serious nature of Daphne's and Loki's injuries. Waves of power and joy exuded through her, from the core of her, and it was fucking amazing. But she could see he didn't believe her. No wonder given her history with covering up how she felt.

But she needed him to believe her now. For more reasons than that she needed to help her friends.

She needed him to believe that she would not try to

cover up anything with him. Not anymore. Never again. But more immediately, she just wanted him to feel this … joy … with her.

Beaming up at him, she said, her voice practically buzzing with emotion, "I feel wonderful. Amazing." He didn't look convinced. She cupped his face and stared into his eyes. "Do I feel exhausted?"

"I—"

"No. Look. At our bond. Feel me through it. Do I feel exhausted to you?"

He stared into her eyes for a long moment before closing his extraordinary leaf-green ones to check their bond. She felt him there, deep inside, stroking the blessed link, testing it for anything that might hint at something other than what she knew he had to be feeling from it: energy.

Untapped, inexhaustible energy.

She was so far from tired, so far from flaring out. In fact, she didn't think flaring out was something that would ever happen to her again because her power came directly from the source of all power. It was like the eternal flame had flared to life inside her. And unless what was oxygen to it, the channel to the Well, was cut off or strangled somehow – and she was pretty certain neither was possible – then she would never run out of the power to do what she'd been reborn to do.

Ever.

It was the most extraordinary, joyful sensation. Only second to how she'd felt when she and Trip had mated.

She would have liked to have the time to appreciate it more, to glory in it with him, but the pandemonium on the other side of the room as Bas shouted instructions at Tamuel, Violetta and Korinna – to help the injured Loki and the traumatised boys who'd come through with them while he tried to help Daphne – was becoming more hectic with every passing second. Made worse by the fact Dawn had started screaming again like something was trying to tear her apart, making it even harder for an injured Jules to settle her and not worsen her own injuries.

Bas was visibly struggling to stay with his patient and not run to his mate.

Korinna had gathered the boys to her but seemed helpless to do anything but hold Gideon as he sobbed uncontrollably, or stop Charlie who, looking terrified, was staring at the place where the claw lay, shouting, "What was that? What was that?" Harry was simply staring around vacantly.

To add to the chaos – and despite the fact he couldn't get up from the floor without risking his guts falling out – Loki was yelling at Bas to, "Just stay where you bloody are and bloody fix her!"

Bas needed help. They all needed help.

Her help.

And for the first time she knew she was the right one – the only one – who could give it. But Trip needed to trust that she wasn't going to hurt herself doing so. She knew his reticence wasn't that he thought she *couldn't* do it, but worry over what it might do to her when she did – because this was a 'when' situation, not an 'if' situation.

Ilia's fingers tightened on his face a little so he'd open his eyes. He did so and she said, "I need to help. I have to help. And I will be fine. More than fine. I promise."

Still he hesitated to let her go. But it didn't hurt like it might once have done.

Because she knew the source of his worry and how to allay it. How to make him stand with her and not try to hold her back for fear of losing her.

"I love you, Trip."

"I love you too."

"Do you trust me?"

"Always."

The flame of her power warmed inside her. "Then trust that I would never do anything that would jeopardise our love and life together. Not anymore. Not like I once might have. I know my worth now. I have a role. Let me fulfill it. For us. For them. For our future. I promise you I know what I'm doing, and I will not be hurt. I will never leave you." It was the truest thing she'd ever said, her words vibrating with the emotion behind them. She was no longer worried that she would have to give her life to save Dawn – to save any of them. She wasn't sure how she knew this, or how to achieve it yet, she just knew it was true.

And Trip must have felt it, must have heard it in her voice, because he covered her hands with his, his gaze intense, then kissed her gently before pulling back and whispering "Do what you must."

He took her hand and led her across the room to where Bas kneeled on the floor beside Daphne.

Her mate's love and trust ... it was everything. She didn't need it to do what she now knew she could do, but it filled up all the nasty, lonely, bitter places she'd nourished within herself over the long years she was trapped in the HeartsBlood Gem and that she hadn't truly let go of since becoming corporeal – not even when she mated. They'd filled her with uncertainty and doubts that she could never rid herself of, no matter how much Trip's love nourished everything else.

But now, her revelation had gouged them out, and Trip's trust and belief added to the fact she got to keep the friends and family she'd found and made, flooded all those now empty spaces with love and warmth and golden joy until she was suffused with light and hope.

A strange feeling for someone who'd lived without hope in the darkness for so long. But one she was never going to let go of.

Trip squeezed her hand as they reached Bas.

The ex-cupid healer was struggling, his power fitting and starting as he held his hands over Daphne's wounds – terrible burns that held the acrid scent of black magic. Something about that black magic was stopping Bas' power from working as it should, even after the incredible boost she'd given him earlier.

He needed a little something else to put that fucker on its arse!

"Let me." As he glanced up at her, she touched his face and sucked all his doubts and exhaustion into herself alongside all that made him a powerful force for good. The flame that was her power ate it up, transforming it into extraordinary energy with every bit of the joy and light and power thrumming through her into glorious, golden healing power that was his true gift. The feeling of it inside her strengthened her, allowing her to strengthen it until it was as strong as tungsten, the strongest metal on this Earth, before channelling it back into him.

He jerked, his eyes going wide, breath a gasp in his throat.

Nothing happened for long, breathless seconds then ...

Light exploded out of him – the golden glow of healing power.

Rays of it filled the room with a brightness that was almost too much to bear and yet, Ilia couldn't look anywhere else but at him. At the radiant sun of healing energy that he'd suddenly become because she'd tapped into who he was in the truest heart of him and ... brought it to the fore.

The light hit everyone in the room, wrapping around them, sinking into them, then flying back out of their wounds as if a new light source had been found. In seconds, wounds closed, burns turned into the pink, shiny skin of a freshly healed wound before becoming normal, healthy skin without a sign that there'd been blisters and full-thickness burns there only moments before.

But it didn't stop just with the physical wounds.

Bas' healing light covered the traumatised boys who stood cowering in Tam's and Korinna's arms. As it washed over them, the youngest stopped his sobbing and the eldest's face was suddenly filled with hope while the middle boy ... he began to laugh with a joy that was contagious because suddenly everyone in the room was laughing too, even as they shielded their eyes from the sun-like glow.

And Daphne – well, her recovery was the most remarkable of all.

The healing light disappeared inside her wounds, settled for a moment and then exploded out of her like bursts of sunlight through a cloud. It was a glittering display of astonishing power.

And it was all because of Ilia's new gift.

She chuckled at the hubris of that thought. This could not happen if not for the extraordinary nature of Bas' natural powers, but it was her unique ability that had brought it out, strengthening it, giving it the courage, the ability, to be what it could have always been if circumstances had only been different.

And that knowledge was fucking amazing!

Everyone else obviously thought so too as, once they were done laughing and blinking through the light glare still bursting out of Daphne, their words tumbled one over the other.

"How ...?"

"What the fuck!"

"Language, Tam! The boys."

"I'm healed. I'm healed."

"That tickled."

"It tastes like honey and chocolate."

"No berries and chocolate."

"Bas, that was remarkable. What did you do?"

"It's not me. It's Ilia. She made me ..." He gestured at himself, at the glow that was still coming out of him, reaching to touch everything in the room, "This." He shook his head, happily bewildered as he looked up at her. "I have no idea what this is."

"It's you," she said. "The purest form of you as you were when you first came into being, before everything else got in the way."

"That's why it feels so fucking fantastic."

A laugh burst out of her as Violetta said, "Bas! Impressionable ears!"

"Sorry." Not that he looked sorry – he was too busy smiling so wide it seemed his face could stretch no more.

"Don't worry about it. They've grown up hearing worse than that," Daphne said as she sat up.

"Daphne! You're okay," Loki blurted out. "Thank me, you're okay."

Ilia couldn't help rolling her eyes as he said 'me' rather than 'the Gods' – trust Loki to make this about him!

"I think you mean, 'thank Ilia'!" Trip said.

Loki didn't seem to hear that, his gaze pinned to Daphne in something close to hungry desperation. "By all the Hells. I thought I'd lost you again."

Daphne's brow furrowed deeply as she turned to see who had spoken and her gaze landed on the mischief God. "Who the hell are you? And why would you have lost me?"

Loki's face fell and he looked down at his hands that were still covered in his own blood. "Nobody worth remembering, obviously."

There was that 'again' again. Obviously a story there that was worth asking about – later.

She certainly couldn't ask now because at the sound of Daphne's voice, the boys tore themselves away from Tam and Korinna and threw themselves across the floor separating them and into her open arms, just missing knocking Bas and Ilia onto their arses.

"Whoa boys. Steady on!" Laughing, Trip pulled Ilia out of the way. "And be careful with your mum. She's only just healed."

Around joyful exclamations, hugs and kisses as she ran her hands over her boys, checking them over, Daphne managed to say, "I'm fine. I'm fine. I'm just worried about my boys."

"We're fine," Charlie said as he pulled back to let her wrap her arms around Gideon and Harry who were sobbing into their mother's shoulders. His gaze ran over her in a way that showed he was still shaken, despite how good the healing had obviously made all of them feel. "We were just worried about you." He glanced at Loki. "If you hadn't arrived and grabbed her away from that thing ..." His voice shuddered to a halt and he shook his head. "Thank you. Thank you so much. I owe y—"

"Uh-uh!" Tam interrupted him quickly. "Never tell a God you owe them or wager anything with them. It is a bargain that will never end well for you. Especially with a mischief God."

"I wouldn't hold the boy to such a bargain," Loki said, sounding curiously hurt.

"Maybe, maybe not," Trip said, clapping his hand on Charlie's shoulder. "But it's always best not to take a chance even with a God like Loki who has been a friend to some of us and has been helping us in his way."

Charlie nodded and turned back to Loki. "Then my simple thanks," he said, sounding far older than his nineteen years.

"That's not needed." His gaze flickered to Daphne. "Not from you. Not for this." He cleared his throat as his gaze seemed to greedily take in Daphne and the boys in her arms. "Not ever."

"Loki – are you okay?" Korinna asked, edging towards him.

CHAPTER

TWENTY

Loki waved a hand at Korinna – a hand still glistening with what looked like fresh blood – and said, "I'll be fine."

"You're still bleeding," Tam said, rushing over to him to pull his other hand away from his stomach – where there was still quite a large gash. Not as bad as it had been, but still there. "How is that possible?" Tam asked of Bas and Ilia. "What you did ... it healed the rest of us. Why not Loki?"

Ilia shrugged – she had no idea.

"It was a Hellbeast, wasn't it?" Trip said quietly, brow raised at Loki.

The God nodded.

"What? That's not possible," Korinna said.

"Why do you say that?" Violetta asked, speaking for the first time as she drew closer to the smoking claw on her lounge room floor. "It looks rather Hellish to me."

"That's because it is," Loki said before coughing, bloody spittle landing on his chin and chest. "It was a Hellbeast commanded by a minion of Perses."

"You said the name!" Ilia accused.

He waved his hand at the ceiling, wincing as he did it. "Shield."

Oh, of course. Did that mean he could tell them everything now? She opened up her mouth to ask but Korinna spoke first.

"It can't be. You have to be wrong."

Loki met the witch's confused – and horrified – gaze. "I'm not."

"But ... but ... it's not possible. They reside in the deepest parts of Tartarus and can only be called – and controlled – by Hades and the Morningstar."

Loki shook his head shakily "Not originally. They were created by the Titans. Hades and the Morningstar inherited them when the Titans were killed by their children."

"Not all were killed," Bas said solemnly.

Loki pointed a shaky finger at the healer. "True. Some were banished into the Void. Hence our little problem now."

"Hardly a *little* problem," Korinna said bitterly as she stared at the severed claw that was as large as the trunk of Trip's sizeable body.

Loki's lips hitched wryly. "True. That bad decision has rather landed us in this pickle, hasn't it?" He winced again.

"Let me help," Bas said, hurrying to his side.

"Save your energy." Loki held up his hand. "You can't help me with this."

"Of course I can. Did you not just see what I did?"

"Saw it and glad of it." His eyes landed on Daphne who was whispering to the boys still in her arms. "But surely you noticed I am the only one it didn't fully heal. So what makes you think it would be different now after all the fireworks have started to die down and the magical smoke is disappearing?"

"Ilia could boost me again."

Loki snorted. "Not a good idea. We wouldn't want you getting addicted to what she has to offer. Besides, I think you need to keep that in reserve. This today ..." he coughed again, more blood speckling his chin. "It was only a skirmish. The big battles are yet to come."

"But ... you're injured badly."

"Of course I am! I snatched my lo—" He coughed again, eyes watering – although Ilia rather felt this cough was more about stopping himself from saying something he didn't want to say. "I snatched that mother from a Hellbeast's claws and got slashed by it for my efforts."

"Daphne was slashed too," Ilia said softly. "And she's healed."

"Yeah, well she's not a mischief God. Unfortunately Hellbeasts have poison in their claws that was designed to keep my kind from trying to 'play' with them."

"Why the fuck would you want to play with them?" Korinna asked.

Loki shrugged. "Search me. Smelly and ugly and vicious isn't my thing. But it was obviously some mischief God's thing in the past, hence the poison."

"It won't kill you, will it?" Charlie asked – Ilia hadn't noticed him drawing closer to the God. "He saved my mum – saved all of us. You can't let it kill him," he said, looking pleadingly from one to the other of them.

"It's fine," Loki said, waving his hand in a very groggy fashion – his face was an unhealthy grey. "It's hard to kill me. It's just going to make me unwell for a time. And take me longer to heal."

"But ... there has to be something we can do," Charlie continued. "He's obviously in pain."

"Well ... it doesn't tickle." Loki coughed again, his entire body shuddering, black spittle flying from his mouth alongside the brighter red of his blood. But his gaze returned to Charlie and he said, "I'm fine."

"If fine means the same thing as looking like shit," Ilia said, "then yes, you're obviously fine."

He snorted. "Thanks for agreeing."

"Almost torn in half and still an annoying arsehole."

Somehow Loki managed a smile. "Glad to be appreciated."

"Idiot." Ilia turned to Bas – she wasn't sure why she was so concerned about the annoying arsehole, but she was. "We can bandage him up or something, can't we? Give him something to help with the pain?"

"Not if the shield keeps us in this room," Violetta said.

Trip shook his head. "The shield covers the entire house, including the library."

"I thought you couldn't make it strong enough if you had to cover the entire house? That's why we were going to move into the kitchen so we'd have access to food and water."

"You can thank my extraordinary mate for that," he said, smiling at her. "My shield is stronger than any I've ever made before even as large as it is. So you can fetch whatever first aid items you need."

"In that case ..." Bas glanced at Violetta. "I'll take him to one of the spare rooms down here."

"And I'll fetch the first aid kit and then make up a poultice to help draw the poison from the wound. Korinna – can you steep some of my pain-ease tisane? I'm not sure traditional pain killers will work on him."

Bas bent to pick him up but Loki said loudly, "Helping me can wait. We've got a bigger elephant in the room that still needs to be dealt with."

They all glanced around – all except Ilia. Her gaze went straight to Dawn who lay listlessly in her mother's arms.

She hadn't forgotten what had brought them here as everyone else seemed to have done – not surprising after what had just happened.

It turned out Trip hadn't forgotten either because he whispered, "Dawn. We have to get that darkness out of Dawn."

"Before it wakes up again and calls to its minions once more," Loki said solemnly.

"They can't get in here though, can they?" Violetta asked, glancing up towards where the invisible shield protected them all.

"No, but we can't get out either," Trip said.

"I wouldn't say that's a disaster," Korinna said, kicking at the claw.

The others agreed with her – all but Loki and Trip, who seemed to understand what had been worrying at her as soon as they'd talked about putting up Trip's impregnable shield.

Because while she was now certain all she had to do was draw out the part of Perses that had got into Dawn the night she was born – like she had unknowingly been doing in smaller sections over the last months – there was one massive problem.

Trip's shield was now up, keeping them safe from the pantheons and whatever had attacked her friends at Trip's farm.

But as had been pointed out, they were now stuck inside it until it was safe to remove – which, by the sounds of things, wasn't any time soon. Which meant, if she drew out the darkness, she had nowhere to put it. There was the Vortex, but something inside her told her it would be a grave mistake to release the amount of darkness still inside Dawn – a darkness they now knew was part of the Titan, Perses – in there to join up with what had already been released into the ley-lines. So that was out. And there was nowhere else to release such a large part of something so monstrous and powerful. She had to keep it within her. But if she did that and had to keep it inside her for too long, it would end up destroying her because it couldn't take her over. And when it had torn her apart, it would be loose in the house with all the people she cared for the most.

The certainty she'd had earlier that she didn't have to give her life hadn't factored that in and yet ... she wasn't going to give up hope.

Trip's face showed that he thought she was not going to be able to keep her promise. She reached for his hand. "I'll think of something."

He shook his head. "*We'll* think of something. We have time."

The words had just left his lips when Dawn started to scream and writhe so hard she almost threw herself out of her mother's arms.

It seemed they'd run out of time.

TRIP STARED at Dawn as she screamed and writhed in Jules' arms, one word repeating over and over in his mind:

No. No. No. No. NO!

They needed more time to figure out why Perses had sent his minions to go after Dawn on the farm. They needed time to ask Loki everything he'd been keeping from them now the shield was up.

A shield that had originally been intended to allow the mischief God to reveal what he had refused to tell them so far; but now was there to keep them all safe from the things trying to kill them.

Fuck!

Loki had to have more information to share – otherwise, why go rescue Daphne and the boys and come back here to lock himself in? Unless he needed to be protected too.

But from what?

Hells!

This was such a mess. There were so many questions – too many questions – and not enough time to answer any of them. Because, the moment had come and Ilia had to take that thing from Dawn and it would be trapped inside her, tearing his love apart.

Maybe he could take it from her? That might work. He wouldn't die if he had it inside him. It would just cause him incredible, torturous pain. But he'd endure the pain and the being torn apart from the inside-out. He could come back from that. She couldn't.

He glanced at her and knew – she wouldn't give it to him. And that was the only way he could take it from her because she was too powerful now for him to take it by force. She'd have to channel it into him. And there's no way she would do that even though she knew it couldn't kill him. He'd seen the look on her face when the small bit he'd had inside him before had caused him so much pain.

His love would never willingly put him through that again.

Not that the darkness that was a piece of Perses would

even let him take it given how poisonous his system was to it. It would choose one of the others to go into long before it ever chose to reside in his body. It wouldn't care that it would destroy them after a time, because even a part of a Titan didn't belong in the body of a human, witch or demi-God, no matter how strong their power. It would just jump from body to body and destroy each of them until it had run out of choices.

Maybe Loki could take it – or part of it.

His gaze snapped to the God. One look told him his hope was useless. Loki wouldn't willingly take such a powerful evil inside himself because his power had a direct tie to Perses' power, which meant that piece of Perses would eventually be able to take over Loki. Faster because of his injuries.

The God didn't look good.

Not that Ilia would allow Loki to take the darkness in. She wouldn't let anyone take it. Even though she had to know it would kill her if she couldn't release it.

This was all his fault. He shouldn't have raised the shield until they'd dealt with what was in Dawn. But then, what else could he have done given the situation?

Rock meet hard place.

But now it was his Ilia who was paying the price. If only she could put more of it in the Vortex – but that wasn't possible. Nothing good would happen if two such signifi-cant parts of the Titan met up in such a place of power. And with the shield up, he couldn't transport her to another place where she could channel it safely after she took it out of Dawn.

If only Loki had told them more than he had, maybe they wouldn't be here. But then, that's what the shield was meant to be for, so the mischief God could finally tell them something that would be more useful than the cryptic shit he'd shared so far.

It wasn't that he didn't understand the need for secrecy – he'd helped Demeter keep quite a few and obscured other bits of information. But when you were on the other end of the stick, it was infuriating. Especially now when they needed more than obfuscation to get through this.

The very thing that was supposed to help them gain some actual, helpful knowledge was now the thing putting his love in more danger than she'd previously been in before.

He couldn't lose Ilia. She was his life. She held his soul together. She kept his heart from becoming a useless husk in his chest; she kept him strong. She gave him more than he'd ever imagined a mate or lover giving him. As he did for her. It was not a one-sided thing their mating, their love. He knew she did not want to give that up for anything.

But this ... it was not something she could refuse to do.

She would save Dawn. She would always save Dawn.

And it was going to kill her because of his fucking shield.

Shields were supposed to protect but his was going to kill.

He glanced, wild eyed, at Ilia. She met his gaze, hers wide and knowing. So sure.

And completely lacking in blame.

It killed him – figuratively because he couldn't fucking die. It stabbed him right through the heart and twisted in a way that made him suddenly understand what the final death might be like.

He grasped her hands, desperate to hold onto her in any way he could. "I'll take it down."

"No! You can't. Not until Dawn's safe from Perses'

minions. And she won't be safe until I've got that piece of him out of her."

"I know. I know," he said, having to shout now above the baby's screams and everyone shouting as they tried to help a desperate Jules and Bas. Desperate not just because their baby was screaming but because she was growing again in front of their eyes. Her features were changing on her face, losing their baby soft-roundness and her body and limbs were lengthening and thinning.

Holy crapping fuck!

If she grew big enough, the bit of Perses that was inside her would finally be able to take her over because it would fully mesh with her flesh in a way it couldn't do while she was still a baby. They'd been afraid of this, but thought they had months, not minutes, to stop it.

Ilia saw what was happening as he did and pulled forward, ready to go to the baby and stop this evil from happening.

He stopped her by grasping her hand tight and not letting go.

She turned to him, none of the sad finality he expected to see in her eyes. "You have to let me go. We can't let this happen. And ... I will make it work."

"How? There is nowhere to channel it to after you take it in." He looked around desperately, the inevitable closing in on him. "Maybe Loki can tell us something that will help," he suggested breathlessly. "He was going to tell us something more after I put the shield up. Maybe it's something that can help you with this? So it doesn't ..." He swallowed hard. He couldn't say it. Couldn't say it for fear of making it real.

Ilia glanced at Loki then back at him, her hand squeezing his – holy Hells, was she trying to comfort him?

Her mouth twisted to the side then she said, "I'm not sure Loki's going to be much use to us right now. He looks like he's a moment from passing out." Her gaze went to Loki again who was still sitting on the floor leaning against an overturned chair, his hand over his stomach where blood still seeped out. His gaze was on the scene unfolding, occasionally flickering to Daphne and her boys where they were in the corner – having edged there to get out of the way. His eyes were glazed with pain and his face was a grey shade of pasty.

Hells – he really wasn't doing well. But ... "We could try. We have to try. He owes us."

She made a moue with her mouth before nodding. "Okay."

He could tell that okay was really a 'Fine. But I'm not holding my breath.'

They were about to move towards Loki when Tam yelled, "Ilia. Trip. Help." He was helping Bas, who had his arms around Jules and the baby, trying to hold them both steady, the panic palpable as Dawn screamed and thrashed and grew.

"Put her on the rug and try to just hold her," Ilia shouted. "I have to figure out what to do."

"Get it out of her!" Korinna yelled as she tossed furniture aside to try and clear enough space in the floor for all of them. "We can't let her grow any more. It will take her over if she gets big enough."

"I know."

"Then why aren't you doing something?" her friend yelled.

TWENTY-ONE

Ilia stared at Korinna, her face showing her turmoil. "I ... want to but ... I'm going to but ... I just don't know what to do with it after I take it in."

"Expel it," Tam shouted as he helped Bas and Jules to the floor with their precious cargo. Jules still held her child in her arms, obviously unwilling to let Dawn go even though she was thrashing around and screaming.

It was awful to watch. So bloody awful.

He couldn't let his mind go there though, so focused in on Ilia as she replied to Tam, "I can't. Not while the shield's up."

"Can't you put it in the Vortex like you did before?" Bas yelled, his voice hoarse with fear and desperation.

"No!" Violetta shouted as she stood there, trying to use her magic to calm the baby to no avail – whatever was happening just deflected any magic aimed at her. "You can't put that much of an ancient Being in the Vortex. It will change its nature in ways we can't predict; except to know it won't be good."

Trip's brows rose, surprised the older witch new this too.

"But she channelled what she had into it before," Korinna said.

"That was only a small portion in comparison," Trip said. "The ley-lines are created to modulate the energy of anything bad that enters them and return it back to the Well, but only in small amounts – like with any of the entities that are in the books and things in that room. It could take care of those easily. But this ... it's an ancient Being, a small part of it more powerful than all of what's in that room combined. The ley-lines would already be struggling to change what we purged into it a few days ago; they would not be able to process more, even if we fed it in a bit at a time. The bit of Perses that remains in Dawn would inexorably change the ley-lines and would take its power – something we cannot afford because with that power it could probably open the Void and let the greater part of Perses that is still trapped in there through into this Realm."

"But you have to help her!" Jules screamed, terrified as her daughter thrashed in her arms. "It's tearing her apart."

And it was. There was blood coming out of Dawn's eyes, ears and nose and a black substance was oozing out of cracks in her skin as she grew from toddler to pre-schooler to school-aged size.

"There's no time," Ilia said, looking up at him, eyes pleading. "I have to take it now."

"But you will die."

"No. I won't. I ... can't explain it but ... I – or we – will figure it out. It has to be that way. It has to. Trust me?"

"Always."

She leaned up to give him a kiss full of all the things

there wasn't time to say, then she broke from his grip and raced over to the baby.

He stood there, unable to move, not wanting to watch – but unable to look away – as his beloved slammed down on her knees beside the baby, shoving Tam aside as she did so. Both of her hands reached for Dawn – one to cover her head, the other her heart – then, eyes glowing in that strange way they did when she used this power, she said, "Come. Leave her now. Come into me. I command you. Come!"

Nothing happened for a moment as everything in the room – even Dawn – stilled. Then there was a rushing sound, followed by a gust of feral wind and Ilia's head snapped back, her eyes going wide as she did whatever it was she did and took the evil from Dawn into herself.

All he could do was stand there helplessly as her eyes turned from a golden glow to liquid black. Her skin took on a ghostly hue as she took more and more of the thing inside her.

Fucking Hells! It kept going on and on and on. How much of it was there?

It was supposed to be only a small part of the Titan that had escaped the Void last Easter – or maybe escape was the wrong word. It looked more and more like Perses had torn this part of himself from the whole and sent it out to do exactly this.

Destroy the very heart of them.

It had meant to take over Dawn because of what she was and what she was destined to do. But how had the Titan known? Korinna had only made her prophecy a few days ago. He shook the question from his head, aware that his thoughts were becoming erratic.

It didn't matter right now what Perses knew or how, or whether he meant to use Dawn in this way or if it was just an opportunistic accident. What mattered was his mate was suffering and he could do nothing for her – the very reason his mind was scattered and chaotic. But he couldn't allow it to be because while she was doing this incredible thing, she needed all of them to work on a way to save her.

Perses couldn't win this day. For if he won this battle, he could very well win the war. Because without Ilia, Trip would be nothing. He would be useless to the others, his powers more open to being used.

"No!" Ilia's voice sounded loud in his mind. *"You will not give up. You will not become nothing. Even if I'm wrong and you were to lose me. Because you must fight for what we love. You must never give up. Not because of me."*

Her voice was so clear in his mind it was astonishing. And reminded him once again just how powerful and special she was. And how, if anyone could, *she* would find a way through this. Because she'd found her way through everything else that had been thrown at her.

He was an idiot for giving up. Something he would never do again. Not when there was Ilia to fight for; their love to fight for; their soul bond to fight for.

Straightening as if to shrug off the desperation and doubt, he said into her mind through their bond, *"I won't need to go on without you, my love, because you are right. We will come up with an answer."* He glanced across at Loki. *"And we have just the mischief God to help us."*

Dawn was no longer thrashing around. She was barely moving at all, her little body limp in her mother's arms. Although, she was not so little anymore. She was the size of a seven- or eight-year-old child, her coltish legs hanging over Jules' arms, a long fall of strawberry blond hair with hints of deepest gold falling almost to the floor. The romper suit she'd been wearing was now torn and hanging halfway down her thighs and upper arms.

Jules was sobbing, silent tears pouring down her face as she stared at Ilia with so much hope and gratitude and fear it hurt to see. Bas sat behind her, his arms around his mate and daughter, his desperate gaze also pinned on Ilia as she kneeled at Dawn's side, head thrown back, her body vibrating with her power and what she was taking in.

For something that was only a piece of a Titan, it was huge. It hadn't taken her anywhere near this long to remove the small portion he'd had inside himself.

He obviously wasn't the only one to think so because Korinna leaned into Tam and said, "Shouldn't it be done by now?"

"Is it too late?" Jules said, her voice a sob. But somehow she was keeping it together, enough to ask, "She's s-so big. Is sh-she too b-big? Did sh-she grow enough f-for it t-to get h-her?"

"Oh Gods!" Tam said, gaze raking over his half-sister. "Please don't let that be true."

"No," Ilia said through gritted teeth. "Not that. It won't let go."

"What do you mean?" Bas asked. When Ilia didn't answer, he asked again.

"I've got ... most of it," she said, face fierce as she pulled more power and bore down. "But there's a bit that keeps ... slipping away." Her brow furrowed deeply, her mouth pulling into a grimace. "I can't get it."

"You can't leave it in there," Jules said.

"I know. I'm trying."

Finally, Trip broke free of his frozen state and rushed across the room to come down at her side. "How can I help?" he asked, touching her shoulder.

She stiffened at his touch and hissed as if in pain. He pulled his hand back but she said, "No! Don't. That helped. It doesn't like it ... when you touch me. It weakens it."

He put both hands firmly on her shoulders. She stiffened and hissed again, but he didn't let go, trusting in her. "You've got this."

She straightened, a smile curling on her lips. "Yes. I do." She pulled more power, her hands pushing slightly into Dawn's skin. "Your power helps shine a light. I can see it clearly now." She leaned in and whispered in Dawn's ear, "You're done, fucker."

Ilia seemed to grow larger before his eyes for a moment, the power she drew on bigger than anything he'd ever felt from anyone or anything before. Dawn let out one, piercing scream – a scream filled with something black and oily from the depths of the Hells – as a roaring sound filled the air.

And as the sound made the chandelier above them shake and rattle, Ilia let go of the child and rocked back suddenly. She would have toppled onto her back with the momentum if Trip hadn't had such a firm grip on her shoulders.

"You got it?" he asked at the same time as everyone around Dawn asked the same.

She lifted her head, gaze triumphant, and said, "I got it." Her head dropped back into Trip's shoulder and she gazed up at him. "Now we have to get rid of it."

"But if you can't use the Vortex, what will you do?" Jules asked, her eyes going back to her child.

"Can one of us take it?" Bas asked.

"No." Her head lolled on Trip's shoulder as she tried to look over to where Loki still sat on the floor holding his wound. "I'm hoping Loki will be able to help me figure out what to do with it."

Everyone's gaze went to the God of Mischief.

"Loki. Wake up!"

Loki's head snapped up groggily. "Who's using manameinvain?" he slurred.

"Me," Trip said. "We need you to help us: tell us the truth about what we face."

"Can'dothat," he said, his words even more mushed together and almost unrecognisable.

But Ilia understood him, as did Trip because he said, "The shield is up, Loki. So you are going to help us – even if it kills you." Trip put his arm around Ilia and turned her to face the annoying God. She was glad of his arm and support as she wasn't certain if she could stay upright much longer.

She *hurt!*

This thing she'd taken from Dawn – it was so much more than she'd imagined. She might have access to endless power but it was also endless in ways she couldn't understand and was taking up every single part of her and trying to take more. It was taking everything she had in her to keep it from bursting out.

How the baby could possibly have held it within her small frame, she didn't know, but it was a testament to the power of the child – a power that Korinna's prophecy had warned them about. Not because, she now realised, Dawn herself was a danger, or even that her astonishing power put her in danger from the Gods because of what she might do with it.

She snorted to herself. It was almost laughable they'd thought a God could hurt her.

No, it was because of what had almost happened. The fact that such power put her in danger from greater, older powers from taking her over in an effort to get back what had once been theirs. She was a gateway of sorts, and none of them had been cognisant of that. They hadn't sufficiently protected her because of it.

But *she* should have known. Not only had she been linked to the baby for months, but she'd been taking parts of that thing into herself for months. However, she'd been so caught up in everything she thought was going wrong for her and how useless she felt in the scheme of things now that her direct link to Dawn was gone, that she hadn't spared a thought for what she truly was taking from the baby. She had allowed it to grow and change that precious girl right under her nose and had done nothing much to stop it. Oh, she'd slowed it down by taking pieces of it into herself, but it hadn't been enough. Not nearly enough.

If only she'd stopped to think, to analyse, to talk it over with Trip rather than keeping what she was doing from him and everyone else. One of them could have helped her to realise what was happening – or in the telling of it, *she* could have realised. Or the knowledge could have tripped a prophecy in Korinna and then they would have known and she could have taken action well before now. Well before it had changed Dawn almost to the point of being able to fully utilise her. Well before it had grown in strength and size and now was inside her, threatening to tear her apart if she couldn't get rid of it safely.

Lesson learned. It was one she wouldn't forget – if she was given the chance to. No more hiding things from those she loved and trusted – because she did love and trust everyone in this room. Well, maybe not Loki but ...

Agh! She bent over double, clutching her arms around herself.

"Ilia! Are you okay?" Trip's arm held her steady and upright.

"I'm handling it." And she was. She tamped down on the ugliness inside her that had already started to tear her apart. Then she imagined a needle and thread sewing the torn bits back together. It worked. It was painful, but it worked. She sighed in relief.

"Are you sure?"

"Yes. For now."

"What's going on?" Tam asked.

"It's tearing her apart. We have to get it out. Loki – we need your help. Now!"

Yes, they did. Because the thing inside her was so much more than she'd bargained for and it felt too big to keep it inside for much longer. She'd stupidly thought she might have some time to figure this out, but it was too far gone for that.

It was a terrible pressure under her skin bursting to get out, slashing at her insides. It was increasing and increasing in a way that made her feel like she was going to split open like an over-ripe banana in the hot sun. She threw shields over it, around it, pushed it down, but it was so big, so strong, breaking through everything she threw at it faster than she could handle.

Holy fucking Hells! It was too much. Too much.

Had she been stupid to believe she could figure some way to handle taking this on? Was she going to break her promise to Trip despite the feeling she'd had that it would work out? It certainly felt like she was going to break it. It felt like she was about to lose everything.

She looked up into Trip's eyes, wanting to apologise, to say goodbye, but the words stilled in her throat. That expression in his eyes ...

No! She couldn't leave him. She wouldn't. Not when she'd had so little time with him. Not when their future was spread out before them if she was strong enough to just reach out her hand and grasp it.

And she was. Strong. Endlessly strong. Not just because of this new power that was hers, but because she had Trip as her mate. And she had Korinna and Tam, Jules and Bas and Violetta as family and friends. Even Daphne and her boys were her family now through Trip.

And because she had Dawn, who needed her and loved her. She intended to be the best auntie to that little girl that ever was.

So, she was not going to let this thing, this part of Perses, take her down so easily. She was going to hang on until they'd found a way for her to get rid of it. "No you don't, you fucker," she said, pushing back at it with every ounce of strength she had.

"What's it doing?"

"Trying to break me. But I won't let the arsehole do it." Sweat dripped down her face and back with the effort as she smiled at him, basking in the glow of love in his remarkable spring-green eyes. "It's not going to win today."

He smiled a smile that was smug and full of knowing pride. "No it's not. Not with you at the helm."

"I love you." The words burst out of her, the sound and feel of them on her lips, in her ears, lessening the pain racking her entire body.

"I love you too," he replied, the full breadth and depth of his emotions in his voice, held in those four words.

The fact of it burst through her as it did every time he said them and gave her strength. She straightened a little more, releasing the death grip she'd had around her middle.

"Can you walk?"

"Yes. With you at my side, I can do anything."

With his help, she began to walk.

They weren't that far from Loki but there was smashed furniture in the way. She moved to go around it, but Trip made a waving motion with his hand and the furniture simply disappeared.

A noise of protest erupted from Violetta as she said, "I could have fixed those!"

"Sorry," Trip said as they passed her. "I'll replace them after we're done here."

Violetta waved the words away. "Don't worry. I can do it myself with all this extra energy Ilia's given me."

Ilia chuckled and said over her shoulder, "You're welcome."

A moment later, they stood over Loki.

"It's time to help," Trip said.

"*Truly* help," Ilia clarified.

He looked up at them blearily. "Leavemealone."

"Can't do that," Ilia said, indicating she needed Trip to help her to the floor. He did so and joined her there, his arm around her.

"I'mdying. Soleavemeinpeash."

"So dramatic!" Ilia snorted. She waved her hand at his wound. "You won't die from this."

"How'dyouknow?" Loki said, head lolling around as he tried to focus on her.

It was no wonder really, given the pool of blood around him that had soaked into the carpet he sat on. He was still losing some going by the fresh blood seeping through the fingers clutching his wound. Not that she had any sympathy for him.

Loki lifted one hand off his stomach, staring at the blood. "Neverbledsomush. Notevenwhen Thor cutmearm orf asha—" He coughed, black and bloody spittle flying from his mouth as his eyes screwed up in pain.

TWENTY-TWO

Loki coughed and coughed and Ilia wondered if he was going to pass out before he gave them more information. But the moment the coughing stopped, he started talking again – obviously even almost dying couldn't shut him up.

"Cutmearm orf ... practicaljoke. Gottha lastlaughtho. HidMirmir. Wasnlaughing then ... washe?"

"Loki. Focus."

"Amfocused. Ondying."

"You're not going to die," Trip said.

"Howdyaknow?" He held up his bloody hand. "Losing-malife's blood, Iam."

"Oh for fuck's sake. You're not dying," Ilia said. "You told us earlier you weren't going to die."

"Did I?"

"Yes. When you told us to save Daphne instead."

"Huh. Me an' mybigmouth!"

She laughed and Trip chuckled.

"Hurtzlika motherfuckertho'."

"I'm sure it does." Given the nasty state of his wound,

Ilia guessed it probably hurt as much as she was hurting –
he'd actually been shredded from the outside-in and she
felt like she was being shredded from the inside-out.

Okay, maybe she did have a little bit of empathy
for him.

She shifted to stretch her legs out because bending
them like they were as she knelt made the skin feel more
stretched and like they might actually begin to split open
with the pressure of what she held inside her.

"Youhurttoo," Loki said, head jiggling in what she
assumed was meant to be a knowing nod.

"Doesn't take brilliance to figure that out given what I
did. But that's where you come in."

"Wi' thabrilliance."

"No. With something actually helpful. How do I get rid
of this?" Ilia gestured at herself, at the greying colour of her
skin, the blackness seeping down from her cuticles that was
slowly changing her nails into something dark and glistening. The room was greying around her, so she was certain
there was also something freaky going on with her eyes.
The Fates had cursed her with this as an end, but she
wasn't ready to lie down and take their using and abusing
her once again.

He stared at her for a moment, somehow managing to
keep his head still. "Looksnasty."

"Feels worse." She swallowed back the need to make a
biting comment and asked again, "How do I get rid of it
with the shield up?"

"Yadon't."

"What?" Trip barked. "You can't be serious."

"Seriousss assa shark," he said, obviously trying to
delineate the words.

"You fucking arsehole! You made me put this bloody

shield up and … did you know it would kill her because she can't get rid of it?" Trip looked like he was going to reach over the space between them, grab Loki and shake him. Ilia put her hand on his leg – the tension in him was palpable and vibrated through her skin and up her arm. Her touch seemed to calm him though – thankfully. She needed Loki compos mentis – or at least as compos mentis as he could be at this point; a shaking would not help matters.

Loki waggled his head. "Toldya toputit up forshafety. Shafetyfor … talking. Shafetyfrom monshtersh attackingush." He looked down at his injury. "Shoulda shtayedhere. But hadtoprotect them."

"Right. And now I have to protect my mate," Trip said fiercely, gripping Loki by the collar and hauling him up before Ilia could stop him.

"Hey! Leave him alone, Trip," Daphne cried out. "He's injured."

Trip turned to stare at his friend, who Ilia knew he viewed as a sister, his eyes wide with hurt confusion. "You're protecting him over me and Ilia?"

Daphne looked taken aback for a moment, confusion crossing her face. "Umm … no. But this isn't like you. To pick on an injured person. I don't like it."

Trip's face fell into lines of apology. "I'm sorry, my friend. I don't mean to upset you. You've been upset enough. But you don't know him like we do. He's a conniving arsehole who wouldn't know the truth if he swallowed it, spat it out then tripped over the remains."

"Hey!" Loki gurgled, blood spraying out on the word. "Wouldn' tripoverit! Notthat clumshy!"

Ignoring Loki, Ilia reached out and put her hand over Trip's. "Daphne's right, Trip. This is unnecessary and unhelpful."

"But ... He needs some convincing," Trip said, turning back to Loki, his grip tightening.

"Idon'," Loki squeaked.

"Apparently you do," Trip said, glaring at him.

"Maybe. Ushually." He coughed, blood dribbling down his chin. "Yerbloodywell makin' mebleed more. Violetta's nevergonna getthishout ofthecarpet."

"You're making jokes? Right now?"

"I don't want you hurting him, Trip," Daphne said. "He came for us ... saved us. I don't want him hurt."

Loki waved his hand in Daphne's direction. "S'okay m'darlin'. Hecan' hurtmemore ... thanalready binhurt."

"Don't call me darlin'. I'm not anyone's darlin'."

Hurt crossed Loki's pain-riddled features. Emotional hurt.

It made Ilia's heart ache for him and say, "She's right, my love. You shouldn't hurt him," When he didn't let go, she leaned in close and whispered. "Trip. Please." She edged around a little so she could cup his face with one hand. "We need him."

Trip's grip tightened further before, with a sigh, he let Loki go. "I'm sorry, my love." He glanced over at Daphne and then back at Loki. "But if this arsehole doesn't help us now and something happens to you, nothing will stop me from making him pay."

"Shteadyon!" Loki said, trying to meet him in the eye and failing miserably – he really was in a bad way. "I'mhelpin. Promish."

"Then help. Say something useful."

"Whatdoyawan metoshay?"

"Fucking Hells!" Trip roared. "I swear, if your injury doesn't kill you, I'm going to."

"For crap's sake, Loki," Tam said, getting up from where

he'd been sitting with his parents to walk over. "Stop playing your games and just help!"

The thing inside her pushed harder suddenly, as if trying to make a break for it and she gasped, clutching at her middle again.

Could it sense other beings here it might be able to use if it broke free?

As if in answer, it pushed harder when Korinna stood from where she'd been talking to Harry and Gideon to join her mate in walking across to them.

Bloody, crapping, fuckity Hells!

She bent double, grasping around her chest and middle as if that would help to hold it in.

"Ilia? You okay?" Trip asked, letting go of Loki to grab her, holding her upright.

"No." Ilia held her hand up. "I'll be even worse if any of you move closer. It's responding to you coming closer."

"Shit. Everyone, get as far away as possible," Trip shouted.

"Sorry." Tam immediately backed up, gesturing for everyone to move back if they could. Given most of them were in corners of the room, the only ones who could back away were Tam and Korinna. Despite it helping to feel Trip's touch earlier, now she wished she could move away from him — and Loki too. But Trip wouldn't abandon her like that and she still needed Loki's help. She needed to hurry this along.

Turning back to Loki, she touched his leg and said, "Please. I need your help." Because this couldn't be her destiny, to lose everything good when she had just started to think it was hers to keep. Those three bitches, the Fates, couldn't weave this as her fate and get away with snipping her thread like this now.

She wasn't going to let them!

On the heels of her plea to Loki, Trip leaned close to the mischief God, her mate's face grimmer than she'd ever seen it, and said through gritted teeth, "She has to get rid of it. It will kill her if she doesn't. And if that's not incentive enough for you, then try this: once it bursts out of her it will be in here trapped with us because of the shield you made me put up. And with nowhere else to go, it will enter one of us, seeking to take over and use us rather than Dawn. And given it will go for the one with a power most like its own, you have to know that's going to be you."

Loki nodded, face paling even more as his lips thinned into a grimace. "Notgonna happen."

"Of course it will happen if she doesn't get rid of it somewhere, you absolute fucking arse." Trip was usually so easy-going and had never lost his temper with Loki once during their encounter with him last year – unlike her – but he really looked like he was about to rip the mischief God in half if he didn't co-operate now.

Loki's head dipped and wobbled, his hand clutching at his bloody stomach. He coughed again, bloody spittle landing on his shirt and chin. Once the cough subsided, his head dipped further down onto his chest as if he'd passed out.

"Loki! Loki!" Trip grabbed Loki's chin, pushing his head up. "You can't pass out yet. You need to help us figure out what to do!"

Loki opened his eyes blearily and said, "Donneed … myhelp. Sheishenough. Totakeitin."

Ilia and Trip shared a confused look. "What does that mean?" she asked him.

"You … trueconduit. Transhmutepower. Transhmute … him."

Ilia stared at the God while trying to process his words, but they still made no sense, no matter how much she tried to figure it out. "Goddammit Loki. Stop talking in riddles. Tell me something I can use."

"Haf tol' you." He wobbled his head to the side in the direction of where Tam and Korinna had backed up to sit next to Jules, Bas and Dawn. "She'lltellyoutoo."

"What?"

"Jushhh ... waitforit."

"Wait for what?"

"Thereshegoesh."

"Rinna! Rinna. Fuck not again." Tam yelled and lunged for his mate as she rose to her feet and into the air, but it was pointless because holding her wasn't going to stop the prophecy from rising out of her.

"What's Rinna doing, Mum? Is she all right?" Gideon asked.

"I don't know," Daphne said, pulling her boys closer to her, eyes wide with fear. "Trip? What's going on?"

"She's a prophet." He shook his head. "I know you don't know what that means, but it's okay. She won't hurt you or the boys. I promise. But just keep them over there, okay?"

Daphne nodded, reaching to pull Gideon back as he tried to crawl forward, his gaze pinned on the woman he'd come to know as family over the past few months.

"Mum! She needs help."

Charlie leaned forward and helped his mum pull his little brother back. "You heard what Trip said. She's fine. Besides, Tam won't let her get hurt. Neither will Trip."

"I won't. I promise," Trip said.

Gideon didn't seem convinced even though he let his brother pull him back. Ilia didn't blame him because Tam certainly wasn't giving off 'she'll be fine' vibes. He was trying desperately to hold onto his love, stopping her from rising higher. But the more he held her, the more she vibrated, her head starting to whip back and forth and side-to-side.

"Tam. Let her go," Jules said. "You hurt her more if you try to stop it."

"It's okay, son. She'll be okay," Bas said, rising to stand next to Tam. "We'll catch her together when she finishes."

Tam didn't let go. Bas put his hand on his son's shoulder. "It's better to let her have the prophecy. She's been okay the last few times. She seems to be getting better at withstanding them." He still didn't move. "She's strong, my son. Believe in her ability to stand what the Eternal Well has given her."

A pause then Tam nodded grimly and let go of his love.

Korinna immediately rose higher into the air. Once she was hovering just below the ceiling, she began to float across the room to hover over Ilia, Trip and Loki – Tam and Bas following in her wake. Ilia knew she should tell them to stay back as she had before – the thing inside her felt like it was trying to punch a hole through her to escape – but there was no chance they'd listen now, so she just bore down on the pain and tried to concentrate on what Korinna was about to say.

If she'd understood Loki, this prophecy was going to be about her.

The witch's eyes were glowing like they had every time she'd uttered a prophecy, swirling with gold and black. A fae wind blew her hair back from her face and shoulders and her pale skin glowed like bone-white porcelain.

She opened her mouth and a low gasp of air came out, shuddering and shaking. Then on its wake she said in that same voice that had intoned each prophecy:

. . .

"She is the flame, she is the light,
Rising as the Phoenix, to set things to right,
Transforming all with night's moon and dawn's ray,
To free Ostara's gifted one of the ancient evil's sway,
To enable her to light up the new day to come,
And take up her role as the prophesied One.
But how when the Fates weave only pain for you?
The answer to that is: be the weaver of fate too.
The Eternal Well's gift is transformative
All you need do is believe and you will live.
In the Eternal Well's blessing, three times three times three
So says the prophet, so mote it be."

THE WORDS RANG in the air like the musical chime of a church bell in the distance before disappearing into silence.

The fae wind stopped blowing around Korinna, her outstretched arms fell to her side and she dropped from her hover – to be caught by Tam and Bas.

"My love? My love ... are you okay?" Tam asked as he swept her into his arms and carried her across to the lounge that Trip and Ilia had been sitting on earlier.

Korinna's eyes opened and she lifted her hand to touch Tam's face. "I'm fine. Just a little dry." She coughed, but she seemed okay.

Thank the Eternal Well for small mercies. Ilia couldn't stand it if someone else was hurt in the effort to stop her from being consumed by what she'd taken in.

"Can I get a glass of water?" Korinna asked when she'd finished coughing.

Bas clicked his fingers and a glass of water appeared in the air in front of Tam. He snatched it, said, "Thanks," to his father and then, "Here, my love. Drink."

"What did she mean?" Gideon's childish voice asked into the silence.

"Good question," Trip said, turning back to Loki even though Ilia knew he was fighting everything in him not to race over to his daughter to check she was okay because of his mate's needs right now. She gripped his hand, sending love and thanks and support through the bond.

He squeezed back, but didn't look at her, his eyes on the trickster God. "What did she mean?"

"Ish obvioushishn't it?" He waved his hand weakly. But when he was greeted with only stares, he said, "Itmeansh ... sheish the ... transhformative ... phoenix." Loki's words were slurred, his voice a husk of a whisper, but they rang through the room anyway.

Ilia started.

A phoenix?

That couldn't be right. And yet ...

She'd felt the flames of power inside her since she'd helped Trip purge the part of Perses he'd taken into the Vortex, but she hadn't understood what they'd meant as they'd licked at her, pleading to be put to use.

Could it be that simple? Could this be what the Fates had actually intended for her all along? Or was this something she'd woven for herself because of the choices she'd made? It felt like it might be the latter – but how could that be so?

She went to ask Loki, to make him say more so she knew she wasn't mistaken – but his head had lolled onto his chest again and it was clear by the way his hands fell to his sides that he was out cold and would be no more help right now. If he was capable of truly being any help at all.

Not that she really needed his help if she understood Korinna's prophecy properly.

All she needed to do was to believe that this was possible; that this was truly her destiny.

Trip's hand clutched hers, pulling her attention back to him. She was about to explain what she thought it meant, but the pain that had been increasing suddenly took a leap and flew past ten out of ten on the pain scale to somewhere in the vicinity of the flames of Hells burning her alive. Or maybe a more accurate description was a Hellbeast tearing into her with claws and teeth from the inside out.

Such an all-encompassing pain coming at her in nauseating roiling waves as the thing seemed to be growing and trying to eat her alive.

"Holy crapping Hells!" She bent over double, gripping her arms around her even more tightly in an effort to keep herself together.

"Ilia! Ilia! Are you okay? Don't stop fighting. We'll find a way. Together. We'll find a way."

She managed to lift her head so she could smile at him – loving his faith in her, in him. She felt the same. But before she said any of that, she had to put him out of his misery. He obviously hadn't heard what she'd heard in the prophecy Korinna had just intoned and in what Loki had said – which was kind of funny given he usually picked up things well before anyone else did. And despite the pain, she needed him to know that everything would be okay. "*We* don't ... need to," she gritted out through clenched teeth.

"No. No! You can't give up."

"I haven't. I'm ... I'm giving over ... to the flame of transformation ... inside me. I'm ... believing in .. a better fate."

Then, before he could ask anything else, before the pain could take her into the dark of unconsciousness, she opened herself up to a truth she should have seen before. What being moon-and-dawn-gifted should have told her. That the regenerative qualities in both wasn't to heal. It was to transform. As they transformed night to day and day to night, so she could transform things, even an enormous power like what was ripping her up inside.

Because she was not simply a daughter of the Well.

She was its Phoenix.

Reaching deep inside, she opened the door to the true core of her power – the Eternal Well – and did what Loki and the prophecy had made her realise she could do.

She changed everything inside her by allowing the transformative power of both the light of the moon and the light of dawn to take her over.

As she did, the world exploded in brilliant light around her. The thing inside her howled and roared, trying to fight back.

It made her smile because it was going to lose just like the Fates that hated her were going to lose.

That knowledge ... it filled her with more strength than she'd ever known before!

Then her world went up in pure silver and brilliant orange flames.

TWENTY-THREE

Trip was thrown back as light exploded out of Ilia and she lifted into the air, her entire form covered with silver and orange flames. "Ilia – no!"

"Protect Dawn!" Jules screamed at the same time.

"Fucking Hells!" Korinna and Tam said as one.

"It can't be!" Violetta said.

"Look, Mum. Korinna was right. She's a phoenix."

"Holy crap!"

"Boys! Stay away."

"Trip! Trip! Don't!"

Hands grabbed at him and he looked down, realising he had scrambled to his feet and was reaching up to grab his mate, but Loki had come to and grabbed his leg, stopping him.

"Let go!" he yelled. "I have to help her. She's burning up."

The God of Mischief smiled a sloppy smile that still shrieked smugness. "Notburning. Transhforming. Ishglorioush." His eyes reflected the flames that were now encompassing Trip's love, flames that were somehow reminiscent of both the moon's light and all the colours of dawn.

In that reflection, the flames looked like wings.

Suddenly he became aware of the sound of flapping.

He looked up and gasped.

Korinna had said she would rise like a phoenix, but he'd thought it a metaphor. Even when Gideon had called her a phoenix he hadn't registered.

It *wasn't* prophecy metaphor.

She *was* a bloody phoenix.

A creature of flame and light and transformation.

Except, she hadn't truly transformed. It wasn't a bird of mythology flying above them. It was Ilia with wings of silver flame and hair like living fire. Her skin glowed with the ever-shifting colours of dawn and her eyes ...

Her eyes.

They had shifted from the awful horror of oily blackness they had become when she'd taken the evil into her and were swirling with all the colours of the light spectrum. That colour began to glow silver, a small spark to begin with that grew and grew as she did whatever she was doing inside her to take the evil of Perses and transform it into the opposite of what it had once been – pure darkness turned into fire and light.

It was beautiful.

She was beautiful.

So fucking beautiful it stole his breath.

And just when he managed to take a breath it was stolen again as the realisation hit him. She was doing something that should be impossible but wasn't. Not for her.

Because she was of the dawn and of the moon.

He shouldn't be surprised and yet he was. Brilliantly,

wonderfully, endlessly surprised. As he would always be with her. For eternity.

He couldn't wait.

The flames surrounding her grew brighter and brighter until it was impossible to look at. But after he'd closed his eyes, Trip could still see the astonishing imprint of a phoenix-Ilia on the back of his eyelids even though the brightness of her as she changed not only herself, but the evil within her, made the usual darkness when he closed his eyes non-existent.

And the warmth of her!

He expected to feel his skin blister and the room around him to turn into a flaming Hellscape as everything burned in the power of her flame.

But it wasn't like that at all. Instead, it was a brush of soothing warmth across his skin, like the water in a warm bath or the softest blanket wrapping around him to give him a hug.

Actually, it was exactly like a blanket wrapping around him. A feathery-soft blanket that smelled of his Ilia.

A brush of fingers across his cheeks followed by the press of lips on his had his eyes snapping open.

"Ilia!"

She stood before him, her entire being glowing, flames still licking around her.

"I did it. I wove my own fate and transformed! Me, the evil, everything transformed!"

"You are magnificent!" he whispered in awe.

She leaned back and smiled at him and as she did, the wings of warm flame she'd wrapped around him slipped away and disappeared. Her eyes stopped glowing with the brilliance of the moon and returned to her usual dawn-tinted violet.

"Trip." She leaned in and kissed him again.

He sank into it, relief and pride and exhilaration shimmering through him as she licked into his mouth and deepened the kiss.

Then passion overtook everything else and he wrapped his arms around her, pulling her as close as he could.

Holy Gods! The feel of her against him, the press of her breasts against the bare planes of his chest, the shape of her hips, her waist, her hips again as his hands ran over her. Then she jumped up to wrap her legs around his waist, allowing him to fully cup her arse ... holy Hells! It was a turn on if the rest hadn't already been. His skin burned everywhere she touched – in the best way.

His cock came rigidly to attention as she squeezed his waist with her thighs and ground her core against him. He dug his fingers into the firmness of those thighs in response and almost came at the way she purred into his mouth then licked the inside of his lips in that way that always made him shiver and his incisors lengthen.

Her glorious scent wrapped around him, filling his head, making his skin tighten. His incisors ached to sink into her flesh so he could taste her and drink her in to his full as she drank him in – because he could feel her incisors lengthening too; could feel her longing for his blood echoing to him through their bond. It drove his need for her blood to a craving he couldn't ignore.

"Whoa! My eyes! My eyes! I'm going to go blind!"

Cold water splashed over them. Ilia yelped and sputtered, her legs slipping from his waist so she could spin around to face Loki, who sat on the floor, an empty bucket dangling in the air to his left. He had his eyes covered – although his fingers were slightly parted, obviously peeping through the gap.

"You arsehole!" Ilia snapped. "What did you do that for?"

He dropped the pretence of not looking and gestured behind them. "Umm ... There are children in the room, you two. Not to mention adults who don't really want to see you getting it on."

Trip's gaze snapped to the others he'd completely forgotten were in the room. They were all still blinking as if to clear their eyesight and didn't seem to have noticed anything at all – thank the Gods. Especially Daphne and the boys! And nobody seemed to be affected by the sexual energy between them as they had been before.

But why not?

Not that he was complaining. It was embarrassing. Both he and Ilia would be so relieved if that problem was no longer an issue.

But still, he was curious.

He sent out a little curl of seeking magic into the room, trying to sense if the magical influence of their sexual energy was anywhere. But it seemed to be nowhere but in the half metre or so around them.

Huh.

So no sexual energy leakage at all.

His gaze went to Ilia. It must have something to do with the way she now used and expelled energy. Because nothing had changed with him except for the fact that he loved her and wanted her and needed her even more now than he did before, no matter how impossible that seemed given he'd previously thought he couldn't love or want or need her more.

"From the look of things," Ilia said to Loki, bringing his attention back to the conversation at hand. "I think the only person who saw anything was you." She began to wring water out of her hair.

"She has a point," Trip said, wiping the water off his face. "We really didn't need the shower."

"From where I'm sitting, you did. I really don't want that image in my head. I have enough nightmarish stuff in here already – I don't need more."

"You're hilarious," Ilia drawled.

Even though he was still very pale and obviously bleeding, Loki smiled up at her. "Thanks for noticing."

"How come you can see and nobody else can?" she asked, frowning.

"For that matter," Trip said, "how come you can talk better now?"

"I'm just that kind of remarkable."

Ilia angled her head and gave him a look that Trip hoped he'd never be on the receiving end of – ever.

It obviously worked because Loki's smile fell from his face. "In answer to your first question, they were blinded temporarily by the light of the phoenix at the end there."

"Oh," she said, glancing around. "Did I hurt them?"

"No. Don't worry. It's not permanent."

Trip stroked her back as she looked worriedly at their friends, their family. "They'll be okay."

She nodded and took a deep breath then returned her attention to Loki. "But you weren't blinded?"

"I knew what would happen so protected my eyes."

"You should have warned them to do the same."

"And how was I to do that when I could barely talk?"

Trip frowned at him. "Which brings us back to the second question – why do you seem better now? Did what Ilia just do then heal you?"

Loki huffed, the sound followed by a small cough. "I

wish. No. The energy you emitted while taking on your phoenix avatar filtered into me a little, giving me a boost of temporary energy which I used to heal myself. Partially."

"So it didn't heal you then?"

"Your transformative powers are not made of healing energy, so while they can be temporarily restorative because of the boost they can give those around you when you change a form of energy into something else, they cannot heal. And they don't last very long. At least, not for someone like me." He started to cough.

"Loki? Are you sure you're going to be okay?" Trip asked, taking a step closer.

Loki stopped coughing, took a shuddering, wheezy breath and said, "Not sure. I don't feel very good." He coughed again, blood spewing out of his mouth as he did.

"Loki!" Ilia shouted as his eyes rolled up in his head and he keeled over.

Trip got there first and rolled Loki over. "Loki. Don't you die on us!"

"He said he couldn't die," Ilia said, kneeling on the other side of him.

"He's been known to lie." Trip pulled back the God's torn and bloody shirt so they could see his wound for the first time. "Holy crap."

"That doesn't look good."

"No."

He had been shredded by the Hellbeast's claws from nipples to almost his groin. Parts of his guts showed through the wound, which was weeping black and yellow puss as well as blood. The edges of the wound were a putrid green-black with striations of angry red rippling outwards – as if it was days old and had gone septic. Whatever was in the Hellbeast's claws that was poison to mischief Gods was doing something terrible to him. "Bas. We need you over here."

"Coming," Bas said, scrunching his eyes and rubbing his lids, but despite his obvious sight difficulties, he began to make his way over to them.

"What's going on?" Tam called, rubbing his eyes while making his way over too.

"Loki is really bad," Ilia said. She jumped up to help Bas over.

"Describe it to me," Bas said as he knelt beside the prone God. "I'm still mostly seeing spots from the brightness of your flaming wings, Ilia." He leaned close to her. "Which was pretty bloody amazing. What did you do with the bit of evil arsehole you took from Dawn? I assume it's gone?"

"Turned into something light and fluffy and sent back to the Eternal Well to use."

"Excellent." He smiled brilliantly at her before returning his attention to Loki. "Now, tell me everything you see."

Between them, Trip and Ilia explained what they saw.

From the look on Bas' face, it wasn't good.

CHAPTER

TWENTY-FOUR

On Bas' instructions, they carried the mischief-God to one of the downstairs guest bedrooms. "I need to be out of this chaos to concentrate and figure out what to do," he said as they settled Loki on the bed. "Thanks for that. Now go and let me and Violetta take care of him wh—"

"But I should stay," Ilia said. "I can help boost you. Maybe that will help to heal him."

Bas shook his head, frowning. "I don't think so. If it didn't help before, I don't think it will now. I don't think any of my magical healing will work on him now. We need to find some other remedy. So while Violetta and I work on him with a more Western medical approach, all of you need to go down to the library and look up information on Hell-beast poison so we can figure out how to cure him."

"Can the boys and I help?" Daphne asked.

"Umm ... I don't think that's a good idea," Trip said, trepidation on his face as he looked at his found family.

"But we want to help."

"We're dealing with magical texts which can sometimes have nasty surprises if you approach them in the wrong way."

"Not all of them can be like that or Jules wouldn't have been able to work on them when she was allergic to magic," Charlie protested.

Trip's brows rose. "How do you know about that?"

Charlie looked a bit sheepish. "We asked Tam and Korinna and Jules about their magic ... I know you didn't want us to get more involved, but as Mum said to you when we found out, you can't put that cat back in the bag. Besides, I kinda find it fascinating."

"Hmm."

Ilia could tell Trip wasn't happy, but honestly, what did he expect with three curious boys who loved him like a father and wanted to know everything about the world he was from and the people he was bonded to.

"I think it will help us all to settle after everything that's just gone on," Daphne said, her arm around Gideon who was leaning into her side, his eyes wide and curious.

"Please," Harry said. "Don't make us go and rest or anything stupid like that. We won't be able to. Let us help."

Trip made a grumbling sound, but waved his hand. "Fine. You can come down to the library with us, but ..." He raised his finger. "You're not to touch a single text until I've checked it for magic and you're not to go running through the stacks or touching anything we don't hand to you."

"Woohoo!" Gideon said, leaping out of his mother's arms to give Trip a hug. "Thank you."

Trip patted the boy's curly mop of dark hair, a smile flickering on his lips. "I need your promise to do as I say, not your thanks, Gid."

The boy leaned back and looked up at him. "I promise.

We all promise. Don't we?" He turned back to look at his mother and brothers and they all nodded.

"We promise," they intoned together.

"Fine." Shaking his head he herded them out of the room. "Who else is coming?"

Tam hesitated, looking back at Loki in the bed. "You sure you don't need me and Korinna, Dad?"

"I'm sure. This is the kind of healing you've had no training in like Violetta, Jules and I have."

"But what if you need anything?"

"I will go and get it," Jules said.

"But you have Dawn to care for." He looked down at his sister. She was asleep in the armchair where Jules had just placed her when she'd followed her mate into the room. The now school-aged child looked truly peaceful for the first time since her birth.

Jules came up beside him and looked down at her daughter. "She is safe now. Thanks to Ilia." She gave Ilia a grateful smile.

"Will she stop growing now?" Tam asked no one in particular.

Nobody answered, but they all looked at Ilia as if she might know. She shrugged. "I am uncertain. The residual magic of what that piece of Perses was doing to her might still be active, so she might grow a little faster than usual for a little while yet. But the bursts of fast growth we've seen should stop. I think."

"We'll just have to wait and see," Bas said from where he stood tending Loki. "Sometimes that's all you can do."

"Yes," Ilia said.

Tam nodded and bent down to give Dawn a kiss on the forehead. She muttered in her sleep and smiled. Jules leaned forward and tucked a stray strand of long, curly reddish hair back from her daughter's face.

"She needs to sleep. The fewer people here talking and making noise, the more likely she will get the rest she needs."

"Do you want me to take her to her bed?" Tam asked.

Jules shook her head in a short sharp motion. "No. I need to keep my eye on her."

"As do I," Bas said.

"Count me into that as well," Violetta said as she came back into the room with a tray of healing herbs and bandages. She placed the tray down on the dresser against the wall and then walked over to touch Tam's cheek and smiled gently. "Don't worry, my old friend. We'll look after your sister."

He nodded. "I know you will." Then his gaze returned to the mischief God lying unconscious on the bed.

Korinna came to his side and, taking his arm hugged it to herself. He brightened as he looked down at her – Ilia knew that feeling well, and she hugged Trip's arm to her as Korinna said, "I know that despite the mischief he has often caused, he is your friend and you are concerned, but the best you can do for him now is to help Ilia, Trip and I look for a cure."

"We will look after your friend as if he were ours too," Violetta said. "I promise."

Tam nodded. "I know you will. Thank you." Then he turned and, Korinna by his side, gestured for Daphne and the boys to follow them and headed down to the library.

Ilia and Trip followed in their wake.

As they reached the bottom step, Trip stopped, his hand on Ilia's shoulder to stop her motion. "Your shields. Your shields aren't up."

"I know." She tipped her head to the side, smiling a little. "Something tells me I won't need them."

"Because you frightened the life out of the ghosts the last time you were down here with that rainbow energy wave?" Korinna asked from where she'd stopped just ahead of them.

Ilia chuckled. "I hadn't thought of that. But yes, that will keep them away for a little while won't it. Crap."

"You don't want them to stay away?" Tam asked.

She shook her head. "I wanted to test it."

"Test what?"

"This feeling inside that things have changed. That now I know my power and how to use it, nothing will ever be able to take me over like they did again."

Trip slipped his hand down into hers. "We'll test it another time." She looked up at him as he rubbed his thumb over the back of her hand, making her shiver in anticipation of what might come later when they were done with this day. "Although, I don't think it will be much of a test. I think you are right. I don't think they'll be able to take you over again."

"Still, we should all be here to help just in case when you do test it – if they don't try something today."

Trip glanced ahead of them into the quiet dark of the library where nothing rustled or stirred. "I don't think they will be coming back today."

"You have ghosts in your library?" Gideon asked, his eager voice ringing in the vast cavern of the library.

Trip continued down the stairs and ruffled the boy's hair. "Yes."

"Cool!"

"I suppose it is. Although, I'm afraid you won't be meeting them today."

"Aww. That sucks," the boy said, face falling as he kicked at the carpet. "I really wanted to meet some."

"Next time."

He looked up at Trip. "There'll be a next time?"

"Undoubtedly." He sighed and met Daphne's eyes. "I'm afraid we're all stuck here for a while until we're certain that minion of Perses and the Hellbeast aren't still trying to get through."

"Oh. The shield is still up?"

"Yes. And protecting us," Korinna said as she turned to face them all. "But that means that while they can't get in, we can't get out."

Daphne's gaze flicked to Trip. "What about the farm? We have to get back to the farm. There's things to do, trees to plant, fields to prepare. We can't just be stuck here for God knows how long."

Trip walked to her and took her hand. "I'm worried about it too, but I'm sorry, we can't lower the shield – not even for a second. That Hellbeast could sense it and if it moved quickly enough, get to us. Or, it could be waiting at the farm for us to come back and attack again."

Daphne's hand went to her mouth. "It could destroy the farm!"

He grimaced. "It could. It probably has destroyed some of it already out of anger and revenge after you all got away."

"My home!" she said, voice wobbling. "What if it's destroyed my home?"

He pulled her to him, wrapping her in a tight hug, his gaze meeting the boys' worried eyes. "We'll rebuild it. We'll rebuild whatever may have been destroyed."

"But ... what about if others come? What if it hurts our neighbours?"

Trip shook his head, his worried gaze meeting Ilia's. She put her arm around him and said, "We have to hope it doesn't. That Demeter or Persephone will intervene finally – because they certainly can't want the humans to see a Hellbeast. I am certain Persephone is telling Hades right now to pull the Hellbeast back to where it is supposed to be caged."

"But what if she isn't?"

Ilia shrugged.

"I'm sure she is," Korinna said. "I know Seph well, and there is no way she'd put up with a Hellbeast being out and about and hurting humans. I'm sure she swept in as soon as we left."

"Really?"

Korinna nodded.

Ilia added, "Although it's far more likely to be waiting in the aether with Perses' minion for any sign that Trip's shields have weakened so it can get in."

Daphne pulled back from Trip a little, her horror-filled gaze going to her boys. "Would they weaken? Is that possible?"

Trip shook his head, his hands going to her shoulders so she looked back at him. "No. They are too strong. The only way for them to go down is for me to take them down, or for me to die. And that is impossible."

"It is?"

He chuckled. "A discussion for another time."

Her eyes suddenly filled with tears. "But ... our farm. Our home! What am I going to do if it's been destroyed and we have nothing. I can't go through that again. I can't."

"That will never happen," Korinna said. "Even if it has been destroyed, you have us. We are your family now. And when we are done with all of this, we will rebuild what was destroyed as Dad said – if it has been."

Ilia said, "And we don't know if it has been."

Daphne looked at Trip. "Is that possible?"

"Maybe. I don't know," Trip said on a sigh. "What I do know is that it's important not to concentrate on what we might have lost. It's that Perses didn't win today. It didn't get you and the boys, or Dawn, Tam or Jules. That's all that matters."

She nodded shakily and pulled out of his grip. "You're right. I'm being ridiculous worrying about things we cannot know." She held her hands out to her boys who all came to her, Harry and Charlie each taking a hand and Gideon tucking in to her side and giving her a hug.

"It'll be okay, Mum," Charlie said as the others nodded in agreement. "We'll work hard and fix whatever's been done if that creature did wreck the farm and our home."

"Trip can fix it with magic," Gideon said brightly.

Daphne looked at him. "Could you?"

He nodded wryly. "That's what I said."

"I thought you meant actual, manual labour."

"We could do a bit of that too if it makes you feel better. But I could do it all with my magic. Starting with repairing the fields and trees."

Daphne gasped. "The field that grew so quickly last Christmas. That was you?"

TWENTY-FIVE

Trip shrugged and looked down at his feet. "Yep. Although, that was an accident. I didn't know who I was or how to control what I could do back then."

"But now you can," Harry asked hopefully.

"Now I can."

"Why can't you just fight off the Hellbeast and that dude in the cloak?" Gideon asked, pulling away from his mum.

"Gideon!" Daphne said.

Trip chuckled. "It's okay. It's a good question." He went down onto his haunches and looked up at Gideon. "My powers, while strong, are not the kind of powers that are traditionally used to attack and fight. I can turn them that way, but it takes a toll."

"A big toll," Tam said gently, coming up behind Gideon. "None of our powers truly lend themselves to fighting, unfortunately."

"Why unfortunately?" Daphne asked.

Trip sighed. "There's a bigger fight ahead."

"And all of us have to stay safe to fight it," Ilia added. "We can't be distracted by fights we don't need to fight. Just as we can't be distracted by other things ... like worrying about those we love and care about."

"Which means," Korinna said, coming up to tuck her arm in Daphne's and give it a pat. "We need you and the boys to stay where it's safe. So even if we were certain the Hellbeast and its master were gone from the farm, you need to stay here for a while until we can find a way of keeping you safe when you're away from us." She nudged Trip's arm. "Or Dad's going to be a mess the entire time worrying about you all."

"They know now you're important to us, so that could make you a target," Ilia said, gaze flicking to Trip as she felt guilt flare inside him. "That's not your fault," she said, waggling her finger at him.

"No. It isn't," Korinna said. "You didn't give it away."

"No. Jules and I did that," Tam said, "when we tried to protect them too. Thankfully Loki arrived. Hang on," he said, frowning. "How did he know to come and help?"

"He's been watching us all for a while," Ilia said. "Maybe he just saw you were in danger and went to help."

"But wasn't he watching us through you?" Trip asked.

Ilia's frown matched Korinna's. "Yeah. He did say that." She shrugged. "Although, he said he wasn't always with us. So maybe he saw them then."

"Maybe," Trip said, his gaze going to Daphne and the boys. "I guess we'll be able to ask him when he's better. And to that end, we really should get on with the research."

"And it's also about time I find out if I'm right about the ghosts." Ilia took a deep breath and stepped down into the library. Nothing happened. No rustles, no moans, no rushing sound coming towards her.

Despite all that had happened, everything that was going on with Loki, all the unanswered questions and all that they still must face, she couldn't help smiling as she walked further into the room. Pivoting in a circle with a 'ta-da!' motion to those who were still standing by the stairs, and going for an air of insouciance – although failing miserably because she was practically dancing – she headed to the kitchen saying over her shoulder, "I'm putting the kettle on. Who wants a cuppa?"

Everyone but the boys put their hands up, so she grabbed a large teapot out of the cupboard and set about making the tea as Tam and Korinna headed off to fetch some titles they both remembered might have some information that could help. Trip started showing Daphne and the boys how to search for titles in the online system and old-fashioned card catalogue that Jules was converting to be both online and in the magical reference book she was creating – an astonishing combination of her new magic and incredible librarian researcher skills.

Harry and Gideon instantly jumped on the computer while Charlie and Daphne got stuck in to the card catalogue. Trip began to call things up in the magical reference book.

Gideon was the first one to start generating titles to search, so Trip stopped what he was doing and went to fetch them, leaving Ilia to join the boys and their mum.

She was surprised to see how well Gideon was doing with the system. It could be used by non-magic users, but got a boost when used by a magic user because Jules had placed a spell on the search engine so that it could read need, want and intent and throw up more relevant leads.

Eventually she planned it to work in conjunction with the magical catalogue book she was creating.

She bit her lip as she watched the youngest of Daphne's boys. Could he have powers? It was unusual for it to show up in someone with a non-magical genetic heritage, and Daphne was definitely non-magical, as were the other two boys. So it was unlikely.

Yet ... she had a feeling there was something there they didn't know about. Maybe it came from his father's side – although it was unusual not to show in the other two boys if that was the case.

She would mention it to Trip when they were through this current crisis and see what he thought. There were things they could do to test the young boy without it being intrusive, or upsetting him or his mum too much over the idea of him having magic.

Going by what she'd seen so far, Gideon would be delighted to find out he was like Trip and Tam – Trip was like a father to him and Tam ... well, the young boy had quickly begun to idolise him from the moment they'd met last Christmas.

Tam and Korinna came back, and seeing Gideon was doing such a good job, he was left to search up more passages and texts on what might help heal Loki while Tam and Korinna went to retrieve them. Trip and Ilia checked the ones they had already brought back for magical content and those that didn't need magic to read them were given to Daphne, Charlie and Harry.

A few times Ilia or Trip had to put a translation spell on the texts so that Daphne and the boys could read them if they were in a different language – although curiously, Gideon didn't seem to need it even though she knew that even on the computer database that some of the titles and descriptions of books and manuscripts he'd sent Tam and Korinna off to get were in a different language. When she pointed it out to Trip he said, "He must be using Google translate." But she was pretty certain that wasn't it.

It was looking more and more likely the young boy did actually have magic. But now wasn't the time to bring it up and distress anyone with what that could mean. It was a worry that could be kept for later.

As was the fact that while they were doing this, they weren't looking for more information on Perses – discovering a weakness was a hope they all had; or finding ways of tracking down Demeter to demand answers and a way forward. But given Loki was part of that way forward, and the fact she really didn't want him to be in pain and unwell – or die, if that was a possibility – then this was the best use of their time right now.

She just hoped there wouldn't be a cost to it at some later date.

Shivering at the thought, she thrust it aside and went off to find a scroll Gideon had discovered with mention of ancient poisons and their treatments.

They worked for hours – so long that Tam organised sandwiches and drinks for all of them, which they devoured hungrily.

Hours ticked by. She hadn't realised how many or how late it was until Gideon and Harry started to fall asleep where they sat.

Trip and Ilia volunteered to take them upstairs to put to bed while the others kept going. Ilia expected Daphne to want to go with them to settle her boys in, but she didn't seem to feel the need at all, just kissing them and reminding them to clean their teeth. Trip promised to make sure they would – there were spare toothbrushes in each bathroom – after he'd rustled up something for them to sleep in, and Daphne had nodded and returned to reading the passage in the old book in front of her.

As they headed up the stairs with the boys, Ilia couldn't help but wonder why it was so important to the other woman to find a way to cure Loki. Maybe it was just because he'd saved her and the boys. She shrugged away the thought and followed Trip and the boys up the stairs.

Fifteen minutes later, the boys had changed into Tam's t-shirts – a better fit than any of Trip's clothes, which were in the vicinity of giant-sized – teeth cleaned, faces washed, and hopped into beds in one of the guest rooms, Gideon letting Trip and Ilia tuck him in. Ilia kissed both of them on the forehead, trying not to tear up as she thought about her own sons whom she'd never got to do this with. Trip's hand on her shoulder, the understanding and empathy she felt through the bond was just what she needed to keep it together and be happy in this moment. Because of course he understood. He'd never got to be there for his daughter's birth or see her grow up, only getting to know her now when she was fully grown and had lived so much life and experienced so much pain he'd never had the chance to help her with. And yet, he never let all that loss, sadness and bitterness mar how he faced the world or enjoyed moments like this.

She had so much still to learn – not only from him but *with* him – and it filled her with a sense of wholeness and oneness that she treasured.

"I've got much to learn with you and from you too," he whispered as they slipped out of the room and closed the door softly behind them. "And I can't wait."

She wasn't even surprised he knew what she'd been thinking and feeling. Their bond was deepening and soon they would be able to hear each other's thoughts and mind-speak to each other at will rather than only in high-stress situations. *"I can't wait either,"* she said into his mind.

He smiled and took her face in his hands and kissed her.

Before she could get lost in his kiss though, the door down the hall opened and Bas and Jules came out.

CHAPTER

TWENTY-SIX

"How's Loki doing?" Ilia asked Bas as he walked towards them.

Bas glanced back at the closed door then shared a grim look with Jules. "Not good. Nothing I do with my magic helps. Violetta is trying some of her magic, but it doesn't seem to be making a difference at all except to help him sleep. Jules and I are off to make some poultices to see if we can draw the infection out a little, and also get what we need to set a drip up – he's quite dehydrated, which isn't helping."

"I don't know what he's been up to in the last few months, but he certainly hasn't been looking after himself," Jules said. "I didn't know a God could get that ... emaciated. He's almost skeletal."

"Really?" Trip frowned. "Loki was always so proud of his looks – it's one of his defining traits. I can't imagine he'd let himself go like that for any reason."

"Well, he has," Jules said. "And the condition he let himself get in is definitely not helping the situation either – it's like he has no God-energy to give to healing."

"You don't think maybe it's the poison?" Ilia asked. "It could be draining him magically and physically."

Bas screwed up his mouth. "It's possible ... although, I haven't heard of any type of poison that can do both so significantly."

"But maybe that's a direction we can look at down in the library," Trip said.

"You haven't found anything yet?"

Ilia shook her head. "Nothing that talks about the Hell-beast poison and its effect on Loki's kind."

Bas shrugged. "Well, even though I don't think the poison is entirely responsible for his condition, it's worth looking into."

"I'll let Tam and Korinna know." Trip closed his eyes and Ilia felt him send them a message with his power. A second later he opened his eyes and said, "They'll include that in their search terms."

"And Dawn?" Ilia eyed the cupid and his witch-mate. "Has she woken yet?"

Jules shook her head. "No. But Bas has checked on her and says she's simply in a peaceful sleep. I ran upstairs earlier to get her favourite pillow, blanket and stuffed toy, so she's comfortably tucked into the armchair." She wiped a hand over her brow and leaned against Bas. "It's a relief to see her sleep peacefully."

"Speaking of sleep," Ilia said, "perhaps you two should get some. Trip and I can watch over Dawn and Loki while you do."

Bas shook his head. "We're fine. Violetta made us drink some regenerative tonic earlier, so we can keep going for now while you all look for a way to cure Loki. The more eyes on this the better."

"Well, you should have something to eat at least," Trip suggested.

Jules smiled. "We were going to grab something while we made the poultices. But enough worrying about us. You have all been hard at it too."

"Tam made sandwiches."

"That was hours ago," Trip said, rubbing his stomach. "I could do with something else. We'll make more sandwiches and take them downstairs."

"Along with a pot of coffee," Ilia said. "I heard Tam complaining before that he was all tea'd out and the kitchen hasn't been restocked with coffee pods for the machine down there."

"And I'll make some more of Grandmama's rejuvenating tea for you all to have," Jules said. "It will do more than the coffee – so tell Tam he has to drink it before he can touch the coffee."

They turned as one and headed to the kitchen. As they set about making sandwiches while Jules made the tea and Bas got the ingredients for various poultices along with what they needed to set up a drip – Jules and Violetta had a fully stocked medicine cabinet that looked like a hospital store-room if it had had a love-child with a witch-healer's herbal room.

"Do you think we should give him some antibiotic through the drip," Bas asked, coming out with two bags in his hand – one obviously of saline and the other, smaller, full of a yellow liquid.

"Not sure it will work on his God body, but it's worth a try," Trip said. "It certainly won't hurt him."

"Are you sure?"

Trip shook his head slowly as he cut up tomatoes. "I'm not sure about any of this. Your guess is as good as mine. I think perhaps you just need to go with your healer instinct added to all the medical studies you did at night while waiting for Julianna to break the curse."

Bas nodded and placed the bags on the tray he was making up.

Jules' lips pressed together and she sighed. Then her gaze slid to Ilia. "You haven't had a knowing about this, have you?"

Ilia shook her head as she put mayonnaise on slices of bread. "Not an inkling."

"What about Korinna? Do you think we could possibly encourage a bit of foresight arrowed Loki's way?"

"I don't think it works like that," Trip said, grimacing over a head of lettuce as he broke it down.

"But we could ask her."

"We *could* ask her, my love," Bas chimed in. "Although, I'm not certain our son would appreciate us asking Korinna to put herself through that voluntarily."

Jules rubbed her forehead with her knuckle as she placed the teapot on the tray for the library, then turned to sort through a box that seemed to have trays full of needles and plastic tubing. "I wish we knew more about her visions so we could help her with that. I can't believe Demeter hid them from her for so long and left her in the dark when she did start having them. I'm pretty certain she suffers more because of it."

"I don't know," Bas said. "Cassandra suffers a great deal because of her gift of sight and she has known since birth that she is a Seer."

"Yes, but Cassandra opened herself up too much to it and now can't turn it off," Trip said. "That's why she suffers." They all looked at him, questions on their faces –

Ilia certainly felt one on hers. Trip simply shrugged and said, "I spent a lot of time with Persephone and Demeter when I was young – they are my mothers after all. I heard things."

"Anything that might help us now would be good."

He bent over and gave his mate a kiss on the cheek. "Wish I was that useful but alas ... all you see is all you get."

"I see a lot," Ilia said, voice dripping with wicked intent.

Trip waggled his eyebrows and said, "I think we'll unpack that later."

She blushed, the others laughed – but the laughter quickly petered away into a silence only broken by the sound of Trip's knife cutting lettuce and Bas stirring the poultice ingredients while they warmed in a pan.

Jules was the first to break the silence. "Do you think that part of the reason Demeter and Persephone didn't want Korinna to spend any time honing her Sight – or know anything about it – was because if one of the other Gods and Goddesses ever heard her utter a prophecy and discovered it wasn't written in the Hall, they would come for her and find out exactly why that was?"

He shrugged. "Your guess is as good as mine. It's not something that could have been known before she was born unless ..." He stopped to chew on the corner of his lip.

"Unless what?"

"Unless Demeter herself saw something in her pond. Or Cassandra croaked something else that Demeter blocked from being written in the Hall so nobody would find out." He sighed. "My mother has done a lot beyond what she ever discussed with me about protecting me and mine from her siblings and the others of her kind, as well as from Perses and his minions. I just wish I could find her to ask her." He clenched his fists and banged them against his legs. "Why would she continue to hide now? She must feel how much we need her."

"Not to mention Loki," Bas said. "He is her ... pet?" He shook her head. "No, that's unkind. He's her favourite lackey after all. Surely she sees he's in danger and would come to help him?"

"Or can't she get through your shield," Jules asked Trip.

His brows rose. "Maybe. Although, I think if she really wanted to, she could get through it. She was the one who gifted me those particular powers after all. So no, I don't think that's the reason she hasn't come to help."

"Perhaps she can't come," Ilia suggested. "Perhaps it will bring more danger. You said she knows things she discusses with nobody else."

"Except Loki. He seems to know an awful lot."

Trip's expression grew more puzzled. "And that's strange in itself. I mean, she trusts him with things she didn't even trust me with. And he followed her orders, hiding away from us all because she deemed it necessary."

"He's not hidden now."

He tipped his head at Bas. "True. But I'm surprised he was able to hide from us for so long given his nature to meddle in everything. But he did it because she ordered it. It just doesn't feel ... normal."

"How so?" Jules asked.

"He's not of her pantheon," Ilia answered for Trip as he pressed his lips together, deeps lines furrowing his brow. "So he isn't bound to follow her orders like he would for one of the Greater Gods of his pantheon."

"You really think he follows their orders?"

She snorted. "No. I misspoke. Of course he would do

exactly as he pleases. But that speaks even more to my point – why would he take her orders when he is known for never doing anything he doesn't want to do?"

"I don't know," Trip said, rubbing her back. "It's a mystery."

"None of this answers the questions we have about Korinna and her prophecies, or any of the prophecies she's spoken for that matter." They all looked at Jules. She waved her hands. "I mean, why did she predict the ones she did at the exact time we needed to hear that information so we could work something out? It's very curious, isn't it? It's like something wants us to win this battle, except the help it's giving is of the kind that could mean we still lose if we don't understand in time."

Something inside Ilia's mind bloomed at Jules' words. "It's the Well. The Eternal Well. The source of all power. It wants us to win this. It wants us to return the old powers to it to be regenerated as should have been done eons ago. The sons and daughters of the Titans got it wrong when they killed or banished them and now the Well suffers." She lifted her head, meeting Trip's gaze. "It's why it made us – all of us – into what we are, so that we could return to it that which always was meant to be returned, and make it whole once more."

"Are you just spouting thoughts, Ilia, or is this a knowing?" Bas asked eagerly.

"It's a knowing," Trip answered for her – she was still wrangling with the enormity of what had just come to her.

"But, how can we do that?" Jules asked, hands wringing the bandage she'd been winding. "How can we make it whole when we can't return any of the Titans to it bar the one trying to break into this world? If we can even do that."

"It's all in the prophecies Korinna has told and will tell soon. We just need to figure out the message that is being given to us."

"Why couldn't the Well just come out and say what it wants?"

"When do Beings with power ever just come out and speak straight on anything," Ilia asked. "Look at the run-around we're getting from Demeter, Persephone and Loki. And they're nowhere near as powerful as the Eternal Well. Also, I don't think it has a brain in the way we think of it – or speech for that matter. It's communicating in the only way it can."

"Damn," Trip said. "I'd never even thought of that before, but it's the only answer that makes sense in this entire shit-show we've all been in for centuries. I thought most Gods and Goddesses in the pantheons were Machiavellian, but they have nothing on the Eternal Well for mastering almost indecipherable machinations."

"I don't think it means to be Machiavellian," Ilia said slowly. "I just think that's the only way it can send its messages to us. It needs our help. We can't fail in this."

"Because if we do, we'll be dead," Jules said flatly.

"There is that," Ilia said, brow quirked as her knowing deepened. "But so will everything else. And not because Perses will destroy everything. He won't be given the chance. If the Eternal Well doesn't get the entirety of what should have been returned to it returned, it will eat itself, consuming all its power to try to continue to exist. Because ultimately, like the cycle of life, it has its own cycle of life and death and rebirth. What it puts out must eventually come back to it so it can remake it and release it again. Without the ability to do this ..." She shook her head as she sucked in a shaky breath. "It will cease to exist. And everything that needs even the minutest amount of energy or power to survive – which is everything – will just stop existing. It will be the anti-big bang. Everything – the pantheons, the worlds, the suns, the Realms, the universes – will just be gone because the thing keeping the spark of life alive within them will be gone."

Dead silence greeted her words and she looked up from where she'd been staring at the ham and salad sandwich in front of her to see utter shock and horror on their faces.

"We better not fail then," Jules said finally, her words breaking the tension with their certainty.

Ilia stared at her, a smile breaking out on her face. "No. We better not fail."

"How do we start?" Trip asked, eyes glowing as he looked appreciatively at his mate.

Ilia lifted a finger. "First, we need to heal Loki. Second," she raised another finger, counting down her points, "we need to get some answers from him. Third, we need to track down Demeter and get the bitch to tell us exactly what she's been doing with all of us and why."

"In the meantime," Trip added, "I need to figure out when I can lower the shield or how I can change it so that we can slip out when needed but nothing can slip in."

"Sounds like a plan," Bas said, looking around as they all nodded in agreement.

Jules actually had a smile on her face as she said, "I think it's time we turn the tables on the Huntress."

"How will you do that, my love?" Bas asked, pouring his poultice into a muslin wrap.

"Once Trip has figured out how to let us out of the shield with nobody the wiser, Ilia and I are going to go Demeter hunting."

Ilia rubbed her hands together, the smile on her face

widening. "Can you teach me how to fire a bow and arrow, Bas?"

"Why?"

"I'm just thinking an arrow in the arse is exactly the thing to bring down this wily bitch!"

EPILOGUE

"Well, that's rude!" Demeter said, stepping back from her pond and surreptitiously rubbing her bottom as if she had indeed been shot in the arse with an arrow.

"What's rude, Mother?"

Demeter looked up to see Persephone striding across the vibrant green grass towards her. "Ilia and Jules are planning on hunting me down. Can you imagine it? The hubris!"

Persephone's mouth twitched. "Don't play the upset card with me. I know you're secretly thrilled. I assume this means they've discovered some pertinent things if they're wanting to come after you in that way?"

Demeter waggled her hand side-to-side. "Some of it. Not all. But enough."

"Did you finally allow Loki to tell them?"

"No. But he did exactly what I thought he'd do when Perses set the Hellbeast after Dawn and Tam and Jules while they were at Trip's farm."

"A Hellbeast! Went after Dawn and Tam and Jules?"

"And Daphne and her boys."

"How could you allow that?" Persephone glared at her mother. "Are they okay?"

"They are fine." She waved her hand dismissively. "And before you ask, yes, I sent a message to Hades and he's already called it back to Tartarus, so no harm no foul. Well, a little foul because he's a bit pissed that it's missing a claw."

"What?"

Demeter waved that away and said, "In answer to your first question, it was necessary to allow the Hellbeast to be used so that Ilia would realise what needed to be done."

"And she did?"

Demeter nodded. "Ilia healed them all through Bas when she tapped into her essential power. All except Loki." Her mouth turned down. "It appears that rumour about mischief Gods being allergic to Hellbeast venom is true. He's not doing so well."

"Then why aren't you down there helping them?"

"Don't you think I would if I could?" Demeter said, her desperation and worry breaking through her carefully crafted facade of cool, calm and collected Goddess. "I love Loki as if he were my own child. I want nothing more than to go down there and heal him. But you know I can't do that. Not if I don't want to give away the entire plan to my brothers and sisters and bring down their wrath on us and everyone we care about, despite the fact it would mean Perses would win."

Persephone nodded. "I know, I know. Because they don't believe Perses is coming back. And even if they did, they think they'd be able to defeat him."

"But they couldn't. Because they are too similar to what he was, where he came from, and what he has become.

Only our band of ... misfits I suppose is the best word for them ... can have a chance of fighting him and winning. They are our only hope and we must protect that at all costs, or more than what Perses will take from us will be lost."

"The Eternal Well," Persephone whispered.

"Yes. Mother and father of us all. If it isn't made whole, it will die and take everything with it."

"How many will be lost in the effort to make it whole once more?"

Demeter looked gravely down at her pond, bent down and waved her hand across it, seeing something there that Persephone could not. "Many. But the sacrifice is necessary. However, only if those we have spent centuries shaping and moulding can do what must be done. For if they can't, the sacrifice of most of the older ones will be but a drop in the ocean of what it sucks back into itself. Nothing will survive."

Persephone looked gravely down at her mother, then touched her shoulder with ice-cold fingers. "We will prevail."

"Not us. Them. *They* must prevail."

"Yes." Persephone turned to look down at the image that still flickered in the water of those few, precious beings on whom everything was pinned. "They *must* prevail."

❦ THE END ❦

Of this one only ...

THERE IS plenty more to come for the Stevens and their friends. **Witch Cursed: Gods Cursed Series, Book 6** is out in

August 2025. This one's Loki's story, so be ready for lots of sexy mischief!

Turn the page to read the first few chapters here ... and after that I have a FREE prequel novel to offer you, so keep turning.

But first, I give you the first few chapters of **Witch Cursed** ...

WITCH CURSED

GODS CURSED BOOK 6

LOKI'S TRUE CURSE

A FEW DAYS AFTER LAST CHRISTMAS

"Demeter. Where are you? Come out and face me!"

Loki stormed through Demeter's palace, determined to find the Goddess. Her handmaidens, mostly Nymphs of one sort or another, scattered as his power crackled around him. The Soteira – her warrior handmaidens – who weren't with Persephone in Hell were all out on various secret missions like the ones Demeter sent him on, so there was nobody here to protect the 'delicate flowers' that she liked to keep around her.

But he couldn't allow himself to care he was frightening them. His focus was all on finding the Goddess who had kept the truth from him. The one truth that would have made so much difference to his life.

His one true love was alive!

He'd been so shocked on Christmas Day when she'd told him the truth of what she'd done as they'd watched Trip and the Stevens celebrate the festival. The shock had made it difficult to think and he hadn't really taken in the full extent of what his mentor had said.

But he'd had two days for the shock to clear. Two days of watching his Callianthe and her boys, Harry and Charlie, plus a third, younger son, Gideon – his son. Two days of longing to go to her but being held back by Demeter's instructions and her – very unclear and wholly unfair – reasons.

And he was furious.

More furious than he'd ever been before in his very long life. Furious enough that the handmaidens who usually fawned all over him were scattering before him like frightened deer before Diana's bow.

He wanted answers. And this time, rather than the usual waffling nonsense about secrets and prophecies that made conversations with Demeter as frustrating and fruitless as trying to reason with his insane mother-father, he wanted answers. Clear answers. And a proper reason for him not to go down to Earth right now to make Callianthe remember him.

"Demeter! You can't hide from me. You need to account for what you did. Demeter!"

"I'm here sweet boy."

He swung around as she stepped out of the secret door that led to the garden where she kept her most guarded treasure – her scrying pond. The one that Cassandra had helped her to magic into existence.

He went to shout at her – she deserved a bit of shouting at after dropping the bombshell on him like she had – but the shout died in his throat as he took in her appearance.

She looked terrible. She often looked like the weight of the world was on her shoulders rather than Atlas' – which it was in an existential sense – but this was different. There was a greyness to her usual dewy complexion, a dullness that blunted the usual brilliant spring green of her eyes, a droop to her shoulders that indicated she carried more than the weight of the world on them. Had she seen something truly terrible in her pond? More terrible than what she had previously seen? Had they missed something? Or done something wrong? Were the odds now truly stacked against them?

His anger, like his need to shout at her, slipped away as he rushed to her side to put his arm around her, feeding a little of his strength into her through his touch. "What did you see?"

She looked up at him – so much sadness and grief welled in her eyes. "I saw you coming."

"You ... what?" He staggered back a little. "You had a vision of me? And it did this to you?"

She nodded gravely, a tear welling in her eye. "I am so sorry, Loki. I am so sorry you are so angered. I am so sorry you had to go through such grief. I am so sorry I could not tell you. And most of all, I am so sorry to ask you now – no to demand from you – a promise that you will not go anywhere near your Callianthe and her boys for much longer than I originally thought."

"But you said they'd remember at the right time. That I had to train Gideon so he'd be ready for the fight ahead."

"I did say that. But things have changed and right now, Gideon cannot know who you are if he is to come into himself in the way we need him to. None of them can know who you are. Not until the right time—"

"And when is that exactly?"

Her shoulders drooped even further and she looked close to collapse. "I do not know. The future is so nebulous right now, too much fluctuation to see clearly. We are not even certain how the Stevens and their mates are to defeat Perses any longer."

"You said it was the hearts curse."

"I did. And that is still part of it. Love will bring Perses down. But to do that, all the Stevens and their mates must come together as one in their powers. Unfortunately the way ahead is not clear. We just have no idea how they are supposed to meld their powers as one only that it must be done."

"Well, shit."

"Precisely."

Loki stared at her for a long moment. "But you said I would know my son and he would know me. As would Callie and the boys."

"Yes I did." Her shoulders sagged further and she sighed. "You know, he resembles you." She touched his face, a small smile curling her lips. "I think it's in the eyes and that straight nose and stubborn chin of his. He's going to be a heartbreaker just like his father."

Her words reminded him of his anger – although in the face of her sadness and worry and grief, it was barely a flickering candle flame. Even so, he crossed his arms, looking down and pouting as he said, "I wouldn't know. I've barely had a chance to look at him given you kept them all hidden from me."

"And I am sorry for that." She touched his arm and he met her gaze. "Sorrier than I can say. But it was necessary. Still is necessary. Not only do we need them in the now to help the Stevens but Zeus would have killed them. Just like he did to Callie's sisters when he found them."

Loki blanched as he remembered the mess of blood and gore strewn around the outskirts of the village the sisters had been about to attack. There hadn't even been body parts, just clumps of flesh. There was no way to tell how many had been killed from what little was left, so he'd believed Demeter when she'd told him Callie and her boys had been slaughtered too. At the time, all of his shock and grief was for what had been done to his love and her boys, but now he knew they were safe, the horror of what had been done to her sisters fully hit him. "I didn't do enough ... I should have taught them better control. Should have hidden them better."

She shook her head sadly. "Oh Loki. You kept them hidden well for the time you were with them, but even you could not have stopped Callianthe's sisters from giving into the nature King Lycaon forced upon them. It is to your credit you kept them hidden for as long as you did. And kept those boys from feeding on the flesh of humans."

He nodded even though, deep down, he didn't truly believe her. He could have done more. Should have done more. Her subterfuge shouldn't have been necessary if his had been better. He was the God of Mischief after all. Who should do subterfuge better than him?

Apparently Demeter. She'd kept the wool pulled over his eyes all these thousands of years and kept Zeus in the dark too.

"But that still doesn't explain why you hid the truth from me. Why tell me they were dead? That Zeus had killed them as he'd killed all the others?"

"Because Zeus knew of your love for her and he was watching you. He could not doubt the rage you aimed his way – rage I only just managed to stop you from following through on. Nor he could doubt your grief after your self-destructive five centuries of wallowing in your sorrow and despair. By the time you came back to me, begging for me to keep you busy, he had long stopped watching. But if I had told you ... well, no matter how much you tried to hide it, you would have given away that your grief was not real."

An ember of his anger flickered to life again. "I am a fabulous actor. I could have—"

"You *are* a fabulous actor. One of the best. It's one of the reasons you are my best operative. But not with this. Your grief had to be real. Zeus would have seen through anything else. Besides, I don't think you would have stopped trying to get to where they were in the future. And that would have spelled disaster because of the secret you hold deep inside. The power vacuum of your missed presence would have created all sorts of imbalances in the life forces that hold the Realms and the Pantheons together."

"If I'd killed Zeus in my rage, it would have done the same."

"True. But I was never going to let you kill my brother, no matter how much at times I want to do the same. However, your absence could possibly have created a crack in the Void large enough for Perses to squeeze through. For the sake of our shared mission, as much as anything else, I had to lie to you. I had to make you believe they were gone. And it worked."

She stroked his face, pushing an errant lock of his messy hair off his brow. "Zeus has no idea Callianthe and her children are still alive. And we must keep it that way. Because he must not know. If he gets wind they are still alive, he will not stop until they are dead. He cannot let what Lycaon did in defiance of him be known. It is too much a stab in his prideful soul to allow others to know that a human under his watch harnessed powers only a God like Zeus should have and created a new kind of Being. Not to mention the threat they posed. Lycaon intended his creations to stand against Zeus and his tyranny. My brother can't allow others to know that is possible."

Loki's lip curled. Zeus. That bastard. Loki would kill him with the cuts of a thousand knives – one of the most painful ways to die so he'd been told – if not for the ramifications on the Realms should a God as powerful as he be killed. It was those ramifications that had stopped him from killing him in the past. Demeter had reminded him how much Callie had loved this world and the humans who inhabited it, and it had been enough to stay his hand – because he had come to love what she loved and it was the only part of her he was able to hold onto.

But that didn't make him hate Zeus any less and he'd spent much of the intervening years doing everything he could to make Zeus' life just a bit miserable. Zeus of course never knew it was him – Loki was that good. But hearing of his rages when things continued not to go his way just made something like happiness burst open inside Loki for short periods.

The only truly good thing Zeus had ever done was killing his father and banishing most of the rest of the Titans and their troublesome children to Tartarus – or in the case of a very troublesome ones like Perses, through the Void and into the Beyond. The problem was, in banishing a tyrant, he had then become one. Although, he was much better at hiding it than his father had been.

Knowing all this was one of the reasons he'd happily gone to help hide Callie, her boys and sisters from Zeus when Demeter had seen they would be important to the future in some way. Of course, he'd had no idea he'd fall in love – practically at first sight – and that protecting her and her remaining family would became such a personal matter.

He'd only left after six months because Demeter needed his unique gifts on a special mission he couldn't even remember now – there had been so many – and she had promised to keep her eye on them and protect them with her shields. He frowned. "I still don't understand how he saw them through your shields?"

Demeter looked for a moment like she was going to cry. "Because I was unaware the sisters had eaten human flesh and so hadn't accounted for their strength and ferocity as the moon rose. The impact of them changing and running under the moon drew Zeus' attention before I realized what was happening. It was all I could do to get Callianthe and her boys out of there. I had seen them in my pond – only the day before – settled in the future with Trip on his farm, so knew that was where I had to send them. I made a decision in the spur of the moment and wiped their memories, giving them new ones, changing their names so they could not be recognized in any way."

"The boys names are almost the same." Charlemagne was now Charlie and Harrar was now Harry.

"Yes. It was easier to get them to accept the new memories if their names were not too different."

"Why did you change Callie's name to Daphne?"

"Callianthe is a flower as is a daphne. Daphne is one of my favourite flowers."

Oh. Well if that didn't fully take the wind out of his sales! But he tried to rally and gather back a little bit of his pissed-offedness as he said, "If you think naming her after your favourite flower makes up for the grief I've endured all these years ..."

His words died as she cupped his cheek. "I know that nothing I can say or do now will make you forgive me for that. But I will say once again that it was necessary. And it had a side-effect I never foresaw."

"What is that?"

"You could have allowed your grief to become everything you were. You could have become embittered by it as so many have before you, yet you didn't. After those first few centuries, you picked yourself up. You endured. Even when in the deepest wells of your grief I knew you would come out of it because you continued to look after those servants and slaves you helped her save. You tried to live up to Callie and how much she loved this world and its people. You took that love inside yourself and claimed it as your own. You have become my best agent in the war ahead as well as my right hand man."

"Right hand God, thank you very much."

She smiled. "Right hand God. Yes. I trust you more than I trust anyone except Persephone. I trust you as equally as I trust her and she is my beloved daughter. You know more about what lies ahead of us than any of my other agents. And you are stronger and more adaptable to any situation than any other Being I know. Which is why, though it is probably the most difficult thing I have ever asked of you, you must stay away from Callianthe and the boys. Not only for their own safety, but for the good of us all."

"Why for us all? Have you seen something else?"

"I have. And it changes what I told you only a few days ago."

"What?" He gripped her arms. "What did you see?"

Her eyes misted over slightly and she said in that prophecy voice tinged with shadow and pain, "What they are flies in the face of everything we know and everything we are. They are different and yet the same. They are more than us. They are the future. They are the way ahead if only those with eyes too blind could see the truth of it. They could be the difference in the fight before us." She jerked as the last words left her lips and the mistiness left her eyes.

"They are that important?" They were that important to him, but to everyone else? It seemed impossible to believe that of a Nymph and her boys who had been made into something that should never have been.

"They are," Demeter said quietly. "They must be protected. And at the moment, the person they need most protection from is you."

"Me?"

"Yes, you," she said, dropping her hands to his shoulders and gripping tight. "Your love would give them away. If expressed in any way it would break the spell I placed on them, and once broken, they wouldn't be able to stop their change. Zeus would see them then kill them."

"I would protect them."

"Yes you would. As would Trip and the others, giving away exactly who and what they are. Who and what you truly are. And then we would be fighting a war on two fronts – one against Zeus and the other major Gods and Goddesses of each pantheon who would take all of your existences as a threat and the other against Perses and his minions as they took advantage of the power fluctuations caused by such a war. So you must stay away. It is the only option right now."

"I could force them not to change. You know I could do it," he said gesturing nebulously at himself, knowing she would understand he was talking about the secret of his true power.

"And you could destroy who they are. There is a reason you suppress that part of yourself, why you hide it away. You can't now think to use it on those you love." She shook her head sadly, reaching out to tuck his unruly locks behind his ear. "You have to trust in me. You have to trust in my visions and what I have told you."

"But the only thing holding them back now is the spell you wove around them. Is that still strong enough?"

"It will be unless you reveal yourself too early and they remember who they are at the wrong time. If that happens, the suppression spell will be broken along with the memory one." She rubbed her forehead and frowned. "If things fall into place the right way, Zeus will be too busy with the repercussions of denying the threat of Perses to worry about going after Callie and her sons. But until that time, nobody in the pantheons can be aware of what they are or what they are capable of doing until the time is right."

"What are they capable of doing?" Aside from the lycanthrope that made them want to feed on flesh – any flesh would do, but the human kind made them more powerful and not a little insane – he was unaware there was anything more significant about them. They certainly hadn't shown any special powers when he had been with them for that six months – the best six months of his life.

"That is yet to be discovered."

"You do not know?"

"Not precisely. But I know it is big. I know it is dangerous to those who wish to hold power to themselves. And I know it will help us in the fight ahead."

Such a nebulous, non-specific answer. He expected that from Demeter after all these years, but right now, that expectation didn't lessen his frustration. With her. With prophecy.

With himself.

She leaned in and kissed him on the lips then pulled

back with another sigh. "I know this is not the answer you came here for. But I cannot give you that answer. I cannot say that you may go to Callianthe and her boys and gain back that which you have lost. I cannot allow it. And I think, if you are truthful with yourself, you cannot allow it either. You always protected them. You must continue to do so."

He wanted to shout at her, to deny her words, but he couldn't. She was right. He couldn't bring danger down upon his beloved and her children – their children – just so she would remember him. Just so he could gain back the love they'd once shared and have the family he had always longed for. The family he'd only just gotten a taste of all those thousands of years ago with her and her boys before they were torn away from him. He'd never had that family with his ex-wife and their children, or his ex-mistress and their children. He'd certainly never had it with his insane mother-father. And he'd been too much of the outsider in Oden and Frigg's household to truly feel like one of their family, no matter how Frigg tried to be a true mother to him.

And now, it seemed, there was a high possibility he would never have the family he longed for more than anything else because Callie and her boys were now involved in the fight ahead and there was a possibility none of them would survive.

It seemed he shouldn't have laughed off the curse that powerful witch, Merriweather Weale, had placed on him a few thousand years ago. He'd played a trick on her – it was his thing after all – when he'd discovered she had a penchant for killing wolves for their fur and to eat their meat for her supper. He'd made her think her husband had turned into a wolf and that she'd killed him and served him up for supper. He hadn't actually done any such thing as he rather liked Petar and had only kidnapped him and put an illusion in his place.

Meriweather had not only received the message, she'd gained a righteous fury on top of it. She stopped killing wolves but she cursed him to wander through his eternal life alone, always longing for the one thing he could never have even though she may be only a handspan away: his greatest love.

She'd said some other stuff at the time that he hadn't really listened to because he'd been too busy laughing – something about mercy because he'd shown Petar mercy. That if he was humbled, or ate humble pie or something like that, and put his love and her wishes first rather than always thinking of himself and his own amusement and what he desired, that he could possibly attain happiness.

It had only made him laugh harder. Not because he wasn't capable of putting someone else first – he wasn't truly the narcissistic God of Mischief he portrayed – but because of the secret he held deep inside that only Laufey, his mother-father, and Demeter knew. He did nothing but put others first because if he didn't, it would mean the end of everything in a way Perses could only dream of doing.

But keeping such a secret – it drove a wedge between him and those he wished to love and trust and have trust him. It was why he could never be close to his ex-wife and ex-mistress and all their children. It was why he'd always held himself a little apart from Callie even though he'd loved her true. Self-sacrifice obviously wouldn't break his curse because if it did, the curse would never have taken root in the first place.

No, his curse had been in place long before Merriweather Weale had come along he realised now. The witch's curse – it had just been the voicing of the curse he'd been born under. The voicing of the curse though, it brought it to the fore. It made the Fates aware of it. It made it a reality and now he was realising just what that meant.

It made him realise all he could never have. All he could never be.

Suddenly he felt more alone than he'd ever felt in his long, lonely life.

"Are you going to be okay, Loki?" Demeter asked him.

He looked at her and shook his head. "I'm fine," he said.

But as he trans-apparated out of her palace and back to his home, he knew he wasn't even close to fine. He was screwed. More than screwed. He was completely and utterly fucked by a curse voiced by a witch that he had no ability to ever undo. Looking up to the ceiling he swore at the three Fates. "What did I ever do to you three bitches to make you hate me so much?"

There was no answer.

Typical.

Now what was he going to do?

CHAPTER

ONE

*KIND OF BUT NOT QUITE ALMOST 5 MONTHS
LATER (LOKI'S TIME IS NOT OUR TIME!) AFTER A
RATHER HEROIC RESCUE (IF HE DID SAY SO
HIMSELF) AND A VERY SERIOUS WOUNDING BY A
POISONOUS HELLSBEAST ...*

"Agh! What are you doing? I'm not a pin cushion!"

Loki slapped at Violetta as she tried to reseat the cannula needle.

She shifted sideways and snapped, "Stop moving around you big sook and let me do this. You need this medication."

Sook! Did she not know who she was talking to? He opened his mouth to tell her when she came at him with that bloody great pokey-jabby thing they said was essential modern medicine. Modern medicine his rather luscious arse! Or it would be luscious if it wasn't covered in bruises from all the other pokey-jabby things she and Bas and Jules had stuck him with over the last few weeks – unfortunately, the only thing helping him to heal after the Hellsbeast attack was human medicine.

How he'd come to this ridiculous piece of ingloriousness, he had no idea. He waved his hand at the pokey-jabby thing. "I don't understand why you have to create yet another hole in me! I would think the Hellsbeast made plenty."

"Which would be far worse if not for all that we have been doing," Violetta snapped, managing to capture his arm and pin it to the bed by sitting on it.

He glared at her – mostly because he was so very frustrated at still being as weak as a mewling human child despite their supposedly fabulous and magic-free modern medicine. Completely unable to fight her off as he once would have done with ease, he snapped, "I think you just like torturing me, witch."

A single brow hiked up into a rather superior arch. "When you carry on like this, you bet I do."

"Well … that's just mean!" He deflated, pouting a little as he did so. "I didn't truly think you wanted to torture me."

She sighed heavily and rubbed her forehead as if she was trying to rub away the headache she said he kept giving her. "I don't want to torture you. I promise."

"But you just said—"

"Words slipped out I shouldn't have let slip out. You do aggravate an old witch so very much."

"I don't mean to be aggravating." She gave him a sideways look and, unusually, he felt not a little chagrin. Shrugging briefly as he looked down at his hands, he said, "Well, I don't mean to be aggravating to you and Bas and Jules. It's just … this is so very humiliating."

She sighed again, this time more sympathetically. "I imagine it is. I imagine you've never felt so … mortal."

"You bet your frilly lilac knickers I haven't."

She glared at him and opened her mouth as if to tell him off but then, closing her eyes, took in a deep breath. "Not reacting to that. Not reacting to that," she said sotto voce.

"You know I can hear you."

"I'm aware." She sighed heavily again and opened her eyes.

"Do you mind awfully getting off my arm? It's starting to lose all sensation."

She looked down, her eyes flaring wide as if she was shocked to see herself sitting on his arm – strange to be shocked given she was the one who sat on his arm in the first place. Purposefully too. And only a minute or so ago. Maybe her short term memory was going. She was old for a mortal after all. Or was she? He kind of didn't have much knowledge about those things. Time passed or didn't pass depending on where he was and what he was doing, so he lost track.

Violetta leapt to her feet and said, "I'm so sorry."

He moved his arm around – it flopped on the bed rather like a landed fish – and then he let out a howl as something prickling and unpleasant started jabbing into his hand and fingers. "What in the name of Hades' balls is going on in my hand!"

She grabbed his hand and started to massage it. "It's called pins and needles, you big baby. And it's not that bad."

He glared at her. "It's pretty bad."

"In comparison to getting gutted by a Hellsbeast? I'd imagine it doesn't even register on the pain scale in comparison to that."

"I was a bit busy rescuing people and being all hero-like to truly notice the pain."

"Probably because you were in shock."

"Shock? I don't get shocked. I give shock."

"I don't mean shock like that. I meant the kind of shock that happens to a body when it's injured badly."

"And this is that? Shock-thing?"

"No. This is simply pins and needles."

"There's no 'simply' about it." He howled in pain as she rubbed his arm harder – although why she was doing that he didn't know because it didn't seem to be helping anything at all. "I don't like it. I don't like it at all."

She made a sound of aggravation. "Nobody likes pins and needles."

"That's such a stupid name for such an all-encompassing pain."

"It describes the sensation – it's like being jabbed by tiny pins and needles."

Well, she was right there – if there were millions of them jabbing at him all at once and were also on fire! "It hurts. And it feels like my arm is about to explode."

She snorted. "You are so dramatic. You could win awards."

"I know." He would have waggled his eyebrows at her except the pain took away his ability to fully play with her in the way he would have done pre-gutting-by-Hellsbeast.

She shook her head at him. "It should be backing off now," she said, continuing to massage. "How does that feel?"

The pins and needles sensation had begun to fade, but he rather liked the massage she was giving his hand and arm. "It still hurts quite a lot. Why did it happen?"

"It happened because I sat on your arm for too long.

Your circulation was cut off. The pins and needles happen when the circulation is restored quickly and the blood rushes back into your flesh."

"Why did you sit on my arm then if you knew that would happen?"

"I didn't mean to sit on it for so long and—" She looked up at him then swore and let go of his arm, dropping it on the bed. "You are trying to play me."

"I think you'd know if I was. We'd be having much more fun." He wiggled his brows at her – possible now the pain was gone – as he flashed a smile. But then the smile fell as she glared at him and he said, "And we are obviously not having fun." He stared down at his arm. "Are you going to sit on my arm again?"

"Why would I do that?"

"To stick that jabby-pokey thing in me once more. Weren't you about to do that when this entire conversation began?"

"You're right. Thanks for the reminder." She picked up his arm and reached for the needle.

"Agh! No." He pulled his arm away.

"What are you doing?"

"Keeping my arm away from you and that pointy-ouchy thing."

"But you just reminded me that's what I was doing."

"Doesn't mean I want you to do it."

"For the love of all that's sacred and magical! You are the most aggravating patient I think I've ever had the misfortune of looking after." She pointed the needle at him. "You know, I wouldn't have to do this again and again if you didn't stop fidgeting and moving around so much. You keep tearing the needle out which means we have to find a new place to seat it."

"I don't see why you need to give the medicine this way. It's barbaric. You know the torturers in the Underworld use needles as part of their program? Souls are genuinely frightened of them for a reason – they're a Gods-damned torture device. And you keep expecting me to be okay with you constantly sticking these foreign metal jabby torture devices into my Godly flesh? You have rocks in your head, witch!"

Violetta rolled her eyes and ran her hand through her hair, sending her usually immaculate bob into disarray, her hair poking up every which way as if she'd had an electric shock. Which given the magic gathering in her might very well be partly true. She didn't fix it though, or the sleeve of her twin set which was tucked halfway up her arm while the other was fully down, but just very deliberately straightened her back and shoulders as she placed her hands on her hips and glared down at him with a look Loki hadn't been given since well ...

The last time he'd seen that look had been on his adoptive mother, Frigg's face after he'd smeared giant filur snot on the senior servants' toilet seat and his nurse had got stuck there and needed Frigg's magic to unstick her without ripping half her flesh off.

Maybe he had gone too far with that one, but he still didn't think he'd deserved that look. It had been a scary look that had made him feel as small and insignificant as the thrips that Frigg loved to squash on her rose leaves.

And here it was again from a woman he very much admired – even though his behaviour and words of the last few weeks might have given the impression he felt otherwise.

He felt ashamed and sorry for how he'd behaved. But what was he to do when they kept torturing him with pokey-jabby things that truthfully were the inspiration for Tartarus' torture devices? Not to mention these 'medications' they kept shoving through the tubes and pokey-jabby things and expecting him to swallow! Not only were they disgusting and made him feel funny, but it was such a blow to his pride that he needed them. Even more so that they were making him a little better every day. Although not enough better for all the ickiness of them he had to endure.

But endure them he must. Or so that look on Violetta's face was telling him. He had to put on his big God pants and God-up. Or Goddess-up. All the Goddess' he admired would have handled this entire situation far better than he had. The one he most admired would probably be looking at him like Violetta was right now if she knew the way he'd been carrying on.

Not that Demeter could know. The shields were still up around the house – the ones Trip had raised to protect them from the Hellsbeast and to stop anyone from knowing about Dawn's powers or Korinna's prophecies or Ilia's new powers.

But still, the thought of a bunch of them standing there next to Violetta giving him that same disappointed-frustrated look was enough to make him swear to the Eternal Well that he was going to behave better and not complain about any of this.

From now.

He smiled up at Violetta – well as much of a smile as he could muster in the face of that look – and held out his arm. "I will behave. I promise."

Violetta's eyes narrowed. She didn't trust him. The fact made him sad in a way that surprised the Hells out of him. He didn't used to care that much about what people thought of him – he knew he was pretty bloody awesome after all so it was easy to ignore when other people didn't see him like that because he knew they were wrong. But now he was here with the Stevens and their extended family – all of whom he'd been watching for so long – it wasn't easy to keep thinking about himself in the same way he'd always done. They were just so ... so ...

Well, he didn't quite have the words to express exactly what they were except that they were more than awesome.

They were everything he had thought to once have with his Callie, her boys and her troublesome sisters – a ready-made family. But that had been stolen away from him so long ago and he'd never dreamed to experience it again. Hadn't even wanted it if he couldn't have it with Callie.

And yet ... she and her boys were here. Here with these people who made him feel like maybe he still did want it. Not that he could have it given the secret that made it impossible for him to truly trust himself with them. And of course there was the witch-voiced curse he was under. That just compounded the situation. But still, his secret and a curse didn't stop him wanting that kind of love and respect and trust more than he'd ever wanted anything else. It was dangling so close and yet ...

It was further away than ever before. Because Callie – Daphne as she was called now – and her boys remembered nothing of their life together. Couldn't remember. Not until Perses made his presence known in a way Zeus couldn't ignore so that he wouldn't have the time to look their way.

So, here he was – exactly where he'd promised not to be – with the woman and her boys that he loved and he couldn't say a thing. Not only could he not say a thing, he had to do everything he could to make sure no part of his being here would make Demeter's spell on them fail. He was constantly on tenterhooks. Which was probably what was making him extra crabby and bad-patienty.

Thankfully being objectionable to everyone who came near – according to Violetta, Bas and Jules – was probably helping his cause. The few times Callie and her boys had come in to thank him for rescuing them and see how he was doing, he'd put on quite the show to ensure that there was no chance they'd remember the loving person he'd once been to them.

But by Odin's hairy balls, them not remembering was tearing him apart.

It made him even more cranky and objectionable. But maybe he'd been a little too objectionable given how exhausted and beyond her wits-end Violetta was.

He didn't want her to hate him. He didn't want anyone to hate him. But he'd been so busy making certain Callie – Daphne! He really had to remember her name was Daphne here – didn't see any sign of the God she'd fallen in love with, that he had perhaps pushed things a little too far.

He needed to make it up to Violetta. And Bas. And Jules.

Which meant he needed to be the kind of patient that got all the gold stars. He lifted his arm higher and said, "Jab that pokey thing into my arm and I promise I won't move or say another word."

She blinked at him, obviously surprised, "You won't?"

"No."

"You won't knock it out after I turn my back?" she asked, obviously suspicious – he didn't blame her.

"I won't knock it out after you turn your back."

"Or complain when I ask you to drink the tisane that will be coming into the room soon."

"I will drink the tisane."

"And you won't complain."

"And I won't complain. Even if it curls my nose hairs and makes my tongue pucker into a prune in my mouth."

"Hmm." She raised a brow, her finger tapping against her arm. "That sounds like complaining."

He raised his arms. "Not a complaint. A simple truthful comment on what might happen – although I won't mention it again if it does because I wouldn't do anything so uncouth. Or disrespectful to your wonderful, healing tisane."

Violetta's glare didn't give up, but her lips twitched in a way that told him she was amused by his nonsense.

Good. He could work with her being amused with him.

He flicked his fingers, using the most basic part of his magic, the only magic that seemed to be available to him right now – at least with any consistency – and a cape swirled around his shoulders. It was sparkly and his favourite colour – scarlet – with the word, 'Superpatient' written in swirly silver script. And to top it all off, he magicked himself up a matching pair of stove-pipe pants with the words 'Big' and 'Boy' written in the same silver script, one word for each leg. He flipped the sheets and blanket down so Violetta could see the brilliance of his sartorial choices and moved the cape around so she could see the word written on it too.

"I'm dressed for the job I want," he said.

Her lips twitched more and she pressed them together tightly for a moment before saying, "And what job is that?"

"Best patient in the world."

"And what makes you think you can be the best patient in the world?"

He gestured at his new clothing. "I have my big boy pants on and am proclaiming myself the best of Superhero Godly types: the Superpatient. Not only am I super and a patient, but I will be super patient and put up with anything you throw at me with that super patience and an equanimity that will put the God Shiva to shame."

"That's rather a big call. How do you think you will manage that?"

"If Shiva could find inner peace and do all that self-discovery stuff, then certainly I can. That God was the biggest selfish dick I ever met when he was a young Godling. If there had been a year book for us young Godlings then he would have been 'Most likely to suck.' So if he could turn into the most boring and pliable God like he did, then I can certainly be a Superpatient. The patient to beat all patients. The patient you wish all patients could be like. You're going to jump out of bed in the morning and you're going to want to rush in here to see me with a song in your heart and a skip in your step and a—"

Violetta lifted her hands and started to laugh. "Enough. Enough. I get it. You're going to be a wonderful patient and I'm going to enjoy treating you."

"More than you've ever enjoyed treating anyone before."

She shook her head, still chuckling. "Well let's see how I enjoy reinserting this cannula and we'll go from there."

He held up his arm. "Superpatient ready and willing to be jabbed at your convenience."

She snorted, but the snort ended in another chuckle and without saying another word, she set about doing what she'd come in here to do half an hour ago.

He managed not to wince or use his limited magic to stop from being jabbed with the miniature torture device. And when she finished and said, "There," he couldn't help but feel a little proud of himself for not doing any of the things that his learned nature was pushing him to do.

Violetta stood and said, "I will just go and get the fresh bag of antibiotics and see what's happened to that tisane."

"Mmm-mmm-mmm, tisane. Can't wait." He smacked his lips.

Violetta chuckled and wagged her finger at him. "Would you say that if I left the honey out of it."

"Honey-schmoney. Who needs it when you've got something that tastes so sweet and yummy – and not like sewer water at all – and you know is doing you so much good."

"Right," Violetta said. "Just don't knock that cannula out."

"I wouldn't dream of it."

She tutted at him and said, "I'll be back shortly."

"And I'll be here waiting breathlessly in anticipation for the best witch-healer there ever was to return to this Super-patient."

"Enough of your ridiculous hyperbole. Just try to rest and if the tisane arrives before I get back, make sure you drink it all down."

"Will do."

Violetta left, closing the door behind her with a soft click.

From his right there was a soft chuckle. A husky chuckle he knew so well. A chuckle he'd never thought to hear again. A chuckle he'd mourned for thousands and thousands of years. He turned his head to see Callie – no, Daphne – standing in the doorway in the corner of the room that led to the adjoining bathroom that was shared with the bedroom next door.

She smiled at him and it felt like the sun had finally come out on a cloudy day after there had been thousands of years of cloudy days. "Daphne," he said softly. Then swore internally at himself for saying it so softly – the kind of softly that was used by lovers the world over.

She didn't seem to notice as she said, "That's my name. Don't wear it out." She pushed off the door, a tray in her hands, and walked across the room in a way that made him want to pant – those shorts she was wearing showed off too much of her lovely long legs. And the way her chestnut-brown hair curled loosely, kissing her jaw – well, he wanted to put his lips there and join in the kissing.

But no. No. That was a bad thought. Bad thought!

Swallowing down the desire that was too eager to rise up and try to catch her attention, he managed to say, "How long have you been there for?"

"Long enough, Superpatient."

She looked down at him, her gaze roving over his cape and then down to his legs in a way that made his cock twitch. He hastily pulled the covers back over his legs and misbehaving groin.

With a smile twisting her lips she said, "Love the big boy pants and cape by the way."

He stroked his cape, thankful for the distraction of it, and sat forward so she could see more of it. "I rather like capes."

"I can see that. And sparkles too," she said, her warm cinnamon coloured eyes dancing as she placed the tray on the bedside table. It was the first time since he'd saved them that he'd seen her smile so openly at him. Admittedly, he'd been such an arsehole, purposefully making her think ill of him, that there hadn't really been a reason for her to smile at him. He hadn't realized how much not seeing her smile had hurt.

Even though he shouldn't smile back, shouldn't engage, should say something to make her leave, definitely shouldn't make her smile more, he couldn't help saying, "Nothing wrong with sparkles."

"Nothing at all. Now," she turned to him, smile firmly in place, a cup of steaming liquid in her hands that smelled like some kind of swamp water mixed with the heroic citrus and honey – heroic because it was doing some kind of feat to partially cover the stench – that would undoubtedly fail to cover the horrible taste no matter how hard it tried.

She held the cup out to him. "Let's see how super you truly are and how well those big boy pants fit." She put the mug into his hands and then stood back, the smile turning a little wicked. "Drink up my big boy Superpatient. Let's see how well you wear your cape."

Loki lifted the cup and almost hurled as the underlying scent of sewage curled up his nostrils.

Her lips widened into a smile as her gaze roved over his face, taking in every twitch of muscle. "Good right? I found a new recipe in one of the healer-witch grimoires that Jules gave me. It's full of everything you need to give you the energy you are currently lacking. And might even help you with your little magic problem."

His brows rose at that. His 'little' magic problem wasn't so little. Being a God without access to the magic that made you who you were wasn't a 'little' problem at all. Especially when he could have used that magic to shore up Demeter's spell and make certain it didn't break. There was also the not inconsiderable fact that he used his regular God magic to keep other, more dangerous magic shoved behind an adamantium-like magical cage inside him. Thankfully that cage was still well and truly intact, but he was keeping a close eye on it.

Of course, Callie – Daphne Gods-damn it! – didn't need to know the ins and outs of any of that right now. In fact, the less she knew the better it would be, because anything that might make her memory come tumbling back could spell disaster.

So all he said was, "Sounds perfect," then lifted the mug to his lips. He didn't stop staring at the woman he'd thought never to see again outside his dreams, as he took a big gulp of the steaming hot sewer water. And somehow – he wasn't quite sure how given this was the worst thing he'd ever put in his mouth – he swallowed the mouthful down without dry retching.

Hoping it wouldn't come right back up, he smiled at her, licked his lips and said, "Yummy."

I HOPE you enjoyed that little sneak peek. There's lots more to come for Loki, Daphne and the Stevens family in this book. I am going to put them through the wringer - as well as give you (and them) some hot, sexy times.

If you want to read more of **Witch Cursed**, you can buy your copy here:

Witch Cursed

https://books2read.com/u/bpoa19

Before you go, as promised, I have something a little extra special (slow burn, friends to lovers, deadly secrets and more) for you right here - a FREE prequel novel for the Gods Cursed Series featuring Tam and Korinna at the training camp where they met.

Just turn the page to find out how you can get your FREE copy of **Fractured Curse** ...

LOVE A FREE BOOK?

Cursed to never be loved; fated to never be alone ...

Cursed cupid Tamuel has been told he will never love or be loved, a fate to which he's long been resigned. Yet from the moment he meets powerful trainee witch Korinna Soteira at the Amazonian and Gargarean training camp, he knows this to be a lie – he loves Korinna like he's loved nothing and no-one in his life. But his curse is right in one respect: he may be able to love, but he can never *be* loved. Korinna will only ever be his friend, a fact he has spent the last twenty years coming to terms with.

However, malignant forces are stirring in the darkest reaches of the Realms. They have plans to use Korinna and her unusual powers – plans that can only be thwarted by the cursed cupid and an impossible love. Yet breaking

Tamuel's curse now could release a force too ancient to destroy – and thus destroy any future.

What if the only way to survive the present is to place the future in peril?

Fractured Curse is a prequel novella to my popular Gods Cursed Series centring on unknown history between two of readers' favourite characters from the series. It takes place 2000 years before the events in ***Love Cursed*** and can be read as an introduction into the world or at any time during the reading of the series.

It's exclusive to my newsletter subscribers, so to get your copy, just follow the QR code or link below, fill in your details and it will be winging its way to you along with other free reads, deals and bookish info.

Get My Free Copy of Fractured Curse Here:
https://www.subscribepage.com/fracturedcurse_signup

JOIN LEISL'S LEGENDS

Subscribe to (or follow) me (via the QR code) at my Leisl's Legends page on REAM—a new subscription app like Patreon except it's designed especially for readers and authors for an amazing reading experience—and you will get early access to *The Huntress and the Vampire*  *King*, my hot enemies to lovers, witch-and-vampire-licious urban fantasy romance that readers over there are already in love with. It's the prequel novel to the first book in the Blood-Rites Series - *The Blood of the Seer*. Be the first to find out where it all began with Anita and Hei's love story.

You will also get exclusive early access to the next book

in the **Gods Cursed Series** and can comment on the story as I write it! Your feedback could be essential in shaping the next book in the series.

Be part of creating the stories you love AND get exclusive access to a whole range of goodies including other WIPs, bonus content, voting rights, signed books and much, much more.

BECOME A LEGEND NOW!
https://reamstories.com/leislleightonauthor

THE HUNTRESS AND THE VAMPIRE KING

She hates the vampire who saved her; he holds the key to her fate ...

Hunter-witch Anita Middleton wants revenge against the violent vampire cults that murdered her father and has worked hard to become one of the best vampire hunters there is. But on a difficult hunt she is caught in an ambush and is mortally wounded ... only to be saved by a mysterious warrior. A warrior with brilliant blue eyes and long silver-blonde hair who fights with a grace and violence like nothing she's seen. It is only after she wakes in the heart of his palazzo that she realises her saviour is a vampire - and according to her brother and mentor, this vampire king is their ally.

Lord Hei rules over an empire of witches, humans and vampires who have been trying to keep the vicious vampire cults, the Wild and Dark Brethren, at bay for centuries. Then he saves Anita and knows with one look she is the prophecied Huntress who could be his downfall or his salvation - and she is also his fated mate. But she struggles to trust him as her hatred of vampires is deep-seated. And she *needs* to trust him because only he can offer the specialised training a Huntress needs so her power won't overwhelm her.

But with the Dark Brethren mysteriously amassing, he has little time to win her over. And Anita must go on a crash course to learn how to control her Huntress magic ... or go slowly and violently insane.

The Huntress and the Vampire King is the exciting action-packed prequel novel to *The Blood of the Seer*.

If you love your vampires hot with a bit of The Witcher thrown in and your heroines as kick-arse as Buffy and even more tortured, if you love fated mates, enemies to lovers, chosen ones and epically hot romance mixed with action and mystery, then *The Huntress and the Vampire King* is what you've been waiting for.

Sign up to Leisl's Legends (via the QR code above) and start reading exclusive early release chapters of it now!

BECOME A LEGEND NOW!
https://reamstories.com/leislleightonauthor

ALSO BY LEISL LEIGHTON

GODS CURSED SERIES

A Love Cursed Christmas Wish

Love Cursed

Soul Cursed

Blood Cursed

Hearts Cursed

Fates Cursed

Witch Cursed

Dragon Cursed

(Coming 2026)

BLOOD-RITES SERIES

The Blood of the Seer

The Blood of the Sire

The Blood of the Son

(Coming 2027)

BLOOD-RITES PREQUEL AND BONUS MATERIAL

The Huntress and the Vampire King

The Middleton Manifesto

(Available now via Leisl's Legends subscription)

~

PACK BOUND SERIES

Pack Bound

Moon Bound

Shifter Bound

Wolf Bound

Witch Bound

(A Pack Bound Series Prequel Novella)

BOX SET

Pack Bound Series Collection Books 1-4

~

DAWN OF THE CURSE

A PACK BOUND PREQUEL SERIES

Soul Bound

Alpha Bound

Hunter Bound

Fae Bound

(Coming in 2027)

ANTHOLOGIES

A Perfectly Paranormal Valentine

A Perfectly Paranormal Halloween

A Perfectly Paranormal Easter

A Perfectly Paranormal Christmas

A Perfectly Paranormal Prophecy

(Coming in 2027)

〜

As well as writing sexy, epic and romantic paranormal novels, I write mysterious and emotional romantic suspense novels too. Check out the following titles for amazing, suspenseful reads:

Storm Haven Series

Need You Tonight

The Devil Inside

〜

CoalCliff Stud Series

Climbing Fear: Book 1

Blazing Fear: Book 2

〜

Echo Springs Series

Dangerous Echoes: Book 1

Books 2-4 in this series, (written by Daniel deLorne, TJ Hamilton and Shannon Curtis) are also available now at all ebook retailers.

ABOUT LEISL

Leisl Leighton is a tall red head with an overly large imagination. As a child, she identified strongly with Anne of Green Gables, and like Anne, is a voracious reader and born performer.

It came as no surprise when she went on to a career as a performer, script writer, script doctor, stage manager and musical director for cabaret and theatre restaurants.

After starting a family, Leisl stopped performing and began writing the stories plaguing her dreams. She now writes emotional stories mixed with mystery and a little bit of what goes bump in the night.

Her novels have won and placed in writing contests here and overseas. She is a passionate advocate for the romance genre, was President of Romance Writers of Australia from 2014-2017 and when she's not writing romantic stories of  redemption, she is helping other authors reach their dreams with her Author Services. You can contact Leisl through her website via the QR Code above or here: https://www.leislleighton.com

And if you want to stay in touch and be the first to find out about new releases, appearances, special deals and exclusive content and giveaways, sign up to her Newsletter and pick up your free copy of *Fractured Curse* via the QR code.

Or sign up to *Leisl's Legends* via this QR code to get *Fractured Curse* plus serialised early access stories and bonus content including a bonus NSFW ending for Love Cursed.

You can also follow her on social media:

facebook.com/LeislLeightonAuthor

instagram.com/leislleightonauthor

bookbub.com/authors/leisl-leighton

amazon.com/stores/Leisl-Leighton/author/B00DBYRGZY

ACKNOWLEDGMENTS

Writing this book was such a joy and yet the path to publication was fraught with many interruptions - my youngest son was in last year of school during the writing of this, then there was the OS trip with the family to celebrate us all finishing the school journey (especially through the last four difficult years of Covid times and my car accident), my migraines playing up, health worries with my parents and my hubby's parents just to name a few! But I was determined to get Ilia and Trip's part of the Gods Cursed series out into the world and I'm so proud of me and then for persisting and getting it done.

So many people, both family and friends, helped out during this time and filled me with love and the encouragement I needed to keep pushing on. Thanks to all of you - you are superstars!

Of course, special thanks have to go out to my hubby, Mark, and my two beautiful boys, Jacob and Nathaniel, and to my parents, Kerrie and Jim, whose support has never wavered and whose love I could never do without. Love you all.

Aside from great family and friends, a writer needs a Coven of writing peeps all their own. Thanks need to go to these special people for encouraging me in this endeavour and giving me the strength to push on through all the highs and lows of doing this crazy writing thing—Anita and Marnie (my writing retreat buddies), Samantha and Helen (my fellow lovers of sparkly unicorns), Laura, Chris and finally Frana. I couldn't have gotten here without you.

Thanks once again to the insanely talented Samantha Marshall for her brilliant covers. Every day I thank the universe for bringing us together and for being able to count you friend.

Thoughts and thanks also to my bestie, Helen, who is always with me and forever in my thoughts, and to the first writing friend I ever had, Liz—a part of you will always live on in my writing because I would never have got published without your helpful feedback and constant cheering support. Both of you will always be a part of my stories.

And a big shout out to all my friends in Romance Writers of Australia—you are inspiration and mentor rolled into a big ball of supportive writerly love. Thank you.

The final person I have to thank is my agent, Alex Adsett, for believing in me and my work and always backing every decision I make. Your confidence in me helps me believe I can actually do this writing thing no matter the path I take. Eternal thanks.